UNCLE SI'S SECRET

M. M. Gornell

Aberdeen Bay
An Imprint of Champion Writers

Aberdeen Bay
Published by Aberdeen Bay, an imprint of Champion Writers.
www.aberdeenbay.com

PUBLISHER'S NOTE

This is a book of fiction. Names, characters, places, and incidents
are either the product of author's imagination or are used
fictitiously. Any resemblance to actual persons, living or dead,
business establishments, government agencies, events, or locales
is entirely coincidental.

International Standard Book Number
ISBN-13: 978-0-9814725-5-3
ISBN-10: 0-9814725-5-9

Printed in the United States of America.

Preface

In 1862, Josiah "Uncle Si" Merrit homesteaded in the Snoqualmie Valley, Washington at the base of the 4,167 ft. peak named after him--Mt. Si. It's reported he grew vegetables, had an orchard, and was a rugged pioneer man. The towns of North Bend and Snoqualmie do exist in this lovely area, but Cedar Valley, The Residence, and all characters are imaginary.

To Madge

UNCLE SI'S SECRET

To John & Family,

Happiness Always!

Madeleine

PROLOGUE

The Third Monday in August

Lana Norris was a beautiful woman--and she knew it.

This morning, as she walked on the Snoqualmie Valley Trail with Max, her Golden Retriever, Lana was simply clad in shorts and T-shirt. A slight breeze disordered her short chestnut hair, and perspiration marred her perfectly proportioned arms and legs. Even her sexually disquieting hazel eyes, set evocatively apart under thick and gracefully arched eyebrows, were hidden behind dark, almost black, oversized sunglasses. Still, Lana managed to look stylish and gorgeous.

Ironically, she and Max seemed to be alone on the trail except for the occasional curious squirrel. So this morning, there was no one to appreciate her natural beauty, and Lana was thankful for that solitude--neither wanting nor needing an audience. For despite outward appearances, she felt extremely strange--not actually ill--but quite unable to put a name to her discomfort. She did know, however, her usually robust and assured stride was lethargic and clumsy this morning--*she'd even stumbled once*--and her mind seemed fuzzy, her thought processes slow. This was *not* a Lana she felt comfortable with, or even knew.

She had enjoyed two mugs of Starbucks French Roast before leaving home--brewed strong, and drunk black. So her malaise and slight queasiness couldn't be for want of caffeine.

But something was wrong.

Even from the start of their walk, Lana had struggled to maintain her stride and not drop Max's leash. Now, almost to Tanner Road, she pushed her sunglasses atop her head, then rubbed her forehead with her free hand. Her skin felt unusually hot and moist.

Could it just be hunger? No, she had eaten the scone Kirby had left for her on the counter.

Kirby. She would decide what to do about Kirby this morning, this walk. No more procrastination and no more secrets.

For a second Lana felt a wave of nausea, but it passed quickly.

She took a deep breath, rubbed her forehead again, then

lowered her sunglasses back over her eyes.

Such a clear blue morning sky offered the possibility of an unseasonably bright and hot August day, and Lana was determined to enjoy her walk in the cool of the morning--*despite* her lack of mental clarity, *despite* her inexplicable queasiness, and *despite* the decision facing her.

Max also seemed determined to enjoy the morning, his tail raised high and busy. "Nice day, huh, Max?" she asked him.

Just saying the words re-affirmed her determination to savor this time for thought.

Max looked back at her for a couple seconds as if he understood and agreed with the rightness of her statement.

Straight ahead of them to the east, and haloed by a pale-yellow rising sun, stood Uncle Si Mountain.

Lana thought nothing could compare to Uncle Si. For her, it stood as an implicit sentinel to the rest of the Cascades as they rose to Snoqualmie Pass. When she and Max were alone like this, it felt like she had the whole valley to herself--*her* summer green meadows encircled by *her* towering cedars, and bounded to the east by *her* ragged cascade outcroppings. Illusory perceptions, she knew. Enjoyable nonetheless.

Lana blew out a breath, deep from within, slow and controlled--releasing tension. This walk was what she needed--the serenity--the time to think. And she was confident that in a couple more minutes, she *would* feel better.

"Today will be the day," she said to Max, "that I change the rest of my life."

Lana had thought about what to do regarding Kirby all night as she had tossed and turned in the spare bedroom.

But now, what a perfect time during a lovely walk to change her life around: beautiful mountain and valley scenery, a sun rising gently into a translucent blue sky above to warm her body, and the air scented with the fragrances of her childhood summers in Chicago--walking with her parents in Washington Park, or lying on the grass in Grant Park near Lake Michigan listening to a Chicago Symphony's end-of-the-season concert. Her life and world had been so simple. Just being a beautiful little girl was all that had mattered.

Then an unexpected snatch of her childhood returned, a remembered conversation with a sixth-grade classmate. A girl Lana had so wanted to be her friend. Sarah. Sarah with the plain face, untamed red hair, and constellations of freckles.

That was an eternity ago, Lana thought. *Why remember now?* Nonetheless, she flushed as Sarah's words returned in the same exacting and hurtful clarity as when delivered years ago while the two girls walked home from school.

"We can never be friends, you know," Sarah had said.

At first, Lana had not understood what Sarah was trying to tell her, or the resentment and envy in her friend's eyes.

But her childhood companion had continued in a voice far too wise for her age, "You're beautiful, I'm not," she said. "And you'll be successful while I'll just stay here in Rockford." Then Sarah had charged ahead, leaving Lana to continue her journey home alone.

Lana remembered starting to cry way back then--but knew she wouldn't now. She was no longer that little girl, and definitely not so easily slighted. She wondered again, why revisit such an old hurt?

Of course! Sarah's words and sentiment had returned because the very next day Lana's father had announced their move to Chicago. Her life *had* suddenly changed. She *had* moved away--almost immediately, and quite dramatically.

And that was about to happen again this morning. She was about to start over, a new life--

Max stopped suddenly, ears and tail alert.

Lana thought she heard something too--but couldn't be certain. Indeed, she felt rather confused and dizzy, not sure what the sounds were. Crunching footsteps in raspberry bushes?

She looked to their rear, and to both sides. Max did the same. Nothing.

Then they both caught real movement to their left, again in the bushes.

A squirrel scurried out--stood motionless for a few seconds--seemingly assessing the threat level a woman and a dog on a leash presented, then shot back into the raspberry thicket cover.

Relieved and slightly amused, Lana wanted to smile at her own silliness, but her mouth wouldn't work.

She heard the noise from behind again. This time more distinct.

What's going on?

Footsteps--she was now sure. Again, she and Max turned to look. Max's tail started to wag. Lana, however saw nothing.

Things are so blurry.

"Must be my imagination," she said out-loud--knowing somehow it wasn't true. For in the next instant, disorientation and fear encompassed her entire being--immediate and raw.

Oh god! She felt as if she were about to collapse.

But why? She wasn't really ill, and they were alone on the trail, weren't they?

Lana couldn't hold onto Max's leash any longer; it had become leaden, and oddly unnecessary. She reached to rub her forehead again, then her eyes, and this time with both hands. Clumsily she knocked off her sunglasses.

And during those last few seconds of Lana Norris' life in this world--and before the .38 caliber bullet ripped through her lovely countenance and lodged itself inside her brain--Lana looked through blurred vision directly into the sun up toward Uncle Si Mountain, and wondered if it was an eagle she saw soaring so magnificently against *her* mountain's southern face.

"How beautiful!" she whispered with her last breath.

PART ONE

Where Fools Fear to Tread

CHAPTER ONE

Several Weeks Later

Monday

"Bella, are you up and decent?"

So early? Barely awake, it took Belinda a moment to comprehend Bernard had come through to see her from his suite on the other side of their office.

"Still in bed, but decent, Bernie. Come on in." She sat up and absently ran her hand through short brown hair as if she could bring order to its curly chaos. Had her brother experienced another one of his weird dreams?

As soon as Bernard plunked down on the end of her bed, barefoot and still in pajamas, she knew what was up. He did his best worrying in the dawn hours between night and day, and his telltale *"I've been worrying!"* demeanor was unavoidable--his brow more deeply furrowed than usual above morose dark eyes.

Belinda was often struck with the cartoonish incompatibility of her brother's brooding eyes with the chubby-cheeked and childlike character of his face, and thought a beard would do wonders to unite the warring components. She knew, however, being cleaned shaved was more suitable to his personality.

She guessed his frown this morning was directly related to the *purple envelope* he was waving.

Damn! She hadn't decided about the murder, and this was definitely not the way she planned starting her morning--but Belinda couldn't refuse Bernard. "What's up?" she asked.

"I've been thinking about Devlin, our architect," he said. "Have we decided to go ahead with the addition?"

"He's called several times now."

"It's rude for us not to get back to him."

More awake now, Belinda smiled inwardly at both their sideways approaches. Bernard seldom pushed hard, even when anxious. Besides, she was the one handling this, and if he made too much stink she might just dump Devlin in his lap. The architect wasn't their favorite person, and the addition was going to cost a hell of a lot of money--added to the hundreds of thousands they had already spent. It wasn't an easy decision. Sure, they had grandfather Bertram's trust fund behind them, but they'd both sworn not to touch it unless dire circumstances demanded.

"Tell you the truth, I'm not sure on this one." Despite her indecisive words, Belinda let her smile show and patted his hand. "But I *have* actually returned his calls. We've been lucky so far and missed him. I left messages on his machine though."

"Then maybe we shouldn't do it?"

She rubbed her forehead and sighed lightly. "I don't know. You're right, we *do* need to give him an answer. But..." She pointed to the purple envelope. "It's that letter you really wanted to talk to me about, right?"

"Yeah, you're right. Are you going to do it?"

"You think I should?"

"Of course you should. He's innocent, Bella, I *know* he is. If I could go and do what you do..." He let his voice fade and looked away, out the window, out toward Uncle Si Mountain.

In the purple envelope was a handwritten letter, purple ink no less, on lilac stationery. The author was Olive Norris. In flowery and precise language worthy of the Victorian era Olive had laid her request out, relying heavily on numerous declarations of her son Kirby's innocence, and lavish praise for Belinda's abilities. She had requested Belinda contact her by last Friday.

"But all the things we have to do here at the residence... " she murmured. "It's not that I don't want to do it. You know how much I liked helping Uncle John those couple times. But without your 'insights,' well, I may not have figured anything out."

The cases had involved embezzlement at a small branch bank and a telephone scam. The investigations had taken a lot of time from her responsibilities at Cedar Valley Residence; and at the end of both "adventures" she had been deadly tired--and so had Bernard.

"I know you plan on taking up a lot of the slack," she said. "But it's not fair to leave everything on your shoulders." Besides, this was *murder!* That scared her.

"I can do the correspondence and pay the bills while you prove his innocence."

Such confidence. It did not escape her notice Bernard had not included dealing with Devlin, or keeping the books. "I guess Martha could do more meal preparation than just breakfast."

His eyes narrowed at her suggestion. "Oh, I think I can still handle lunch and dinner. Not that Martha isn't good."

They had hired Martha Milton four years ago as *sous-chef* to Bernard, and Belinda had never regretted their decision. Belinda thought Martha's bakery creations the best she had ever tasted.

Oddly, their *sous-chef* had been a business woman with a brokerage firm before becoming a chef; and consequently was also extraordinarily competent in kitchen management. Indeed, Belinda considered her invaluable to Cedar Valley Residence's success.

"Speaking of whom," she said, and dramatically sniffed the air. "I don't smell anything."

Extremely unusual. Since Martha specialized in pastry, every morning the aroma of cinnamon coffeecake, or Danish, or Kringle, or some other equally enticing offering floated up the stairs and into the resident suites.

This morning, nothing.

"I better go check," Bernard said. In seconds he was off to his domain, the kitchen.

Belinda never forgot her grandmother Glory Jones' admonishment. "You don't love *things*, Bella dear," she had said. "Love is reserved for people."

She knew it had been said with kindness to an impetuous and headstrong granddaughter--and at the time just a skinny wisp of a girl--because Glory Jones had been a loving woman who had wanted her only granddaughter to carry forward her gentleness of heart and spirit.

Nevertheless, the grownup "Bella," *did* love Cedar Valley Residence. She couldn't help it.

From that first cold and rainy day she and Bernard had walked up its creaking front porch stairs and taken refuge under its leaking veranda, the building had spoken to her; and she had responded with instant ardor.

Sure, it had needed work.

A lot of work.

But she and Bernard had made an offer that first morning, five years ago.

This morning, within seconds of Bernard's departure to the kitchen, Belinda's bedside alarm clock went off at 6:00 A.M.-- precisely as planned. There was a lot she needed to do.

Cedar Valley Residence had become a demanding lover.

She stretched and sat up straighter in bed to get a first look at the morning developing outside her bay window.

Her "suite" (as Bernard had insisted on calling the rooms), had an eastern exposure with a view of open pasture and Uncle Si Mountain in the background. She seldom closed her shutters. Who was to see or even care? A few munching horses, a couple goats?

Besides, summer was short in Cedar Valley and Belinda wanted to soak up as much sun as she could while it lasted.

Bernard had left her door cracked, and their dog Naja- -who evidently had slept the night with Bernard--took the opportunity to saunter in and jump up on Belinda's window seat.

"Now you come to see me." Despite her chastising words, seeing Naja looking out the window pleased Belinda and she smiled warmly.

Naja also seemed to enjoy the early light and view, though her interest appeared to be the occasional passing dog along Cedar Valley Trail rather than the mountain.

Belinda figured she and Naja made good companions, since they both liked mornings. She had come to them the day after they had moved into Cedar Valley--a stray with mischievous eyes and a thick black coat--probably chow, lab, and heaven only knew what else. Naja had immediately made herself at home, and now clearly considered herself queen of the residence.

"Time to get up, Naja girl."

Typical of a morning person, Belinda was able to hop out of bed and *do* something without caffeine or much wakeup time. Her runaway ex-husband, a.k.a. "The Bum," had been a night person. In retrospect, she now believed this biological disharmony had been a blessing, and a curse.

It only took Belinda moments to get up and don her swimsuit. A quick look in the mirror caused her to reflect for a moment. Time did what it wanted--no matter how much she wished otherwise.

She had not forgotten how dissimilar she and Bernard had looked as children, and this morning her mirror reminded her how pronounced these physical differences were becoming as they marched through midlife. While she was tall for a woman, 5'8" with a thin and willow-like figure, Bernard, though equal in height, was stocky in build.

"Sure, we both have brown hair," she had joked with Bernard and others in the past.

Her brown hair, however, was thick and curly, while his hung flat and thin. Her face was oval tending to longish, his round and cherubic. And even though both had dark brown eyes, Belinda was aware hers were smiling and comfortable, Bernard's serious and gloomy.

Quickly she slipped down to the residence's lap pool out back and swam thirty laps, her body on auto-swim, her mind on residence business and Lana Norris' murder.

The pool had been Bernard's idea and every time Belinda used it she mentally praised his good sense and sent a *"thank you"* his way.

When Belinda returned to her suite, it didn't take long to shower, dress, and head next door to their office.

She could hear and feel her stomach juices gurgling, *may we eat now?* But the sooner she got routine business out of the way, the sooner she could work on the figures for the addition.

No, breakfast could wait an hour.

And the *purple letter;* that could wait also. Maybe forever.

Belinda unlocked the door leading into the hallway and opened it wide as was their custom. The bottom desk drawer was always locked--that was where they kept their aged Iver Johnson .38 inherited from Glory.

Belinda considered the gun a laughable excuse for *real* protection, and knew it was a bizarre keepsake. But having it with her at the residence was a way to keep Glory Jones close; and it brought her comfort whenever she unlocked the drawer and took a peek.

Her calendar and daily to-do list were on the computer and she had barely sat down and turned the machine on when the uncertain and whispery sound of Miss Shirley's voice floated in from the doorway.

"Am I too early, Dear?" she asked. "You opened the door and I've been anxious to talk to you this morning."

"Come in, Miss Shirley, your timing is perfect." Only a small lie. The bills, the bank account, the deposit, the supply order--all could wait. Miss Shirley was one of her favorite residents. "Have a seat."

Their office, like much of the residence, was paneled; and two walls were dedicated to bookshelves. The paneling stain was a light cherry which Belinda hoped kept the room from being too oppressive given the mass of books packed into the bookshelves and the weightiness of the furniture. A gigantic claw-footed mahogany desk dominated the room and was flanked by two equally massive leather wing-chairs. Both desk and chairs had been passed down from their grandparents and were cherished.

Miss Shirley tried to perch herself in the wing-chair closest to Belinda but was instantly swallowed into its massive burgundy depths. "Do you have a couple minutes for me?"

"Of course I do." Sometimes Miss Shirley put Belinda in mind of her grandmother, especially the way her presence managed to be formidable and genteel at the same time.

In her seventies, five seven or so, sturdily built with a wiry and athletic carriage, Miss Shirley was not waif-like. Still, the aged armchair managed to engulf her. Her style of dress tended to long jumpers, mules, and turtle necks reflective of Eddie Bauer and LL. Bean. She wore large round glasses, her eyes behind the thick lenses brownish-black, and her wavy hair almost a matching color except for haphazard patches of gray.

Belinda watched as Naja, who had followed her into the office, climbed up into her second favorite spot, the other wing-chair. The sight, sound, and smell of Miss Shirley started Naja's tail thumping.

"This is so difficult for me, Dear." Miss Shirley breathed in deeply. "I'm afraid I'm going to have to leave Cedar Valley Residence." She let her breath out. "There! I've said it."

No, not Miss Shirley. "But why?" Belinda demanded.

She could still picture the morning Miss Shirley had appeared, a year ago, a bewildered look on her face, broken glasses perched on her nose, no identification, and a pile of cash in her purse.

"You know all that money I had?"

Belinda nodded. *How could I forget.*

"I've spent it, you see." She gestured with opened hands and a shrug. "Things are expensive."

Before thought, Belinda blurted out, "Well don't worry about your rent for awhile. We'll see if we can work something out."

Miss Shirley smiled. "You *are* a sweetheart, Belinda, but you know as well as I, you can't run a place like this without paying residents."

"You still have several weeks paid up...and where would you go?" The poor woman was still no closer to knowing *who* she was. Maybe she could get welfare assistance, but didn't that take a long time? "Promise me, Miss Shirley, you won't just disappear on us. Bernard and I will try to work something out."

Miss Shirley stood up, reached across the desk, and patted Belinda affectionately on the hand. "You and Bernard are dears."

Behind her brave words Belinda could see fear in Miss Shirley's eyes. She would have to do something about this.

But what? Early on they had put an ad in the newspaper, talked to the police, and even tacked flyers on telephone poles. No one knew who she was or where she had come from--and Miss Shirley certainly didn't know. Both Doctor "D," their favorite local physician, and a colleague of his at Harborview Hospital had agreed--temporary amnesia. She probably would come out of it. But when?

"Oh yes," Miss Shirley said as she left the office. "Did I mention about my Chinese print scarf?"

"Ah..."

"The one I like to wear to dinner with my blue dress?"

"Ah..."

"The one you and Bernard gave me for Christmas?"

"Of course. I'm sorry, Miss Shirley, I was just trying to figure out some way you could stay on. Yes, I remember the scarf." Belinda had special-ordered it from the Metropolitan Museum of Art. "Does it need cleaning or something? It was silk, right?"

"It's gone missing. Two days now. Phoebe believes Vera's great-granddaughter, what's her name..."

"Kaitlin."

"Yes, Phoebe believes Kaitlin stole it. I can't believe that. Vera's too nice to have a thief for a great-granddaughter. But Phoebe says I'm too naïve. Well, maybe..." Her voice faded.

Olive sat across from her son with her back to the jail guard. So what if the guard was tall, heavy, and unfriendly. He didn't scare her.

She said, "Not to worry sweetheart, I've hired our own investigator for you. They say she's good." A small exaggeration, but she needed to keep his spirits up.

She leaned across the metal table and caressed her son's face--her eyes locked into his--refusing to look around at their bleak surroundings. Kirby's lawyer called it an interview room, but it still felt like a prison cell. Cold and colorless, and something else quite unpleasant that she couldn't put her finger on.

"Our private investigator will find the evidence to get you off." Olive didn't tell Kirby that Belinda Jones had yet to say "yes." No need to depress him further.

Olive squeezed her son's face tighter in her hands. "I'll get you out of this."

"Excuse me, Ma'am." The guard shifted his position. His voice was deep and his delivery firm. "Touching isn't allowed. Sorry."

She released Kirby's face and sat back with a controlled sigh. "Don't worry son," she said softly. "God will help us."

Indeed, Olive prayed every night on bent knees to the baby Jesus and the Virgin Mary that this horrible mistake against her son would be rectified. The Blessed Virgin and Jesus would in turn save her Kirby. She knew they would.

And Belinda Jones would be their instrument.

During this visit, Kirby spoke very little to his mother. She understood--the denials, apologies, and strategies had all been gone over before--many times. Consequently, Olive didn't stay her full allotted time and the same guard escorted her out through a labyrinth of corridors Olive had yet to gain mastery over.

Finally, she was deposited outside King County Jail onto Fifth Avenue.

This morning Olive noticed no reporters or photographers lurking, waiting to grab a photo or sound-bite. Kirby's predicament, for the time being, had evidently fallen from primetime grace.

She would have to change that.

It was barely 6 A.M., cool, and a clear blue sky. Fall nudging at the last days of summer.

Calvin "Senator" Pope, Kirby's astronomically priced defense attorney, had arranged these early morning visitations for Olive. She had prevailed upon him that being able to see her son in a room without all the other riffraff was paramount. At least he had accomplished that one thing for her.

Once outside, Olive greedily breathed in fresh morning air and vowed out loud that Kirby too, one day soon, no matter the cost to her, would breathe free again.

The brass plaque above the arched entrance to Cedar

Valley Residence's dining hall read "The Cedars." The room itself had a high ceiling, massive panels of glass, and mahogany stile-and-rail paneling. It was the jewel of their residence and Belinda and Bernard had loved bringing it to life.

For Bernard, it was his favorite room.

"There he is now," Phoebe Farmer twittered from a window table where she sat with Vera Price.

As usual, Phoebe, in her early sixties, was a flutter with nervous energy. She reminded Bernard of a bird, but he had yet to pinpoint exactly which one. Her small oval face was surrounded with tight bleached blond curls reminiscent of the early 1940's. Her hair color and deep olive skin were a mismatch, but Phoebe was not deterred. It was a style she had started in youth, and was now reluctant to abandon--regardless the vagaries of fashion and appropriateness.

She waved anxiously to Bernard, arms flapping, curls gyrating. "Over here, Mr. Jones, over here."

Bernard smiled and headed toward their table. He was used to Phoebe's easy excitability. This morning though, Phoebe's companion, Vera, also seemed jittery. No, not jittery, he corrected himself, Vera wasn't the type. More like she was upset. No, that wasn't quite right either. Perturbed. That was it. Vera was most definitely perturbed.

"No, need to make a spectacle, Mrs. Farmer," Vera admonished Phoebe while looking directly at Bernard. "I'm sure Mr. Jones sees us quite easily and has quickly recognized our distress."

Vera, who insisted on being addressed as *Mrs. Dr. James Price* even though Dr. Price had been buried twenty years previously, was ninety plus a few. She had been born not far from the turn of the last century, to a "good" Atlanta family. The story of how she ended up on the West Coast was elaborate and involved her husband moving his practice, his wife, and his two daughters to Seattle in the fifties.

Bernard had never seen Vera with a silver-white hair out of place. Usually she was dressed in nylons, pumps, and a two piece suit. This morning, though groomed accordingly, the very proper Vera was not her usual composed self. Most significantly, her facial expression directly reflected her displeasure.

"Good Morning!" Bernard could hear his cheeriness was overdone. He was aware of his morose aura and occasionally over compensated.

"Something's wrong," Phoebe proclaimed. "It's been half an hour, at least, since we last saw them."

Bernard continued to smile indulgently with raised eyebrows, hopefully showing appropriate attentiveness.

"Something terrible must have happened." Phoebe pointed toward the kitchen.

The two swinging door panels stood motionless. Patrick Tody and MaryAnn Johnson, their student waiter and waitress were nowhere to be seen. The kitchen was silent and ominously bereft of tantalizing aromas.

Bernard glanced at his watch.

"Exactly," Vera stated. "Six-thirty A.M. Breakfast service should have started at six."

"I'll go see."

The kitchen proper was indeed silent, but not empty. Patrick and Mary Ann, both in their wait-service uniforms and looking particularly youthful and anxious, were huddled together at one of the prep tables. In the distance, back in the alcove--usually an oasis of calm--Bernard caught the discordant edges of banging and cursing. Ironically, the alcove had single-handedly been brought to life in the early days through Martha's hard work and desire for a tranquil space of her own making.

So, Bernard surmised, Vera and Phoebe had definitely been right, something was amiss, and he feared trouble awaited just a few feet ahead. He directed Patrick and MaryAnn to take some tea, coffee, juice, and toast out to Mrs. Price and Mrs. Farmer; he would handle whatever was going on with Martha.

The two young people scurried off, evidently quite happy to oblige and get out of harm's way.

He knew their reluctance to confront Martha wasn't because they didn't like her personally, or because she actually was a hard person to get along with; but rather the thought that after all, she was a *Chef*--and everyone knew how chefs were!

"Darn, darn, darn!" Martha paced the small area around the alcove dinette. "I should have been more careful."

She turned as Bernard entered. Her eyes, on the verge of tears, glistened. "Why was I so stupid?"

How could he answer a question like that? "Mrs. Price and Mrs. Farmer are getting hungry," he sidestepped. Bernard knew letting hungry residents sit in the dining room unattended was not Martha's style.

"I can't find Buster." Buster was a large black dog; probably a retriever-lab-chow mix with a big head, long spotted tongue, and a wonderfully gentle personality. He was about ten months old, and had been adopted into the fold by Martha.

Ah, her behavior was now understandable. Bernard knew Martha was not silly or hysterical by nature. When it came to her animals, however, she was fanatical.

"What do you mean, you can't find Buster?" He thought it a reasonable question.

Martha's tone indicated she thought he was being dense as a post. "I mean, he's nowhere in the residence. I've looked all over. Unfortunately I left that door open," she pointed to the exit leading to her back garden, "when I went out for basil this morning. I think he followed me and then wandered away. And now he doesn't know how to get back home."

"Buster's not a dumb dog. I'm sure he recognizes a good thing when he smells it." Bernard wanted to ease Martha's distress. "That dog isn't about to leave the comforts you've provided him. Especially all the treats he gets."

She gave him a doubtful look.

"If he has indeed sneaked out for a walkabout, he'll soon be back. Not that I'm not also a bit concerned..." He too had grown fond of Buster.

"...and just when he was getting settled," Martha said.

"Settled" had entailed a doghouse inside the pantry so he would have a place to call his own, a dog bed in Martha's suite, another in the game room, and another in the office upstairs.

"I really don't think he's run away, Martha. Just taking a nap somewhere..." As Bernard said the words he walked into the pantry, bent over, and peered inside Buster's doghouse. Two large sleepy and puzzled hazel eyes peered back at him.

Seeing the smile on Bernard's face, Martha insisted, "But

I looked in there."

He shrugged and gave her what he thought was a nonchalant yet emotionally neutral look.

Obviously PO'd, Martha proclaimed, "We better get breakfast back on track. We shouldn't keep our customers waiting you know."

Buster had followed Martha out into the garden, but he had also returned with her to the safety of the kitchen and his comfy inside doghouse.

When Martha had looked in, Buster's eyes had been closed while he pondered.

For he had come upon a secret.

And clever as he was when it came to hearth, home, and food--*this*--he didn't know what to do about.

After Miss Shirley left, Belinda worked in the office until 8:00 A.M. or so, paying bills, preparing the bank deposit, updating her accounting software, and doing "what if" calculations for the addition project.

She and Bernard *wanted* more suites, but was it a sound financial decision?

Complicating the matter was her distaste for the architect--too brusque and snooty and a real jackass to Belinda's way of thinking. His designs, however, were great.

Her final numbers seemed to show they wouldn't breakeven until after they had increased their revenue base for two more years--if they did in fact grow. What a god-awful long time.

"Well, Naja girl, let's go tell Bernie we can add rooms." She would have to lie or else he'd worry himself silly. Well, not actually lie, just not mention the two year part.

Oddly, Naja didn't seem eager to go with her. Belinda patted her head. "Hope you're not getting sick on me."

Once downstairs, Belinda ran into Theresa Bacera in the

foyer.

"Hi, Mrs. Jones," Theresa greeted Belinda with one of her generous smiles.

Belinda thought she was an attractive young woman, with dark olive skin, large round hazel eyes, and thick shiny dark auburn hair, often worn in a ponytail: and when she smiled her entire face lit up. Theresa was petite, but curvaceous, and this morning was dressed in her usual costume of jeans, T-shirt, and light jacket. She had told Belinda her parents had emigrated to the US from Ecuador in the seventies, but she was born in The United States.

"Beautiful morning, huh?" Theresa added.

"You know, I don't mind you calling me Belinda. In fact I hate the title 'Mrs.' Even when I was married, I used 'Ms.', and Jones is my maiden name."

"Good grief, I sure got the name thing all screwed up. So sorry. All this time you've let me go on with the Mrs. stuff." She shook her head in apparent dismay, "'Belinda' it is, from now on."

Theresa started to go upstairs, then evidently remembering something, stopped on the first step and turned back to Belinda. Her expression was serious and her voice lowered, "I hate bringing this up, Mrs…, I mean Belinda, but I've looked and looked everywhere, so I feel pretty confident I've got it right."

She took a few steps closer to the young woman. "Got what right?"

"Well," Theresa exhaled a short breath of exasperation. "It's my pen set. It's an ink pen, you know the old fashion kind that you have to fill? And a mechanical pencil. They're in a leather case and I always kept them by my bedside. They've disappeared."

"You believe they've been stolen?" Belinda hated saying the words.

The whole character of Cedar Valley Residence would change if the residents thought there was a thief among them. She prided herself that up to now residents seldom bothered locking their suites, even occasionally leaving the doors open.

First Miss Shirley's scarf, now Theresa's pen set.

Possibly seeing something in Belinda's face, Theresa quickly added, "Maybe they'll still show up and I will have made a stink about nothing. Anyway, I'm off to take a shower then come back down for breakfast. See you in a bit."

Belinda watched as she headed up the grand-staircase. *To be young again.*

When Belinda entered the dining room, Bernard was waiting for her at the first table inside. From this particular table, one could see the front door and the reception desk.

This was one of their little habits Belinda found most comforting. Having coffee or tea in the dining room after she came down from her morning office work was an event she could count on. Just like she could count on her brother.

Fortunately, she knew Bernard was able to have these morning moments free because breakfast was Martha's bailiwick, and unless they got really busy (the Residence dining hall was open to the public), his assistance was not usually required.

In addition, her brother had his own way of doing things. Unlike many chefs, Bernard was not fanatical about purchasing ingredients himself. Instead, he had an arrangement with the chef at a local Italian restaurant to also shop for him.

Francesca, even though Belinda found her brusque, was extremely particular about the freshness and quality of her ingredients.

"Did you get the bills paid?" he asked as soon as Belinda sat down.

"Yep."

Their dining chairs were plush for restaurant use and cost more than they should have spent; but every time Belinda sat down in one she was glad they had gone overboard. The dining room was now warm with enticing aromas comforting her senses.

"Are we still solvent?" he asked.

"Barely. But yeah, no emergencies like last month." July had been horrible--leaks in two bathrooms and the bread-oven had died. Belinda added, "We should never buy secondhand appliances again." It was wishful thinking more than a dictate. New restaurant equipment was pricey, while used could be purchased at a substantial discount.

He leaned forward and lowered his voice almost to a whisper. "And the upstairs addition?"

She smiled and nodded, easily neglecting to mention the two year break-even point. "If we keep eighty-percent full we should be able to meet our mortgage obligation, and if we just make the regular payment every month we'll have it paid off in ten years."

On the good side, they already had a loan with the Cedar Valley Credit Union. Devlin Stephens, their barely tolerable architect had name recognition, and the institution had been eager to finance the addition once they had seen Cedar Valley Residence owner's financials and found out about Devlin's involvement.

"Great." Clearly relieved, Bernard fell back comfortably in his chair.

Belinda hated spoiling the moment, but he had to be told. "Miss Shirley is leaving."

"What? No..."

"She's run out of money."

He sighed. "I guess we should have known it would happen one day."

"Yeah, I know. But I hoped we would have found out who she is by now. Someone, somewhere, must know."

"What will she do? Where will she go?"

A thoughtful silence hung between them for a few moments before Belinda suggested, "We could just let her stay for awhile longer. Couldn't we? I mean since we aren't full up anyway."

"You're right, we still have a vacancy. But if we get full up again..."

"Excuse me." Patrick was at Belinda's side. "Did you want some breakfast, Ms. Jones? Martha sent me to ask."

Belinda had forgotten she was hungry, but with the sensory comforts of her surroundings and the mention of breakfast she became instantly ravenous. *Bless you, Martha,* she thought.

"Yes, Patrick, I'm definitely ready to eat. Anything new?"

She liked this young man better than a lot who had come through. Patrick was starting his final year at the University of Washington in September. After that he planned on going to Gonzaga Law School in Spokane. So, this was his last summer with them, and Belinda was sorry to lose him.

"Well, Chef Milton is preparing French omelets this morning. I'm not sure what makes them *French*, but I had one earlier and they're great, light and tender."

"What's in them?" Belinda asked.

"Nothing except some herbs. It's amazing."

She looked to Bernard who said, "I'll explain all about French omelets later. Take Patrick's word for it, Martha makes a lovely omelet."

High praise from Bernard.

Belinda ordered an omelet but also insisted on American style hash-browns, toast, and orange juice of course. Bernard ordered a refill on his tea.

As she had hoped, while they waited, brother and sister discussed the addition in more detail, each feeding on the other's ideas. It had been that way from the start of Cedar Valley Residence, a collaborative effort, and to her mind well worth the hassle of give and take.

Not until after her food had arrived and Belinda had taken her first bite and declared the offering excellent did Bernard explain how Martha whipped the eggs to fluffy perfection with a whisk, how she slow cooked them, spreading them just so in the *French* manner, half folding them before leaving the skillet, and the final fold with a flip of the wrist and skillet.

Belinda--not a cook, much less a chef--didn't follow most of what Bernard was saying. She smiled encouragingly though, ate on, and praised the gods her brother had become a chef and Martha had sold her brokerage firm and come to them.

As Belinda finished her omelet, Kaitlin Melon-Price, Vera Price's visiting great-granddaughter, sauntered into the dining room, looked around, then went to a rear table and plopped down in a chair with her back to the room.

"She can probably sense we don't like her," Bernard said.

"I never said I didn't like her. I can't say I much care for that Goth look, but she's a teenager. She can't help being horrid."

"Not all teenagers are horrid. That's not a fair statement."

"Tessa's kid was." As soon as she said the words, Belinda regretted bringing their disagreeable L.A. cousin into the conversation.

"But Gillian grew up eventually. Don't forget she's in college now and doing well."

True enough, Tessa's daughter Gillian, as far as they knew, was now doing well after some very bumpy teenage years. "Yeah, you're right. And at least 'Goth' to Gillian suggested architecture."

Belinda stared at Kaitlin's back for a few moments wondering. She was sixteen, her hair jet black, her clothes and shoes jet black, her eyes jet black (contacts), and her lipstick blood maroon. Two studs adorned her pierced nose and three dotted each of her ears. Double rings decorated every finger and her nails resembled claws, painted with black nail polish of course, and studded.

Weird, Belinda thought, but did that make her a thief?

Kaitlin *did* seem to be in another world. A world encapsulated by earphones seemingly surgically attached to her head. She seldom spoke to or acknowledged anyone around her. When she did fleetingly enter the realm of adult mortals, her utterances were monosyllabic.

Yet again, did that make her a thief?

Belinda pulled her gaze away from the young woman. "Did Phoebe or Vera mention Kaitlin this morning?"

"No. They just wanted to know what was going on in the kitchen." He drained the last of his tea and made an unpleasant face. His tea had evidently gone cold.

Belinda leaned across the table and said *sotto voce*, "You are so prissy sometimes."

"Humph. There's nothing *prissy* about wanting your tea strong and hot."

"Miss Shirley claims Phoebe thinks Kaitlin is stealing things."

His expression darkened. "The LeBeaus sat down at the same table with Phoebe and Vera before they finished and I eavesdropped a bit." His eyes betrayed his concern. "And they were asking Vera about Kaitlin. You think they're thinking the same thing?"

Belinda would not have considered Morris and Anna LeBeau, residents from the first day they had advertised, malicious or gossipy.

"I don't know." This was not sounding good.

"Well, I didn't hear them say anything about missing items, but they *were* asking nosey questions of Vera. Like, 'Do you know where your great-granddaughter is all day? Do you give her an allowance? When is she going home?' Stuff like that."

Belinda laughed outright, "Good grief, you sure managed to hear a lot."

"I was setting the table next to them."

Belinda cleared her throat, lowered her voice again, and leaned forward. "To change the subject, I ran into Theresa coming in this morning. You know it's not the first time we've noticed her coming and going at odd hours. What I find particularly interesting is there doesn't seem to be an exact time pattern." She straightened back up. "Of course it isn't any of our business, but still, I *am* curious."

Theresa's rental application had simply stated she was a recent UW graduate living off an allowance. Parents? Trust Fund? Theresa hadn't volunteered further details. Her credit had checked out, so Belinda hadn't seen any problem or pushed for more information.

Maybe she should have? But asking her now seemed awkward.

Belinda had, however, worked up various scenarios for Theresa's comings and goings--from a variable shift worker at Boeing, to a prostitute on the night streets of Pioneer Square. Belinda didn't know much about Boeing's factory schedules, *or* prostitutes, *or* Pioneer Square; but her mind required explanation and order for the world around her, and an unemployed ex-student on an allowance didn't adequately explain Theresa Bacera.

She certainly didn't buy Bernard's simplistic conclusion offered during a prior discussion that Theresa was rendezvousing with a married boyfriend in secret places at secret times.

"Truth is," Belinda conceded, "she pays her rent on time, doesn't cause trouble, has a pleasing and lively personality, and the other residents like her. What is there for either of us to complain about?"

"I'm not complaining. You brought Theresa up."

"Well what do you *really* think? I don't believe your affair theory."

The bell at the front desk rang, causing sister and brother to look at each other in surprise.

"Did you see anybody come in?" Belinda asked. She certainly hadn't. But oddly, Belinda thought she smelled the faint scent of lavender.

"Nope."

She sighed, then pushed her plate away and her chair back. "I better go see."

The supply list still awaited her; and she neither needed nor wanted another interruption. But then again, maybe it was a new resident, always an exciting event. There was a suite available and they certainly could use the money.

A short round woman with a puffy oval face haloed with thin overly permed white hair and a substantial bosom stood firmly and resolutely at the reception desk.

She wore sensible flat shoes, and was dressed in a fifties style "go to church" suit; the blouse was silk and lavender colored, the suit, dark purple linen. Hanging from her arm was a suitcase size lavender leather purse, the initials O. N. burnt in scroll across its front.

Olive Norris.

Olive concluded in a quivering voice and with pleading eyes, "So you see, Ms. Jones, given the resources I have left and my son's desperate circumstances, you are our last and best chance."

Belinda took Olive's comment as a complement and a genuine request for help, though she was not so naïve as to think Olive would have chosen her if money hadn't been a concern. Calvin "Senator" Pope was top of the line and cost a pretty penny.

She couldn't help feeling sorry for Olive--her only son in jail, possibly facing the death penalty; and according to Olive, her savings nearly depleted, house mortgaged to pay his lawyer, and no help from her other son.

Still, Belinda had not warmed enough to Olive to say "yes."

She had taken Olive on a tour of the residence, partly stalling for time, partly to get a measure of the woman. Tour concluded, Olive had delivered her plea for help as the two women sat in the parlor alcove looking out onto the front porch.

Belinda had instinctively chosen this less formal setting over the upstairs office. Here it would be easier for her to decline Olive's request.

"Maybe if you could talk to my son, see him in person," Olive added. "Then you'll know he couldn't possibly kill anyone. You'll see it in his eyes. Kirby is innocent." Olive's voice cracked and her eyes watered. "He's expecting you. I saw him this morning, and at first he barely spoke to me. I know he's depressed and he's given up hope, you see. But when I told him you were coming, he was much more animated." She reached down and fumbled for a Kleenex in her gargantuan purple handbag knocking the monstrosity sideways. "You could see him this afternoon." She leaned forward earnestly. "Please?"

"I do care that an innocent person might go to jail," Belinda admitted.

"He *is* innocent!" Olive re-asserted. "I know he is. A mother knows things like that about her son."

"But the gun, the panties..." Belinda had read in the newspaper the murder weapon and Lana's panties had been found in the wheel-well of Kirby's trunk.

"I told you, he's being framed! Can't you see that?"

It was possible.

Belinda did want to get involved, but the addition and the recent thefts weighed heavily in her decision. If a resident was stealing, it could destroy the residence. No one would stay, and the addition would be money down the drain. She needed to pay attention to her and Bernard's dream before trying to solve other peoples problems.

Even at this moment Belinda could hear the edges of a conversation in the parlor proper between the LeBeaus and Phoebe. She was sure she caught Kaitlin's name and hoped Vera was elsewhere because they were talking rather loudly.

"I'll go see Kirby later today, Mrs. Norris," Belinda finally agreed. Even with that concession, she hedged her commitment. "Only if I think he's innocent will I get back to you this evening and make some kind of arrangement."

"And then you can talk to Senator, then to my son and daughter-in-law..."

"Whoa." Belinda held up her hand. Olive was a force indeed. "Mrs. Norris, I'm not promising anything. Yet."

"Yes, yes, Ms. Jones, I understand."

Belinda knew Olive did *not* understand and would push and push. She was Kirby's mother after all, and Belinda could see in her eyes that he was her life; which caused Belinda to wonder how such all-encompassing devotion sat with the other son Olive had mentioned. Evidently there wasn't a Mr. Norris in the current picture. Divorced? Deceased? No need to pry further unless she took the case.

"It's terrible." Again Olive's voice cracked. "Not only losing a beautiful daughter-in-law in the prime of her life but facing the possibility of losing your son too."

"You liked Lana?"

"Of course!"

Olive's response sounded forced to Belinda's ears and she doubted any woman would be good enough for a son so adored.

"Lana was always giving me presents," Olive continued. "She knew how Reverend Norris spoiled me."

"Reverend Norris?"

"My late husband." She dabbed at her eyes. "So many tragedies in such a short time. We lost him two years ago."

How odd, Belinda thought, to call your husband by his professional title. "I'm so sorry." She then cleared her throat and squirmed. Time was up.

Maybe Kirby Norris was innocent like Olive claimed--*or*--he was a cold-blooded killer who had drugged, strangled, and shot his wife.

Now, she, Belinda Jones, was about to plunk herself right in the middle of it.

Involuntarily she shivered and hoped Olive hadn't noticed.

When Olive first arrived, Naja had come downstairs to check out the "stranger," but kept her distance in the corner.

Buster also stuck his head in to take a peek, but she growled him off.

Cedar Valley Residence was still her domain, alone; no new canines need apply. Bad enough she had to put up with Miss Kitty, the Morris's calico.

"I don't expect you to believe me." Kirby allowed himself a small wry smile. "But Mother insisted I talk to you. And what Mother wants, Mother usually gets." His smile grew. "But you probably already know that."

Belinda very much wanted to give Kirby the impression she knew what she was doing--though she actually felt quite wobbly. She had never been in King County Jail proper, and on the surface, the interview room they were in was neutral and impersonal--cream walls, a high small barred window, a dingy fluorescent ceiling lamp, one grey table, two stiff backed wooden chairs--but there was a bitter and desperate coldness exuding from the pores of the place.

Added to that, seeing Kirby in person for the first time progressed what had started as a crazy *idea* to solve a murder into the realm of reality. A mental exercise no longer--she was actually interviewing a flesh and blood accused murderer.

"Well, yes," Belinda said, hoping her voice was coming across neutral, but strong. "Your mother is a formidable woman.

She very much believes in your innocence."

"Do you," Kirby asked, "believe in my innocence?"

She sidestepped his question. "I'm here at her request."

"Ask whatever you want. I didn't kill my wife." His denial flowed easily.

Considering the physical aspects of the man across the wooden table from her, Belinda found it astonishing Kirby and Lana had ever linked up.

The photos Belinda had seen all indicated Lana had been a beautiful woman--classical features enhanced by large hazel eyes, a generous mouth, smooth complexion, and stylish haircuts. In one picture Lana had been standing, and Belinda guessed her to be around 5'8" and maybe 120 lbs. maximum. Belinda concluded Lana also had had a darned good figure.

In contrast, Kirby was short and round in a way that made him look like he was bursting out of his clothes--even in his loose fitting jailhouse coveralls. His face was also round and fleshy with inadequate lips, crooked nose, and asymmetric washed-out brown eyes.

Lana must have seen something special in Kirby beyond the physical.

"If you didn't kill your wife, Mr. Norris, then how did your gun and your wife's panties get in your car? You hadn't noticed your gun was missing?"

"You sound like Senator. I really don't think he believes me either." He shook his head resignedly. "Hell of a thing when your own attorney doesn't believe you. Now you."

"Don't you lock your car?" Belinda insisted.

"Yes! Yes! I lock my damn car."

Good, Belinda thought, there was still a little fire left in Kirby. He wasn't completely dead like Olive had led her to believe.

"So how could someone get into your car without breaking the lock or using a key? I understand the police didn't find any evidence of forced entry."

"No, they didn't." Kirby ran his hand through his hair.

A ridiculous looking gesture, Belinda thought, given the dearth and lifelessness of said hair. She had to force back an urge to laugh.

"But," Kirby continued. "I tell you, Ms. Jones, I didn't put them there. I swear."

"Why don't you call me Belinda?" An easy concession that could help win his confidence.

"Sure. And Kirby is fine with me."

"Okay. Now, Kirby, tell me about the gun." Belinda leaned forward, wanting to expand her feel for the man. She needed to see the man Lana had loved, and the son Olive believed was innocent.

"Nothing much to tell really. Lana and I kept it in the desk drawer in our study. The study is on the first floor at the front of the house, easy access for an intruder. But the gun's been there for ages. I've seen it often. We bought it after a home-invasion incident in Seattle a while back. Don't really remember when, but Mother insisted I get guns. One for the house, and one for her apartment. Are you going to the house and check things out?"

Despite his predicament and current surroundings, Belinda thought she caught a hint of childlike eagerness coloring his question.

"I'll go where the trail takes me." She quickly added, "That is, if I take your case."

The room they were in was the same one Olive had visited her son in that morning; and like Olive, Belinda wasn't keen to look around. Too awful. Nonetheless, Belinda took a couple seconds pretending to take in her surroundings--stalling to form her next question before returning her gaze to Kirby.

"Were you and Lana getting along?"

Kirby stared into Belinda's eyes for a long moment. "Not really. We were pulling away. Seems like we were spending less and less time together."

Belinda forced herself to ignore his scrutiny. She couldn't let him take control of her interview. "Fighting?"

"No, not fighting. Just not as lovey as we used to be."

"So the sex you and your wife had the night before she died was...?"

Kirby continued to hold Belinda in a hard tight gaze. "Consensual, if that's what you're asking. Lana and I had our differences, more and more recently, but that doesn't mean we weren't getting along well enough not to have sex." His face relaxed, his eyes shifting to the guard at the door, then he smiled. Tight lipped, but a smile nonetheless. "We both have strong libidos." His smile vanished as quickly it had appeared. "*Had*, that is." A flicker of sadness crossed his face. "Funny thing, we ended up having an argument the night before…and Lana slept in the guest bedroom."

Kirby looked down at the table and fell silent.

Belinda waited, and after another moment he continued, his voice somber. "Not like mother and father. Always agreeable, never a fuss or a fight that I can ever remember. The perfect couple." He shook his head. "I don't think they ever had sex again after I was born. Mother is old fashioned in that way. Sex is for God's creating. Not for fun."

Belinda seldom thought about Clive "The Bum" anymore, but Kirby had hit several raw truth nerves. She and Clive had been romantically and sexually involved until the day he took off for parts still unknown. One of the many reasons, Belinda figured, why she still called him "The Bum."

Decades earlier, Glory Jones had advised a teenaged Bella, "*Never confuse lust with love, sweetheart.*" Belinda had regretted many a time not having more closely heeded her grandmother's words of wisdom.

She cleared her throat and memories. "You and Lana didn't have any children?"

"No, she was never interested. To be fair, I wasn't either. Not the parent types, I guess."

"And your brother and sister-in-law? No children either?"

"No. Not a prolific family it seems."

Belinda wanted to ask what his brother Walter thought about all this, but hesitated. She had gotten a clear impression from Olive that Walter was "second-string."

"Walter thinks I'm guilty," Kirby said before Belinda could find the appropriate words. "It's okay, you know. In fact, he should actually hate me. Don't think he does though, Walter's a good guy." A thin ironic smile crossed his face. "I was the baby, and mother always preferred me. At least he found Melissa. I think they're actually happy together."

Belinda was not yet sure why, but she found herself warming to Kirby. "Who do you think killed your wife?"

"I've thought a lot about that, you know. Either it's some crazy serial killer, or it's one of those two guys the police picked up and then released."

"Do you think it's possible your wife was having an affair?"

He didn't hesitate. "Well, maybe. Actually, I'd say probably. Lana was flirtatious. Our marriage though was not 'open' enough for her to confide in me. Melissa would probably know. Whether she'll tell you or not is another story."

Belinda sat back in her chair and took another moment to further assess Kirby.

In turn, he also sat back, seemingly content to await her judgement.

She found it unusual for a man to be so casual about his wife having an affair. Probably faking his nonchalance--or just maybe covering for a dalliance of his own? And he did seem stressed, but not on the verge of a breakdown as Olive had claimed.

It would be a considerable stretch to consider Kirby handsome, but somehow he managed to exude charm and even sensuality through his facial expressions and physical mannerisms. And the eyes she had found so washed-out and bland, were somehow captivating.

He was an odd man, she concluded, maybe even interesting. But was he also a killer?

She asked, "What motive do the police think you have?"

Kirby smiled again, this time accompanied with an ironic chuckle. "A million bucks."

"You find that amusing?"

"Damn straight." he answered. "You see, I wouldn't have gotten that stupid insurance policy if Lana and my mother hadn't insisted."

She nodded.

"My wife didn't work, as you probably know. So it made sense I have life insurance. But mother insisted Lana should have insurance too. Stuff about women's value in today's world being as much as a man's. And Lana agreed." He scoffed lightly. "It didn't make sense to me in that Lana didn't work. But mother and Lana ganged up on me. I got the policy to please them." He raised his eyebrows and waved his arms in a sarcastic motion directed at the "grandeur" of his current surroundings. "Now look where I am. And the damn policy cost me a bundle on top of it."

"You pleaded not guilty, right?"

"Yep." He lowered his voice to a whisper. "But my hotshot lawyer wants to change to temporary insanity. Can you believe that? He's the one that's insane. I told him in no uncertain terms I'm not spending the rest of my days in a loony-bin for something I didn't do."

"Anything else you can think of that can help me find out who killed your wife?"

"Well, there *is* something that's been bothering me. But when I mention it to Senator he ignores me. It's the ring. Mother's ring. A gigantic fake ruby in an antique-gold setting. The darned thing goes back three or four generations I think. Mother gave it to me and I gave it to Lana. She seldom took it off. Well, the ring wasn't on Lana's body and the police can't find it in our house."

"You think your wife's murder was a robbery gone bad?" Belinda made a mental note to find out if the ME found bruising on Lana's ring finger.

"I don't know what I think, but it is curious. What the hell happened to the ring? And why take the ring and leave the money? Doesn't make any sense. It should prove to the cops it wasn't me. But they aren't listening."

"What money?"

"My wife never left the house without at least a hundred bucks on her. It was a thing with her."

"Even on her walks?"

"Yep, carried it in her shoe. Senator said the ME found two one-hundred dollar bills still in her right shoe."

Belinda next asked Kirby to go over his movements the morning Lana was killed. She watched him closely as he laid out his activities and couldn't detect any telltale eye blinking or lip moistening--an interview observation tip passed her way by Cedar Valley's Sheriff, her Uncle John Thomas.

Kirby told Belinda he'd gotten up at 5:30 A.M., before his wife. "I didn't even kiss her goodbye." He also told Belinda he'd gotten ready for work and left at 6 A.M., turning the hot water kettle on as he left.

"Lana always needed a cup of coffee to get her going before her walk. She brewed it in a French-press and liked it strong."

He arrived at his office around 6:30 A.M., he further explained. "Not sure on that time exactly because I stopped at the twenty-four-hour Safeway in North Bend and got a cup of S&B for myself before heading into Bellevue. And I didn't check the clock when I got to work."

Once at his office he remembered getting his notes and briefcase together; he was heading into Seattle for an auditor's association meeting. At the meeting, his group ate breakfast, there was some association business to conduct, then they had a guest speaker with a presentation and a film. The whole meeting went from 7:00 A.M. to around 10:00 A.M. He arrived back at his Bellevue office around 10:30 A.M. and one of the first things he did was call his mom.

"She stays there on the property with us, but she has her own separate living quarters. Morning ritual, you see, she likes me to check in on her."

"Daily?" Belinda hoped her voice was neutral. *But really.* Every morning? Lana was right there on the property. Why couldn't *she* make sure her mother-in-law was okay?

"Yep," Kirby responded, seemingly unperturbed. "Then the police called me around one in the afternoon, and maybe fifteen minutes later they came to my office to tell me in person Lana was dead."

"I gather there are people who can substantiate your alibi."

"Every minute. Even in the car. I carpooled to the meeting with a colleague."

"What did your wife usually do to fill her time?" If Kirby didn't kill his wife, somewhere in the details of Lana's life was a motive for murder. Who though? And why?

"She took exercise classes somewhere. Don't know anything else. As I told you, our lives were starting to go in different directions."

"Anything else I should know?"

He hesitated a second before answering. "No," he eventually said.

It was obvious Kirby wasn't telling her everything, but she would push him later--if there was a later.

"Nope, nothing at all," he restated. "You see, I didn't do it. And that's the truth."

After she left and stepped out into a glorious summer afternoon in Seattle, Belinda welcomed the fresh air and freedom. It felt so good to be back outside.

She could almost taste the sensation.

On her way home to Cedar Valley, about forty minutes east from Seattle, Belinda had time to think. She found it a pleasant drive; Interstate 90 was wide, and the lower Cascade scenery winding up toward Snoqualmie Pass was spectacular in spots--trees and hills, hills and trees--and not a billboard for miles. It was an easy stretch during the daytime and on dry pavement to put her body on auto-pilot and ponder life, love, and murderers.

Belinda needed the time out; she was tired. Her interview with Kirby was the culmination of what now felt like an exceedingly long morning and afternoon.

After her meeting with Olive earlier, Belinda had returned to the office and worked the rest of the morning trying to get the supply list together. It took forever because her thoughts kept bouncing back and forth between the thefts and her upcoming meeting with Kirby. Finally, she gave up on completing her list and went down to an early lunch.

Bernard and Martha had prepared salmon croquettes with a cayenne pepper sauce, baked miniature red potatoes tossed in herbed olive oil, and endive salad sprinkled with Gorgonzola cheese. Some of her favorites.

Not wanting to deal with Phoebe, Vera, Anna and Morris, Belinda ate alone at a back table near the kitchen. In particular, she didn't want to hear anything more about items gone missing. Kaitlin, thank goodness, wasn't anywhere in sight.

Morris LeBeau, however, came over to her table for a couple moments, and in his best southern gentleman style asked if she might allow him a couple minutes of her time later that evening. They agreed upon 9:00 P.M. after Bridge, in the office.

After talking to Morris, she reluctantly, yet resolutely passed on dessert--peach cobbler with home-churned vanilla bean ice cream.

She then went to her suite, grabbed her canvas bag, and headed out to downtown Seattle and King County Jail for her meeting with Kirby.

Now, long hours later, as Belinda drove back to Cedar Valley, her mind sorting through the day's happenings, again flitting between concern for Kirby and thefts at the Residence, she desperately wished for cobbler and prayed Martha had leftovers.

As she passed the Highway 18 exit, about halfway home, Belinda finally decided she would take on the Lana Norris investigation for Olive. She knew it was a big decision and a big challenge.

She also knew she was scared. Perversely and inexplicably scared of taking on this case now that she'd started, and most importantly, scared of failing.

But Kirby, she now felt, was innocent.

And though tired as she was, with that decision about Kirby behind her, Belinda smiled to herself and tried to enjoy the scenery.

When Belinda arrived back home, she found Bernard in his suite, fully dressed, stretched across the bed sleeping. Buster was beside him crunched against his back, also asleep and snoring gently.

She glanced at his bedside clock, 3:15 P.M. Most days, somewhere between three and four Bernard took a twenty-minute power nap before the evening crowd. Dinner was their biggest meal of the day for both resident and walk-in attendance, and he liked to be what he called "fresh and revitalized."

It was amazing to her how he could sleep for such a short time and wake up ready to go. Her naps were never shorter than two hours, and often produced a sluggishness she had a hard time shaking off. Despite that risk, she decided to likewise indulge in a nap and headed to her own bed. She would set her clock to keep it short. Once in her suite, Belinda found Naja had started without her, in the middle of the bed, on her back, legs in the air, also snoring.

After her nap, when Belinda eventually went down to dinner, Phoebe was waiting for her just outside The Cedars' arched French doors. Near the end of their renovation, Belinda and Bernard had felt the doors, twelve feet in height and extremely pricey, were necessary to accompany and accentuate the dining room ceiling. The glass-lights in the doors were etched with simple *fleur-de-lis* done by their cousin Tessa.

"Do you have a minute, Belinda?" Phoebe touched her lightly on the arm. "I just wanted a word in private before I go upstairs and freshen up. Tonight's bridge," she fluttered. "But you know that. Why am I rambling on?"

"Of course I have time for you, Phoebe. Is there a problem?"

"You know, I just hate doing this. I'm not the kind of person who likes to start trouble, and it isn't valuable, but it's such a treasured keepsake."

Oh no, Belinda prepared herself. "What…"

"It's my brooch. You know the one with the cameo, the one you so admired at Vera's birthday party?"

"Yes, I remember it."

Phoebe took a deep breath and with a pained expression continued, "It will break Vera's heart to find out her great-granddaughter is a thief. But I just don't know who else it could be. Young people these days."

"It's gone missing?" Belinda wanted to make sure she understood Phoebe.

"I can't find it anywhere. I know I'm scatterbrained sometimes, but I tell you, Belinda, I'm sure I left it on my night table last night. I keep it in a nice velvet sachet. Wouldn't want to scratch the cameo. It's so pretty I think." Her eyes watered over for a second. "It's one of the few things I kept from the past when I moved here...after George passed on."

Belinda had heard the story many times of Phoebe and George Farmer, sweethearts since college, married forty years. He had passed away a year ago due to complications of lung cancer.

"I'll do everything I can to get to the bottom of these disappearances." Belinda took Phoebe's trembling hands into hers. "Don't you worry. Bernard and I are going to make these thefts our number one priority." She spoke with unjustifiable bravado, but Phoebe looked so pathetic. Even her springy blond curls seemed to have plopped with the loss of her brooch.

Belinda watched Phoebe ascend the stairs. Probably going for a good cry, she guessed.

When Belinda entered the dining room, she saw Vera and Kaitlin sitting at a table near the door and the front windows. Patrick was just leaving their table, a pile of dirty dishes on his tray. He smiled at her and hurried on back to the kitchen. Belinda returned his smile--he must have won the toss tonight. She was aware Patrick and MaryAnn had an ongoing ritual of flipping a quarter to see who bussed, and who washed dishes--dishes being the more onerous of the two tasks.

Vera waved her hand daintily and with a nod indicated she would like Belinda to stop and talk. Kaitlin was slumped in her chair, a pout engraved across her face.

It was still a tad early for dinner, and other than Belinda, Vera, and Kaitlin, the dining room was empty.

"Good evening, Vera, Kaitlin." It had taken a much longer time than with Phoebe for Belinda to break through the "Mrs. Dr. James Price" barrier; but now they were also on a first name basis. "Nice to have daylight so late. Summer."

"Yes it is. In fact I'm planning on a little stroll with Morris and Anna before bridge." She added, "Not on the trail of course."

"And wise not to go alone, Vera," Belinda agreed. If

Kirby hadn't killed his wife, there could still be a maniac on the loose.

This evening Vera wore a two piece heather-green suit and a cream blouse that she must have purchased in the fifties. Of course they were in pristine condition. "Well maintained," Bernard called the look. And as usual not a piece of silver-white hair dared to stray.

"I know you're here for your dinner, so I won't keep you. But I needed a word with you while the others aren't around."

Belinda assumed the *others* were Phoebe, Morris, and Anna. Her other two residents, Theresa Bacera and Janice Tanner were younger and weren't part of their Bridge group.

"We seem to have the place to ourselves." Belinda sat down next to Vera and across from Kaitlin. "Nice to see you, Kaitlin," she added with a smile. *Soon, even Kaitlin will get older,* she reminded herself.

Kaitlin managed a grunt in return. The pout lingered.

"I'm afraid Kaitlin is not happy with me," Vera began. "You see, Belinda, I know they think she's stealing their keepsakes." Seeing Belinda was about to speak, Vera held up her hand. "No dear, you don't have to soften the blow. And who can blame them?" She eyed her great-granddaughter with dismay. "The way she dresses, hardly ever talking..."

Kaitlin interrupted, "I ain't nicked any doodads."

Too much BBC Belinda conjectured.

"Why should I?" Kaitlin further defended herself. "My dad gives me plenty money to get whatever I want."

Vera sighed. "That's exactly the problem, Kaitlin dear, and that's exactly why you're here spending your summer with your great-grandmother instead of on the Riviera with your sister. Your parents have finally realized what excess is doing to you."

"I haven't stolen anything." Kaitlin said loudly and jumped up from her chair, almost knocking it to the ground. "And Lila's a jerk!" With that indictment against her sister, Kaitlin ran toward the foyer and presumably upstairs to their suite.

"You're excused, Kaitlin," Vera said to her great-granddaughter's retreating back. "You know she's a math genius. She gets straight A's, always has. Never see her study. That's why her parents indulge her so much." Vera exhaled a tiny and dignified whiff. "She's also in line for several scholarships. She's studying British culture as part of a summer project. That's why the linguistic affectations. One minute it's cockney, next minute Oxford educated upper-crust toff."

Belinda glanced outside, her thoughts however, remained on Kaitlin's behavior. *Nothing is ever black or white.* So easy to put Kaitlin in a box--self-indulged spoiled brat--but that type usually didn't get good grades and scholarships.

"But beyond all her bad behavior," Vera continued, "I don't think she's stealing things. It just doesn't fit with her personality. Of course she could be a kleptomaniac, but I really doubt that."

Belinda frowned, shook her head, and shrugged. She knew very little about teenagers in general, and nothing about Kaitlin in particular.

"I don't want to point the finger," Vera said. "But I ask you, Belinda, how much do you really know about the young woman Theresa Bacera? She's seemingly a lovely young lady but there's something odd about her comings and goings, don't you think?" She leaned across the table conspiratorially, "I saw her in town once talking to some ruffians."

"Ruffians?" Belinda hadn't heard that word since Grandmother Glory had admonished her about "fraternizing" with public school "ruffians." Because of that snobbery on Glory's part, she and Bernard had been sent to private schools through college.

"Scruffy looking men, you know."

"Homeless maybe?" Belinda suggested.

"Well, more like members of the criminal class." She gave Belinda a knowing look.

Belinda wasn't certain what Vera meant exactly, but it sounded unkind. However, she would let it ride for she liked Vera and recognized the generation from which she came. If dirty homeless men scared her, she could understand that.

Further, Belinda also refrained from pointing out to Vera that Theresa herself had been victimized.

*   *   *   *   *

After dinner Belinda was able to get in an hour or so of sorely needed office time, during which she completed the supply list except for a quick check of the communal room. Their second floor comprised seven single suites, two doubles (the LeBeaus' and one vacant), the office, and a common room that contained limited kitchen amenities, laundry facilities, and resident storage compartments.

Pleasing to Belinda, Naja kept her company from after dinner on, dogging her steps from the dining hall to her suite to freshen up, and then back to the office.

After another half hour or so, Buster hesitantly joined them. When he first stuck his head in the door Naja growled him off. Finally, after encouragement from Belinda, he screwed up his nerve and slinked in, head and ears down, tail between his legs.

"Come on Buster-buddy," Belinda coddled. "Naja just thinks she's queen of the pack. It's okay." After a few minutes he laid down under the desk at Belinda's feet and took his after-dinner nap.

To Naja, Belinda admonished, "You know Buster's a sweet dog. You're going to have to accept him sooner or later."

Her anthropomorphic interpretation of Naja's return look was, *"That's what you think."*

Belinda remembered it had been the same at first with Miss Kitty, the LeBeau's calico. But after a couple weeks, and after a lot of watchfulness and cajoling from her and Morris, both feline and canine had come to terms.

A tap on the open office door stopped Belinda from heading down to the common room to finish her supply list.

"Do you have a moment now?" It was Morris LeBeau, and he didn't look happy. His signature and perpetual aroma of Mixture 79, the only tobacco aroma Belinda actually liked, proceeded him.

"Sure, Morris, come in. Are you alright?"

He dropped heavily into the armchair opposite Naja like

a defeated giant of a man. Morris was actually of medium build,
spry for eighty, and usually had a suave ladies-man charm. It
was as if he had metamorphosed into a different person.

Morris and Anna were both from rural Louisiana bayou
communities and had known each other from high school.
Morris told Belinda their marriage in those days was unusual for
members of such closed communities hell-bent on retaining their
ethnic identities. He claimed Creole heritage and she claimed
Cajun. The difference, he had explained to Belinda and Bernard
one rainy winter afternoon over snifters of brandy in the parlor,
was mainly where your French ancestors came from--France
or Canada. And then there was Spanish, Indian, and African
intermarriage to be accounted for.

"But," he had thoughtfully added, "that was a long time
ago. Times and people have changed. Now there's even Zydeco
music which combines Cajun and Creole influences with some
Caribbean and Blues rhythms thrown into the mix."

Except for a few Bach and Vivaldi concertos, Belinda
was not musically inclined or sophisticated. "Tin ear," Glory
had called it. But Belinda remembered that evening well
because Morris had been so ebullient, full of life and himself,
eagerly spouting off about his heritage. While this evening, his
skin looked lackluster, and his usual twinkling eyes--he was an
incessant flirt--were dull and lifeless.

"I've been putting off facing up to what I have to tell
you," he said. "But I can't stall any longer." A flicker of the
octogenarian's teasing manner resurfaced for a second. "This
is our secret. Can't let Anna know." Then with a heavy sigh he
was back to the task at hand. "I can't put off telling her much
longer, though. I just hate breaking her heart like this."

He looked close to tears. "Morris," Belinda said quietly
as she got up from her desk, came over and sat in the chair next
to him--pushing Naja out in the process--and took Morris's
hands into hers. "Whatever you have to tell me can't be that
terrible? Can it?"

Oh my God--one of them must have cancer!

He responded by squeezing her hands in return, and
holding them tight. "Promise me you won't tell Anna. It will
be our secret. I'll tell her when the time is right. She has always

counted on me, you see."

"I promise," Belinda whispered.

Morris released his grip on Belinda, exhaled and flopped back into the recesses of Grandfather Jones' well-worn armchair. "My pension fund has collapsed. You know they're indicting..." He mentioned an investment corporation CEO Belinda had heard about on the business news channel. "His company managed our pension. The money is gone. Everybody's suing of course, but we know what that means. Lawyers will make a killing and Anna and I will get very little if any of our investment back."

Belinda held her breath, waiting for what she feared was coming next.

"And," he continued, "the union at the company I used to work for negotiated away our retiree medical insurance."

"Can they do that?"

"I don't know, but they *did.*" He spread his hands, palms up. "I guess there will be another class action suit. Again, we know where that will lead."

This should not be happening to Morris and Anna--not at this point in their lives.

"You have Social Security, right?" As if Social Security would pay Cedar Valley Residence room and board.

"I'm afraid, Belinda, next month will probably be our last. We've enjoyed living here..." his voice cracked and he stood. Then quickly pulling himself together, Morris seemed taller, more chipper, like his old self--one heavy burden accomplished. He still had to tell Anna.

"By the way Belinda, my pipe, you know the one with the diamond inlay on the stem and meerschaum bowl? Well, it's the strangest thing. It seems to have gone missing since this morning. You will keep your eye out, won't you?"

He turned to leave, then turned back to Belinda. "And, Anna thinks she left her keys in the parlor. You know the ones with the little leather fob?"

Belinda nodded that she did.

"They aren't there now. We're guessing the cleaning service picked them up."

"I'll call and ask them," Belinda offered--knowing full

well if their weekly cleaning service had found Anna's keys, they would have already turned them over to her.

Belinda sat quietly for awhile, wondering what the heck was next? *What* next was the telephone rang--requiring Belinda to leave the padded comfort and emotional security of Grandmother Glory's armchair and return to the desk.

It was their cousin, Tessa Harrington.

As she hung up with Tessa, Bernard--looking quite worn out--dragged in and flopped in the chair Morris had just vacated. Naja, who had sulked out of the room, now returned with Bernard and reclaimed her rightful throne.

"Long day, huh? For both of us," Belinda said sitting back down behind their desk.

He explained ten or so diners had come in late, ordered full course meals, and lingered over coffee and desert. Consequently, Patrick and MaryAnn had had to leave before they were able to completely clean the dining room and kitchen. Martha was taking a few hours off now, like him; but both would be back in the kitchen later to prep for morning breakfast and make sure the tables were set.

"Are you going to help Kirby?" he asked anxiously and without preface.

"Yes." She watched his smile return. It pleased Belinda she could give her brother *that* good news at least--one less worry for him to fret over in the wee morning hours.

She hated bringing him the accompanying *bad* news. Nonetheless, he needed to know. "Looks like Morris and Anna are leaving too."

"Oh jeez. How come?"

"Lost his pension."

"That's awful."

"Yeah, but take care what you say. Anna doesn't know yet."

Bernard nodded.

They fell silent for a moment as Belinda looked around for an animal count. Only seeing Naja she asked, "Buster was just here; did you see him leave? Is he doing okay now? No more walkabouts?"

"Oh yeah, he's doing fine. He probably headed to the pantry to snooze in peace."

How nice to be able to go hide away in your own dark and comfy little dog house. Lucky Buster.

Belinda was tired, disappointed, excited, and eager-- all at the same time. It had been a long day for her also, and it wasn't yet ten, her usual bedtime.

"You must be really tired." She smiled at Bernard fondly. "You were in my room with the dawn this morning."

"I am tired," he admitted. "Do you still think we should go ahead with the addition now that Morris is also leaving?"

"That's the same thing you asked me this morning. Except for the Morris part." *Eons ago.* Quickly she changed the subject--too tired to deal with money decisions. Maybe in the morning. "Did I say yet that Tessa called?"

Bernard rolled his eyes comically. "No, you didn't. So what's the latest L.A. suburban crisis? Did one of her 'movie industry' friends go on a new diet? Oh. Oh. I know." He was being tired-silly and enjoying it immensely. "One of Gavin's buddies missed a cocktail party!?"

"You know Gavin has done well for himself and his family," Belinda admonished ever so lightly. She and Bernard were of the same mind when it came to Gavin Harrington. "She's coming for a visit."

"What? Did you say Tessa's coming for a visit?"

"Yep."

"When?"

"Wednesday morning."

Bernard jumped up. "That's day after tomorrow-Wednesday, right? We've got to get the vacant suite ready, and order some fresh flowers, and I need to make sure we have avocados, you know how she loves them...."

Bernard continued talking to himself all the way down to the kitchen, only stopping once in the front entrance to say goodnight to Theresa, who was leaving, dressed in black from her cap to her toes.

He barely noticed.

Martha Milton had returned to the kitchen from her suite in back. She loved her arrangement at Cedar Valley Residence. It was perfect. At least for now.

Buster had indeed come back downstairs but he was lying in the pantry doorway, not his doghouse. She now realized Buster had come to believe the pantry was the source of all goodness--warmth, safety, his doghouse, his dog food, and his treats. She was glad.

She collected ingredients from the pantry, stepping over Buster in the process, and brought them to her prep table. Then she started mixing dough--by hand--in her favorite giant stainless steel bowl.

"I think this will be a rich roll dough." She liked the solitude of her kitchen. It was home, and a friend.

Now in her mid-forties, Martha had graduated from The University of Washington School of business with an MBA at twenty-three, then opened a financial advisory business in Bellevue--a business she and some very smart employees turned into an extremely lucrative enterprise in a span of five years.

Problem was, she eventually realized, most of her staff had worked sixty-plus hours a week and lived and breathed stocks or clients from their first waking moment into their dream-time at night. It had been all-consuming.

Thinking about those past times prompted her to inform her kitchen and Buster, "God, am I glad I'm here."

And for a moment, Martha allowed her mind to wander back to that spring morning when she decided she'd had enough--and within two months sold the whole business to several of her former employees. Within another week, she had enrolled in the California Culinary Academy in San Francisco, and in thirty weeks earned a Bakery and Pastry Arts Certificate.

And to her relief and delightful surprise, she loved cooking, especially pastry.

Her certificate had led to jobs in L.A. and Vegas restaurants. Luckily, each job-change was to a better and grander establishment. But the pace, the personalities, the long hours, the stress--again it all became too much. Martha succumbed to what her friends dubbed a "nervous breakdown." Remembering caused her to shudder, and in turn, Buster to look at her anxiously. For two years she was in limbo, then four years ago, she, Bernard, and Belinda hooked up, and the rest, as the *cliché* goes, is ancient history. *Thank God.*

She was kneading dough when Bernard joined her in the kitchen and grabbed a clean chef's jacket from the linen rack by the door.

"One day we're going to get caught," he said while pulling up a stool at her pastry table and inclining his head toward Buster. "Thank God all the residents love animals, but if a stranger--"

"Isn't that former chef friend of yours still letting you know when the inspectors are coming?" Martha was not ignorant or stupid when it came to health department regulations, but she was not overly worried. She even had a hunch the current inspector, who had five cats herself, knew about Buster coming into the kitchen, but was letting them slide by. "But maybe you're right. I figure I can shoo him back into my suite if we get surprised."

"Bread or pizza dough?"

"Bread for tomorrow's dinner rolls," she answered.

"Well, did Belinda take the case?" She had followed Lana Norris' murder from the very beginning; and on first seeing Kirby's picture in the newspaper had emphatically declared, "He didn't do it."

"Yep, she talked to Olive and Kirby Norris today." He pulled his checklist for tomorrow's ingredients out of his shirt pocket. "Where's the other pantry cart?"

Martha pointed to a spot between the two refrigerators. "I rearranged a bit so we'll stop banging those doors together. Now they don't hit each other and there's a nice little spot for the carts."

"Olive was actually here at the Residence today. Did

you see her? The purple woman?"

"No, I missed that," she said, laughing. "I gather you mean she was dressed in purple."

He tsk'd at her frivolity. "I think she really loves her kid and is willing to sell everything she's got to help him."

"He's not actually a kid." Martha covered the dough with a towel so it could rest and pulled up a stool across the table from Bernard. "Belinda is going to charge Mrs. Norris, a fee, right?"

Bernard shrugged. "I hope so. We need the money." He proceeded to tell her about Morris, Anna, and Miss Shirley leaving.

"Damn." This was terribly bad news. Maybe she could help somehow? "You want a glass of wine?"

He nodded.

Martha cooled all her wines, red and white. She took opened bottles of Beaujolais and Tawny Port, Bernard's favorite, out of the refrigerator. One of the things she liked about Bernard was his lack of wine snobbery.

If any Beaujolais remained after tonight, she would use it in a reduced wine sauce for the stuffed mushrooms on tomorrow's luncheon menu. She was thrifty in that way, and wanted little waste in their kitchen.

Martha also placed a plate of leftover sliced cheese on the table between them. "Well," she said after a generous sip of wine and lifting her glass in a toast, "here's to Belinda figuring everything out. And soon."

Bernard poured himself a scant couple ounces of Tawny Port. "I'll drink to that." He raised his glass to hers.

Martha knew that for both of them, it was a pleasant moment in a long day, and she stared thoughtfully at her Beaujolais, its rich ruby tranquility beckoning her mind to wander again from kitchen tasks. "Have you noticed Janice Tanner seldom comes to meals here? She pays for board right? But she doesn't use it."

"No mystery there, I think she works very long hours. Someone," Bernard looked to the ceiling, "I can't remember if it was Phoebe or Vera, told me she works odd shifts."

"And Theresa?" Martha had also noticed her odd

hours of departure and arrival. "Does she work a night shift or something?"

"Possible. But she claims she has an independent income--whatever that means."

"Well, I think she has a secret lover and they sneak off to a little mountain *pied-à-terre* when they get a chance. Maybe up at Snoqualmie Pass." The thought appealed to her romantic side.

Bernard's eyes widened in amazement. "That's exactly what I told Belinda."

"Do you think that Kaitlin child is actually going around stealing our resident's possessions?" Martha, like Belinda and Bernard, didn't have any children and also found Kaitlin's behavior mystifying. "It would be so easy for her to get caught," she said. "Although," she handed Buster a piece of cheese under the table. "I don't think she's a dumb-bunny. I'm guessing a lot of the 'Goth' stuff is camouflage to keep from getting hassled."

"Camouflage," he said, mulling the word over out-loud. "What?"

"Oh nothing. Did I mention cousin Tessa is coming to visit?"

"When?"

"Day after tomorrow."

"Not a problem." Martha finished her wine with a quick last swallow; she needed to finish her dough and prep for breakfast before calling it a night. "It's so terrible when you really think about it."

"You're talking about Lana, right?"

"The poor woman is taking her dog for a walk in the morning--who knows what she was thinking about. Maybe what she was going to have for breakfast. Maybe planning a vacation. Maybe thinking about her husband." She shuddered. "Bernard, it's just too terrible. Your life snatched away from you like that. And she was a young woman, well, our age at most."

"Yeah, I know." Bernard also finished his wine. "If Kirby didn't kill his wife, and I'm sure he didn't," he said, and looked meaningfully at Martha. "Then, there's still a murderer running around Cedar Valley."

Martha shuddered again and mentally prayed Belinda

would figure out who had killed Lana Norris. She also returned to her earlier thought of somehow helping on some front--either catching a murderer, or catching a thief.

No, she couldn't just stand by and let the residence fail.

It was a clear black sky that night, and to the naked eye, the stars twinkled like a sparkling evening ocean. Up in her room Belinda took a moment before climbing under the covers to sit on her window seat and stargaze. Naja jumped up next to her and uncharacteristically also gazed toward the heavens.

"The world doesn't look as good as it did this morning, does it, Naja-girl?"

Naja's eyes glistened with apparent interest, encouraging Belinda to continue her woman-to-dog conversation. "I so want to help Kirby, and Bernard is so confident I can. But I'm not sure I'm actually capable of figuring out who murdered Lana Norris. Or dredging up any evidence Senator can use to establish 'reasonable doubt.' Maybe I'm just kidding myself."

Of course Naja couldn't answer, but Belinda could indeed still hear Glory Jones' voice across the years as she had admonished a tentative teenage Belinda, *Self doubt, my Dear, is like a garden weed. Snatch it out, or it'll take over.*

Smart words, brave words,

So easy to say.

But not so easy to do.

Cedar Valley nights were cold, no matter the season.

Phillip "Philly" Towers didn't mind chilly temperatures. In fact, the cool night dampness invigorated him. Made him feel alive, confident he could take care of himself. If he could survive on his own under the trees and stars, rain or shine, well, that said he wasn't so dumb, now was he? Not everyone could make it living rough like he did.

Sure, group homes had been okay, but there was

always someone telling you what to do. Like you were stupid or something. Sometimes even telling you you're crazy, just because your eyes are different colors. Couldn't help that, now could he? And the rules--they were endless. He liked his hair long, and why shave anyway? Even his dad had told him a beard made a man. Nope, being out on your own--that was the ticket.

Tonight Philly was excited. So excited he arrived early at the Tanner Road Trailhead. No one came here at night and it was one of his favorite spots. A man could be alone with his thoughts. Just the occasional stray dog and he usually had some scrap handouts ready to appease.

All that, though, was about to change. Philly had seen something important; and a very special and nice person was going to reward him for that. Tonight, here, and in just a few minutes.

He had had a nice dinner at St. Francis. Monday evening was spaghetti night and they always made him welcome even though he couldn't pay. Then the night manager at Glenn's truck stop had let him use a shower. A good day and evening so far, and things were about to get even better.

He'd had a few drinks, of course, it always helped to have a few drinks, even though he wasn't supposed to with his medications. But he never saw how just a few nips hurt anything. Besides, the liquor mellowed him out and his benefactor had given it to him free.

When his benefactor finally arrived at Philly's special Tanner Road spot, his new friend also brought Philly a nice warm thermos of hot chocolate. Oh yeah, there was a little brandy in it, Philly could taste it. What harm was a little brandy? Besides, they were celebrating Philly's new-found wealth--lots of nice green money for keeping his mouth shut. It was a special night.

So, when the blow smashed the back of his skull, Philly was almost asleep, dreaming of buying a brand new sleeping bag. He'd never had a new one, and he was imagining how it might smell and feel.

CHAPTER TWO

Tuesday

Belinda came down to breakfast early because her night had been so rotten--and consequently she was at the right place at the right time to bring in the morning newspapers.

Gordy James delivered them between 4:30 and 5:00 A.M. every morning--fifteen copies in a plastic wrapper bound with a convenient little bow-knot that slipped loose with the tiniest of tugs. It wasn't a large bundle; the Cedar Valley Dispatch struggled daily to fill its meager five pages.

Belinda loved the service Gordy gave--old fashioned competence and reliability.

Over time, she had found out he was a retired school teacher and delivering the Cedar Valley Dispatch perfectly suited his new artisan lifestyle (woodturning); and the added income nicely augmented his pension. He and his wife Dorothea (Thea to everyone) had lived in Cedar Valley all their lives.

Indeed, Belinda occasionally envisioned Gordy stealthily leaving their stack of papers on the porch at the foot of the planter by the front door in that ethereal gray time betwixt the blackness of night, and the glow of a new day. Inexplicably, it was an image she found oddly romantic.

The planter was a convenient spot too. For the house rule was, whoever passed the front entrance first: brought in the newspapers, untied them, took them out of the plastic, and then placed them on the reception desk.

Another big plus for her and Bernard was that Gordy and Thea were experts on Valley history and politics, including who did what to whom, when, how, and why; and all the information and advice Gordy and Thea had given them had been very helpful, especially in the early days.

Even now, Gordy and Thea were frequent diners at the residence, and were easily enticed to talk about "the old days" and give continued advice. Both were in their sixties, with rounded bodies and white hair; and beginning to look very much like each other as some longtime couples do.

As Belinda picked up this morning's papers, for some odd reason she recalled one such piece of advice, offered numerous times by Gordy. "Make sure you stay away from County Inspectors. I'm telling ya', they'll drive you crazy and send ya' to the poor house. Do it right, but do it alone." Belinda was sure if they went ahead with their addition, Devlin Stephens would be the one dealing with County Inspectors. If not Devlin, the general contractor. So she wondered for a second why the remembrance popped in her head.

Maybe her mind just hadn't cleared from last night's sporadic dreams about Lana's dying moments? Belinda knew she was probably reaching for a "rational straw" to explain this morning's seemingly haphazard thoughts and images.

Besides the dreams, Naja and Miss Kitty had hogged most of the bed, leaving her to wake up stiff, out of sorts, and sad. Why Miss Kitty would want to leave the comfort of the LeBeau's suite was unfathomable.

A quick shower helped, but hadn't cured.

Belinda also hadn't been able to shake a disconcerting and uncomfortable feeling she found difficult to articulate--but nonetheless quite real in its impact. An awareness somewhere through one of her senses--which she also couldn't identify--that something terribly wrong had happened during the night. In response, she had immediately and instinctively desired a pot of tea for succor.

With that goal in mind she had dressed quickly in loose blue cotton slacks and a long-sleeved and high-necked blue shirt. After her ragged night, the feel and smell of soft freshly laundered cotton was a minor but pleasant comfort.

And her current trademark loose fitting "cotton casual" usually flattered her lean body. This morning, however, Belinda's world was a-tilt, and dressed as she was, her appearance put one in mind of a scarecrow.

As she now placed the newspapers on the corner of their stalwart faux Edwardian desk--also their foyer guardian and reception counter--Tuesday's headline stopped Belinda in mid-action, one hand undoing Gordy's bow-knot, and the other holding the papers.

Phillip 'Philly' Towers was dead.

She grabbed the top newspaper and hurried into the dining room on her way to the kitchen, almost passing through the still vacant Cedars in a blur. But she stopped for a moment, and a piece of Belinda's psyche "looked" outside through The Cedars' large bay windows--and in that blink of time, she fancied night lingered a few seconds longer than physical concepts dictated before its inevitable fade into dawn.

An infinitesimal salute from the fabric of time to acknowledge Philly's passage?

Belinda doubted the truth of her fanciful and impossible perception. But it was a unique experience--quite comforting-- and held her for several mesmerizing moments.

In the kitchen, Belinda found Martha, up for hours she guessed, fully clad in chef-whites, and preparing for breakfast.

Martha was putting freshly shaped cinnamon buns in a pan, but stopped long enough to give Belinda a quick glance. "You look awful."

"Thanks for the complement. Must be the hair."

A wisecrack, but in truth, Belinda was aware her curly crown *did* look frazzled and wild--probably intensifying her scarecrow imagery.

"I didn't sleep well," Belinda explained. "For some bizarre feline reason Miss Kitty decided to bunk with me again instead of with her owners. And then Naja..." she let her thought and words evaporate with a weary sigh. It wasn't important.

Philly's death--now that was important.

Martha gave Belinda a more scrutinizing once-over before gilding her cinnamon creation with a generous sprinkling of raw Turbinado cane-sugar.

Belinda usually enjoyed their bantering repartee. She felt their personalities complemented each other, with Martha often providing a calming influence. This morning's exchange felt a little off.

If I could just go back a day. But she couldn't. A man had just died and there was no way she could make it not true. She pulled up a stool across from Martha, put the newspaper on the worktable, and turned it around so Martha could read the headline. "Look at this." Martha wiped her hands on the white kitchen towel hanging from her waist and read the headline out-loud, "Local Vagabond Found Dead." Then she read on to the text:

"Phillip Towers, known to many in Cedar Valley as 'Philly', was found dead at Tanner Road Trailhead at around midnight by the county street cleaning crew."

"Oh, no." Her eyes moist, Martha looked up from the newspaper and brought a hand to her mouth. "That was just last night. They barely had time to get it in the paper."

"Yeah." *Just last night.* Belinda had heard of Pieta, the paper's night-reporter. Her reputation as a diligent miracle-worker with printing deadlines was legendary among old-timers like Gordy and Thea. A reputation evidently well deserved.

Martha said, "The poor man. He was so damn nice. You know I gave him food at least a couple times a week. He wasn't a bother, not really, and he didn't come by that often…" She returned to reading:

"As yet the police have not issued a formal statement; and Sheriff John Thomas stated last night that it was too early to speculate on cause of death."

Martha's tone was speculative, "I'm guessing from the words he used, John thinks Philly was murdered, doesn't he? If it was an accident, he would have just said that, wouldn't he?" She looked to Belinda. "Is there anything you can do? That's two deaths right here on our little trail. *Two deaths.*"

"Yes. Two *murders.*" From the moment Belinda had read the headline, she had someway *known* Philly's death was connected to Lana's murder.

"Why do you say murder? That's what I think too, but

do you know something in particular?"

"My gut *knows*. My mind will just have to catch up."
There was no way she could explain to Martha the feeling she
was experiencing right then. Nevertheless, Belinda was sure,
without a doubt, and without any further knowledge, Philly had
been murdered. Murdered because he knew something about
Lana's death.

For her *sous-chef's* benefit, Belinda added, "This is
terrible. I need to figure out what I should do. Is it okay if I fix
myself a pot of tea and an English muffin? I don't want to get
in your way. And do we still have some of Thea's jam?" Thea
James always made sure Martha and Belinda received a few jars
when she got in the "canning zone."

"No problem, stick a muffin in for me too will ya?"
Martha went back to work and removed a cantaloupe and a
small watermelon from the refrigerator. "So you believe Kirby
is innocent and the murderer is still out there killing people?
Killing Philly?" Her face betrayed her actual emotional state;
and quickly, Martha brushed away a tear before starting to cut
melon wedges for breakfast garnishes.

"Yep."

"Are you still going ahead with the addition?"

Belinda was relieved at Martha's abrupt change of
subject. Philly's death was just too damn sad.

"You sure are full of questions this morning. Bernie
must have told you that Morris, Anna, and Miss Shirley might
have to leave." She had yet to get up and start the muffin
process.

"Yeah, *Bernard* told me last night." Belinda's slip-of-the-
tongue use of "Bernie" didn't pass by Martha unnoticed.

Belinda smiled despite her sadness. "He's sort of silly
with the name stuff, isn't he?"

"Why doesn't he like 'Bernie'?"

"Bernard was named after our Uncle Bernie, Tessa's
father and our father's brother. I don't think Bernard much likes
Uncle Bernie. He lives out in the Mojave Desert somewhere in
southern California. Can't remember the name of the town right
off. There was a movie made there about a café, or something."

"Back to the addition." Martha started putting melon

slices in a covered plastic dish to go back into the refrigerator. "Did Bernard tell you Devlin called twice yesterday while you were out? God is he arrogant."

Devlin usually tried reaching Belinda on her cell phone, a direct line from god to his subjects sort of thing. She had stopped answering his calls two days ago. "He called here at the residence number?"

"Yep, said you must not know your cell phone isn't working." Martha shook her head in amazement. "I guess he can't imagine you don't want to talk to him."

Belinda wanted to run the remodel numbers again but she intuitively suspected the worst. "Bernard really wants the addition, and I guess I do too. It would mean more residents and maybe *one day* we might make a profit. But we've got to be able to pay the bills first."

Bernard, wearing reading glasses and waving another copy of the morning paper, burst through the kitchen's swinging doors. "Have you guys seen this?" Then he saw the newspaper on the table. "I guess you have." He dropped down onto a stool next to Belinda. "This is terrible. Because of Philly's death, no one is going to want to live in Cedar Valley. Especially not near the trail." Evidently he caught a look in Belinda's eye or sensed something in her body language. "You think Philly was murdered, don't you?"

"She sure does." Martha answered for Belinda.

"Hard to keep ahead of you two," Bernard said with a shake of the head. "I guess you have it all planned what you're going to do today to get this all sorted out. Anyone for an English muffin and tea?" Catching himself, his face and mood turned instantly sombre. Even his shoulders slumped. "That sounded so..."

"Life goes on," Belinda said, trying to comfort. But it didn't go on the same, not really. *"Death always changes your life in someway, Bella Dear,"* Glory Jones reminded across time. Glory had been talking about Belinda's parents at the time, and trying to comfort a grief stricken little girl.

Now in the present, Belinda understood and internalized for the first time in all the years that had passed, how deep Glory's own sense of loss must have been--losing a

son and daughter-in-law so tragically. While at the time, all
Belinda had thought about was her own grief.

A few moments of silence passed before Belinda said,
"I was just going to do the same thing, Bernie. And no, I'm not
sure what's next until I talk to Calvin Pope and Uncle John. I'm
not as organized as you sometimes think brother-dear."

Bernard ignored Belinda's caution and made himself
busy starting the tea and pulling muffins, butter, and jam out of
the refrigerator. "Where's Patrick and MaryAnn?"

"They're not due for another half hour or so." Martha
inclined her head toward their large round kitchen clock.

The clock's white schoolhouse face showed it was barely
a few minutes before 6:00 A.M.

"Seems later, doesn't it?" Belinda said.

"You *know* it's murder?" Bernard demanded.

Again, Martha answered for Belinda, "Her gut *knows*."

Once back upstairs in her suite, Belinda took a few
moments to look at herself in the mirror, physically and
emotionally.

Indeed, her eyes were tired and strained, her skin
limp and dehydrated, and her hair was corkscrewing itself in
multitudinous directions. She looked and felt her age, plus
some.

Ordinarily, she was not inclined to spend much energy
on her appearance; and fortunately her features were strong and
her skin tone usually vibrant. She didn't have the time anyway--
Cedar Valley Residence was a dawn-to-dusk endeavor.

However, after this morning's reality check, she figured
a little effort and time spent on appearance might be wise before
she ventured out into the world. If she looked too much like the
Wicked-Witch-of-the-West, she probably wouldn't get much out
of Kirby's lawyer. Another of Glory's maxims had been, "*First
impressions, Bella Dear, are lasting impressions, good or bad.*"

Quickly, Belinda rubbed a dab of oil through her curls,
brushed a smidgen of blush on her cheeks, and applied a touch
of lipstick. Minor, but they helped a lot in obtaining a more

positive self-evaluation. Hopefully, Calvin "Senator" Pope, considered one of the most dapper defense attorneys around, would find her appearance acceptable.

Next Belinda tried working off any residual negativism by running remodeling calculations. At 9:00 A.M. she shut down her computer, tucked a notebook in her canvas carryall, and prepared to drive to Kirkland for a chat with Kirby's lawyer. She also checked that her cell phone was in her bag--not that she really wanted to answer Devlin's calls. Maybe she should just let him wait.

On her way out the front door, she noticed Theresa standing at the reception desk reading a copy of the *Cedar Valley Dispatch* and said, "Hello."

Theresa held up the newspaper and shook her head angrily. "Have you seen the headline?"

Belinda nodded.

"Poor man. Bashing his head like that. So often it's the innocent that get the short end of life's stick. I wonder sometimes." She exhaled a disgusted sigh, put the paper back on the stack, and headed upstairs.

Much like the day before, Belinda watched as Theresa ascended their grand stairway. This time however, Belinda was further saddened by hearing such world-weary thoughts from one so young and vibrant.

Adam Mason-Martin was well aware how important it was to dress well and have a "good" business address.

Today he had worn his best navy blue pinstripe suit, a pale pink shirt, and an *avant-garde* gold dotted maroon tie. He thought this particular suit made him look leaner and more athletic than he actually was; and the shirt and tie combination clearly showed his daring and complemented his dark brown eyes and well-tanned skin. At least that's what a lady friend had told him when he had worn a similar combination on a dinner date.

Adam also thought dressing well pulled attention away from what he considered his overly large and rather rough-hewn features. Of course his attire and looks certainly couldn't match Calvin's--but he figured good enough to impress Belinda Jones.

On the "good" address front, Calvin "Senator" Pope's office suite in Kirkland on prestigious Vermilion Pointe was in an upscale business complex fronted to mimic semi-attached British countryside cottages.

Entry was through a mammoth wrought-iron gate into a lavishly landscaped courtyard accented with boulders, cobblestone walkways, and an oversized Tuscan-styled fountain--pooling and cascading from three levels.

Adam had seen, first time and regular entrants alike--stop, look, and take account--seemingly no longer aware of the traffic streaming down Lake Washington Blvd to their rear. He imagined the overwhelming smell of greenery, the insistent and soothing sounds of water in movement, and the Mediterranean ambiance might almost capture and take them to another place, another time.

Almost. Adam Mason-Martin regularly took a moment to ponder when entering this unique place, and his conclusion always came up the same--good address or not--old-world European ambiance could be copied with distressed bricks, imported artifacts and their ilk. The real and hard-earned markings of culture and history, however, just could not be duplicated--no matter how clear the designer's vision or how limitless the builder's resources.

On the backside of the building, Lake Washington--incessant and loud--lapped at generously sized wooden decks adorned with teak furniture and specimen-sized potted-plants. Adam had seen the architect's brochure with its glossy pictures depicting amiable waterfront entertaining. The decks, however, were seldom used; and Adam thought them lonely, damp, and inhospitable.

This morning, however, as he looked out his office French-doors facing the lake, a bright blue sky and a brilliant late morning sun had momentarily appeared, showering the decks with congenial warming sunlight, and perversely mocking his thoughts and mood.

He knew Calvin planned to dump Belinda Jones on him--and Adam wondered yet again--why the hell was he still working for Calvin? And how soon would he feel confident enough to leave? His distaste for his self-absorbed boss would soon be palpable, no matter how hard he tried to push it back. He needed to leave before that bridge-burning point arrived. Not that he hadn't learned a lot from Calvin, much of which was in the "I'll never do that" category. Nonetheless, on-the-job courtroom experience was invaluable.

Adam guessed Calvin was somewhere around sixty and at least twenty-five years his senior. Consequently, as his uncle Major Garrett Martin would put it, he was learning a lot from Calvin's "time-in-grade," especially when it came to courtroom logistics. Adam's personal feelings would have to stay in the background a bit longer--at least until the Kirby case was over.

Then he would move on.

Adam had graduated in the top percentile of his class at the University of Chicago Law School, then put in several years as a clerk in a prestigious New York law firm, and several more at an equally prestigious Los Angeles firm--both specializing in criminal defense.

He was not considered a dummy by former employers, colleagues, friends, or enemies. Only Calvin, Adam occasionally mused, seemed unaware of his abilities. One of Adam's main strengths was preparatory research. He found surprises exactly what they were meant to be--off-putting.

He had gone over the Kirby Norris case with Calvin numerous times. Still he arrived early this morning to again review his notes. Adam also planned on obtaining a research folder on Belinda Jones sometime this morning.

For now, before anyone else in the office arrived, he had time to go over his notes; and for once, the decks facing Lake Washington seemed an ideal spot to refresh his mind. Good light, not too much heat, not too much wind, and the place to himself.

Once outside, Adam took off his suit jacket and stretched his lean frame between two teak high-backed deck-chairs in the shade of the building's overhang, then opened Kirby's folder.

"Nice to use this silly deck for once," he said to several sea gulls cautiously eyeing him from atop one of the deck's massive pinions.

It had been easy gathering the information on Kirby. Most came from the newspapers, some from a friend in the ME's office, and some from Patience, an old flame--now a big muckety-muck in the DA's office.

Waves clashing against the deck's edge caught his attention for a moment as he remembered Patience. Sometimes, in moments like this, Adam wished his relationship with Patience had worked out. Indeed, *she* had broken it off--claiming age difference as her reason.

"But it was only a ten year difference," Adam further informed the sea gulls. From his perspective, Patience's maturity had been intellectually, emotionally, and sexually enticing and stimulating. Sometimes he missed her terribly. Fortunately, not often.

Adam yawned. Maybe he should make a quick run to Starbucks a few doors down before Calvin and the others arrived.

First, though, he'd finish going through his notes-- snatches of information and thoughts--written on yellow legal paper in a precise large scroll, often prefaced and organized by a question, and the things he wanted to do underlined. It was how he organized his thoughts when collecting information. He had of course transcribed everything into the computer; but when reviewing, he preferred his hand-written notes.

Kirby and Lana?
  - Married fifteen years--no children--lived in large log cabin on Millbrook Rd. in Cedar Valley--expensive and upscale--he works--she didn't--must have good salary
  - Lana walked Max everyday--always in the morning- -usually on the same route--Snoqualmie Valley Trail--no witnesses came forward--<u>should talk to line-workers</u>

Adam *had* talked to Bull Morton and Pete Naldeen. Both men had steadfastly claimed they didn't see Lana and Max walk past their work-site after 9 A.M. when they reported to work. Thinking back, Adam remembered feeling that their story was truthful: and he considered "feelings" an integral part of decision making. What *he* felt, a jury would probably also feel.

Time of death?
- Bull and Pete claim they were at Meadow Street until Noon
- Housekeeper Mrs. Keyes said Lana wasn't at home when she arrived at 7:30 A.M. and didn't return before she left at noon
- ME at scene reported lividity and rigor mortis indicating time of death between 7 and 10 A.M--later official report said same

Suspects?
- Kirby--most likely suspect--but iron-clad alibi--except waiter at Sheraton won't swear to presence all the time--talk to brother and sister-in-law (Walter and Melissa)--grand jury indicted without a problem--no bail--his mother refuses to believe he's guilty
- Gun and panties found stuffed behind rear left taillight assembly in wheel-well of his trunk--Kirby claims no idea how got there
- Jake West--couple-acre farm backing on trail--supposedly anti-social and belligerent--court filings to stop trail--held Lana responsible--told everybody who would listen he hated her--police didn't hold--no evidence--had motive though and no alibi
- Phil Towers--slept rough on the trail--Jake West called him "Town Idiot"--stint in Western Washington State Hospital--then group-home--then drifted into "homeless" status--got meals and clothes and blanket handouts at St. Francis--police didn't hold--this time, no motive--but no alibi either

Condition of body and forensics?
- Jogger, Bob Tomian and dog Ebony found body--dog contaminated ground for footprints--Tomian

puked, but not near body
- Lana found face up--breasts exposed--shorts and panties off and not at scene
- Sexual intercourse within last twenty-four hours-- ME couldn't swear as to consensual or not--Kirby DNA match on rape kit--Tox screen showed high amount of Librium--Lana had prescription for 25mg a day--level at death 200mg--she had also been strangled.
- Actual cause of death was gunshot to head--rifling grooves and lands on bullet removed from Lana's skull indicated six shot Colt .38 Detective Special with a two-inch barrel--same gun as one found in Kirby's car.

Adam had a copy of the ME's report and several duplicate crime scene photos. He didn't re-read the report, but he did stare at Lana's crime-scene photos for several long minutes. In particular, he was emotionally held by the first photograph taken of Lana's body--a pool of dried blood caking her thick brown hair and surrounding her head in a gruesome halo.

He turned away from Kirby's folder for a moment, stared out at Lake Washington and wondered at the personality needed to be a crime scene photographer. The picture showed part of Lana's face destroyed, with one open green eye still visible.

Involuntarily and without forethought, Adam simultaneously shuddered and released a raspy and guttural, "Ugh."

Probably become immune, his mind rationalized. "Hell of a way to make a living," he said out-loud.

Startled or confused by Adam's movement and words, his sea gull buddies departed; and Adam returned to his notes.

Max?
- Found safely at home locked in backyard
- But neighbors swore saw Max leave with Lana

Adam wondered who had Max now while Kirby was in jail? Olive? Melissa and Walter? He hoped the darn dog was okay. After he made his coffee-run, maybe he'd make a couple calls and find out.

The interior of the two suites comprising C. Pope Law offices were decorated by Calvin's wife's personal designer, eclectically furnished through his brother's import business, and spoke of understated elegance.

The suite Calvin claimed as his private office was divided into three "areas": his desk and working area, a mahogany encased and embellished library, and a sitting alcove with floor to ceiling glass looking out onto his section of rear decking and Lake Washington.

In the alcove were three leather recliners that looked more like works of art than functional chairs, three side tables, and a coffee table. The walls were mauve and the area rug underfoot was Tibetan, circa 1850.

Calvin sat comfortably in the center recliner, his favorite, his long legs stretched out and crossed at the ankles, one manicured hand resting on his chair arm, and his other holding a cup of Starbucks coffee. He had imported the chair from Italy, personally contoured to the nuances of his figure by a Turinese craftsman only a few knew about. Like most of his possessions, the chair had cost a fortune. His gray suit was Armani, his gray leather loafers Gucci, his blue shirt and gray socks, Ralph Lauren. Calvin's fragrance, Giorgio Armani's Black Code, was noticeable but not overbearing. Even his sunglasses resting on the table beside him were from Yves Saint Laurent's latest collection.

To match this perfect office and stylish wardrobe, Calvin's countenance offered the beholder symmetrically deep set dark green eyes, a sculptured nose, and strong sensual lips. Behind those perfect lips were straight and even sparkling white teeth, his own he was proud to point out--without mentioning the caps and years with braces. Over his life, Calvin had paid minor fortunes to dentists and surgeons to look the way he did.

To his mind--money, time, and inconvenience--all well spent. Now, when Calvin smiled, juries were dazzled. And when juries were dazzled, Calvin won cases. High profile cases.

He even provided Adam Mason-Martin, his number one gofer, his own small, but still opulent office (standards had to be maintained, even for underlings!) through a connecting door.

This morning, Calvin had asked the younger lawyer to sit in on his meeting with Belinda. His plan, not yet mentioned to Adam, was to dump the amateur detective on his junior assistant. Then he could spend the rest of the morning contemplating invitees to the Mediterranean cruise he and his wife Emelda planned hosting in the fall. If he could only remember where he put the damn brochures.

Why couldn't he just have his memory fixed like his teeth? Maybe he *should* see another doctor. Get a second opinion, like his wife wanted.

Adam had selected the armchair to the left of and at right angles to Calvin. Belinda would also have to sit at a right angle to Calvin and would be facing Adam.

Just like Calvin had planned.

Adam sighed, making sure Calvin didn't notice. While he and Calvin waited, Adam looked over the dossier he'd been provided only minutes earlier on Belinda and Bernard Jones. Not only did he need to prepare himself fast--no surprises; but it was also imperative he make his own assessment. Calvin's judgement certainly could no longer be relied upon.

He remembered in particular an onerous Calvin rant from just a couple days earlier. "Does the Norris woman really believe her son is innocent? Mothers! The statistics scream it's always the husband in cases like this. What the hell, Adam, we'll just have to humor this Jones woman Olive Norris has drudged up. Who knows? She might bring me a case one day. Not that there's ever any shortage of work for Senator."

Reliving his boss' insensitivity, Adam almost visibly shook with distaste.

Forcing himself back to neutral, Adam returned his

attention to the dossier. On top was a recent newspaper clipping photo of Belinda, Bernard, and Devlin Stephens standing on the porch of Cedar Valley Residence. The occasion was the announcement of their engagement of a nationally known architect for a planned expansion.

At first glance, Adam was surprised the two were sister and brother. But the next clipping was a close-up taken four years previously. Again, it was Belinda and Bernard, but this time with Martha on the announcement of her arrival as *sous-chef*.

Here, Adam could see the resemblance--the eyes. Both sister and brother were staring unabashedly into the camera lens. Two people seemingly comfortable with themselves, each other, and what they were doing. True enough, Bernard's eyes betrayed a moroseness not seen in Belinda's, but Adam also astutely saw a shared vitality he wondered if they knew they possessed. For a second, then another, he envied them--then wondered why? He hadn't even met them.

The dossier, mostly newspaper clippings and articles, was arranged chronologically and covered back through grammar school. Adam jumped to near the end and read about a Mr. and Mrs. Bertram Jones Jr. being killed in a hit and run accident. There were also pictures of their grandparents on the day the court awarded them custody of the children. A friend was also present--John Thomas. He knew a Sheriff Thomas in Cedar Valley and squinted at the picture, wondering if it was the same man he now knew--many a year later?

As Adam came forward through time, there were yearbook pictures from high school, a small Bellevue newspaper article touting Belinda's great success in the stock market in the nineties, an equally small article on the sale of Bernard's last restaurant in Seattle, and one interesting article in the *Cedar Valley Dispatch* mentioning Belinda's assistance in unraveling an embezzlement scheme. Sheriff Thomas was giving her a community service award. Seeing Thomas in the more recent photo refreshed Adam's memory and allowed him to connect the dots. It was the same John Thomas.

Adam figured he had an incomplete and splotchy picture of the Jones sister and brother. But it was enough to give him a slight feeling of preparedness. It was also enough information to tickle his curiosity. Adam wanted to know more.

Ah well, he would be meeting one half of the brother-sister act in a few minutes anyway. He was looking forward to it, and again, wondered why?

This time the surprisingly odd answer came to Adam immediately--he liked the look of Belinda. Unsettling, since he had yet to meet the woman.

"Are you sure about the coffee, Mrs. Jones? The coffee shop is right next door." The words were right, however Calvin's intent was clear. His offer was a polite formality--he had more important things to do--and the quicker this was over, the better.

Belinda smiled pleasantly and hoped she was speaking in her best no-nonsense business-like manner, "No thank you, Mr. Pope, and it's *Ms*. Is there anything you can tell me about the prosecution's case that might help me?" It would have been easier for her to look and talk to Adam, especially since the young lawyer was not hard to look at.

Not as tall as Calvin, and leaner, Belinda thought everything about Adam projected vitality and intelligence. His dark brown eyes were lively, his mannerisms energetic and fluid. She conjectured he was the one always chosen "first on team." His suit, shirt, and tie weren't from the pages of *GQ*, but were smart, looked like good quality, and hung comfortably on his frame. Nevertheless, appealing as it might be to talk to Adam, Belinda turned herself sideways in her chair and spoke directly and pointedly to Calvin. Adam was only the junior partner, and just a kid really.

Calvin sighed rudely. "I know Mrs. Norris thinks you can help her son, *Ms. Jones,*" he said. "And my client himself thinks his alibi is going to win over a jury." He shook his head incredulously.

Then, quite abruptly--as if some kind of mental or psychological switch had flipped--Calvin's demeanor changed and he produced a big toothy smile. "May I call you, Belinda?"

It was asked rhetorically, and in what Belinda guessed to be Calvin's version of an endearing tone. "Clients pay me hundreds of thousands of dollars to defend them and then often want to second-guess me." He spread his hands in wonderment.

"So, *Calvin,* you think Olive is trying to second guess you?"

"Of course. Kirby killed his wife. And now it's up to me to convince a jury he didn't."

"How will you do that?"

"I won't."

Caught off guard Belinda said, "Excuse me?"

"I need Kirby to plead temporary insanity and then I can plea bargain him down to a lesser sentence."

Belinda forced her features to remain neutral; inside she was seething. Calvin Pope was not only arrogant and callous, but he was also stupid. How on earth did he ever win so many cases? "It seems to me if Kirby did kill his wife, the circumstances of her death certainly would indicate premeditation."

Again Calvin spread his perfectly manicured hands, "I know, Belinda, I know. Insanity is the last defense of--"

She leaned forward and demanded, "You really think Kirby is guilty?"

He sighed again. "Here are the circumstances." He ticked the items off on his fingers: "Kirby recently took out a million dollar policy on his wife; they have sex but hardly do anything else together; he knew she was taking Librium; their housekeeper has heard them have some real donnybrooks-- usually about her spending; and the murder weapon and her panties were found in *his* car."

"Why would he put the gun and panties in his *own* car? Doesn't that look like a frame-up to you?" It seemed obvious to her. The Kirby she had met was not a stupid man. "And what about his alibi?"

Adam cleared his throat. "I can help you there. I interviewed Tony Alvarez. He's the waiter at the Sheraton where Kirby was in an association meeting. Mr. Alvarez says Kirby was there for the breakfast part alright. Then they had a speaker with slides and the lights were dimmed, then there was a film and the lights were completely out. He says he can't swear Kirby was there the whole time."

Belinda asked in rapid succession, "Did Mr. Alvarez see Kirby again at the end? How long did the slide presentation and movie take? How far and how long from the Sheraton downtown back to Cedar Valley? Half an hour each way I would guess? Have you interviewed the other people at the meeting? And, what the heck were they talking about that early in the morning?"

Adam responded equally fast and succinctly. "Yes, the waiter noticed when Kirby got his coat at the end and stood at the elevators with the others. The meeting room, you see, is on the top floor. There's also a service kitchen, bathrooms, and cloakroom on that floor. Mr. Alvarez only had this one group to worry about. Three hours for the presentations, and yes, half an hour each way for the drive to Cedar Valley. It would be tight though, and he'd barely make it." Adam leaned forward a little, talking directly to Belinda. "Nevertheless, it can't be ruled out and I'm sure the prosecuting attorney won't miss it. I didn't personally interview the fifteen other people at the meeting, but the police did. Everyone saw Kirby when things got started and at the end when good-byes were said. No one will swear he never left nor testify they saw him leave. The meeting was about computer security and fraud."

Belinda had attended meetings herself at the top of the Sheraton. Consequently, she knew the layout. A person *could* sneak out the back of the room--assuredly they closed the blinds for the presentation--so it would be fairly dark. And the elevator bank was sufficiently far away from the meeting room that one could go down unnoticed and unheard. Still, it would be a bold and tricky maneuver.

Belinda turned back to Calvin. He would probably succeed in fobbing her off to Adam, but she was going to make darn sure he worked for it. "Are you sure about the time of death?"

"The housekeeper comes at 7:30 A.M. and had to let herself in. She left at noon and Lana hadn't returned. Talk to her yourself if you want, won't help you with the time though. And there are the two electricians." He inclined his head toward

Adam. "What were their names, Bill somebody..."

"Bull Morton and Pete Naldeen." Adam smiled at Belinda.

Calvin continued, "Those two were right there on the trailhead, can't ask for better eyewitnesses."

Belinda made a mental note that she did indeed want to talk to the housekeeper and the electrical guys. "Do you have any pictures? Of Lana? Of the crime scene?"

Adam responded again, "Yes, pictures of the Norris family members, their house, and the dog. There are crime scene photos I can show you." He looked to Calvin. "If *technically* you're working for us on the case."

Calvin waved his hand, clearly indicating he didn't care if she got copies or not.

Belinda smiled graciously. "Well, you aren't paying me, but you could say I work for you if anyone asks, like the DA, and I wouldn't contradict it. I want to see everything I can." She noticed she was again looking at Adam, and forced herself to turn back to Calvin. "If Kirby didn't kill his wife, and I'm convinced he didn't, the answer is somewhere in the details of their lives." Which reminded her of Lana's ring. "Calvin, what about the ring? Why would Kirby take that off her body? He could have taken it anytime he wanted to at home."

"What ring?"

The man really is an insufferable fool. "The ring Lana was wearing at the time of her death. It's disappeared."

Again Calvin waved his waved dismissively. "Irrelevant. Anything else I can do for you?"

"Phillip Towers. Did you know he was murdered last night?"

"Phillip Towers?" Calvin turned to Adam questioningly. "Wasn't he..."

"He was one of the men the police picked up right after Lana was killed. They released him quickly. Homeless gentleman I believe, down and out." Adam looked at Belinda. "I read the newspaper article about his death this morning and I don't remember any mention of murder."

Belinda was unapologetic in her response. "I know he was murdered." She turned back to Calvin. "Don't you find it

strange that a man who hangs around the very trail Lana was
killed on dies suddenly right before Kirby's trial is scheduled to
begin?"

"It is unfortunate, poor man." Calvin shifted
impatiently in his chair. "People do die however, and it's not
always murder, my dear."

It was useless.

"Thank you, *Calvin*." Belinda stood to leave and turned
to Adam. "When can I get the pictures, *Mr. Mason-Martin?*"

Not until Adam left did Calvin allow himself to relax.

He went to his desk, collapsed in his custom leather
swivel chair, and with a deep heavy sigh, pulled a folder out of
his bottom desk drawer. He pulled *the* letter out and reread the
pertinent sentences again.

"Jesus," he sighed to himself after rereading what he
already knew by heart.

He was having to fake it more and more these days--
though he didn't think the Jones woman had picked up on it.
She did, however, seem smart. No telling what she might dig
up, given enough time.

He rubbed his face and sighed again. He was weary of
the mental charade, but not yet resigned enough to throw in the
towel. He had never been at the top of his class, but good grief,
he should be able to figure out something better than an insanity
plea. Where had the sharp and intelligent Calvin he knew as
himself disappeared to?

"And where the hell *did* he put that brochure Emelda
gave him?"

Back in his own smaller office, Adam allowed himself an
amused little smile. Score one for Belinda Jones.

*   *   *   *   *

The straightforward and seemingly logical way to go home from the Kirkland/Redmond area was to hop on I-405 south to I-90, then head east to Cedar Valley. However, after dealing with Calvin, Belinda was in a contrarian state of mind, and decided to head home via surface streets through Kirkland and Redmond, then cruise home through one of her favorite rural areas via Redmond Fall City Road.

Neither Belinda nor Bernard were car fanciers, preferring to maintain their older autos for as long as possible. They did keep a newer minivan as the Cedar Valley Residence car, but Belinda's Nissan Altima was a twelve year old front wheel drive five-speed, and she liked the way it hugged the curves.

There was traffic, especially through Redmond, which required constant shifting, but this was something she could manage; and for the moment, no rain. Not like Calvin--so slippery and slimy--and maybe even downright crooked and unethical. Well, she wasn't ready to go that far, not yet.

Belinda understood politics and it's role in driving the prosecutor's office to move fast--despite the weakness of their case. But what was wrong with Calvin? Why wasn't he trying to find out who really killed Lana Norris? He was throwing in Kirby's towel without any kind of fight. In their early days, Clive "The Bum" was fond of watching lightweight boxing from The Forum. "No *cuhunas*," Clive would have wised off about Calvin.

Belinda was not so sure--too easy an answer. She could hear Grandmother Glory. "*Easy answers, Bella dear, are often wrong answers.*"

For a moment, sitting in bumper-to-bumper traffic on Cleveland Street, and remembering Glory, Belinda could almost smell her scent. Gardenia.

Poor Glory was overly liberal in splashing the stuff upon herself, but to an impressionable young child like Belinda, the sweet floral scent had enhanced her Grandmother's adult stature and endeared her even more.

Even now, several tears surprised Belinda. Quickly she brushed them away.

Eventually she made her way out of downtown

Redmond. She hadn't come this way for a year or so and was astounded at the rate of new development overflowing into the pastoral section of her drive home--the part she loved and made going through all the traffic worth the effort.

Development after development, and their accompanying strip-malls now left far fewer miles of rolling greenery for her to enjoy.

This particular back-road, historically known as "The Sunset Highway," had always sung to her heart, even as a child, and especially in summer when the nine months of Pacific Coast dampness gave up its bounty of lush foliage. The two-lane highway wound its way southeast and ran through hillside stands of cedar, fir, and hemlock to the east. To the west, vibrant green pastures balanced the landscape, and usually worked magic on her soul.

Not this morning.

Redmond-Fall City Road had become a dangerous stretch, especially in heavy traffic; and after several oncoming homicidal drivers executed hair-brained passing maneuvers, Belinda realized this was not going to be the relaxing intermission she had envisioned.

First Philly this morning, then Calvin, and now this cherished memory shot to hell.

A crappy day so far.

On the positive side, at least Adam Mason-Martin seemed intelligent and reasonable. Even likable.

He had suggested he make copies of pictures she requested and bring them to lunch at the Residence. *Good.* Maybe he could offer some insight into Calvin's behavior.

Her cell phone rang. She took it out of the ashtray where she had stowed it while driving and looked at the number blinking on its face.

Devlin Stephens, the architect. Belinda let his call go to voicemail.

Sheriff John Thomas was on his way out when Belinda arrived at his office.

"Going on a call?" she asked--hoping he wasn't. She had decided at the last minute to stop by and see what she could find out about Philly's murder.

"Nope, just hungry. Heading for DQ." He smiled. "But you know I always have time for my niece, hungry or not."

They weren't actually related, but John had no children and the closeness of his friendship with her parents and then grandparents had matured over the years into honorary "Uncle" status. These days John was nearing mandatory retirement age-- but wasn't in a hurry.

Together they went back inside and headed to his small office in the rear of the three-room building. The Cedar Valley Sheriff's Office wasn't much; and since age had not diminished John's stature, still over six feet, and solid, his presence made the place seem even smaller.

Belinda had always considered John a handsome man. Now time had grayed his moustache and the hair above his ears; and creases marked the corners of his mouth and eyes. However, as happens with some, aging had bestowed upon him a rugged sensuality that only appears with maturity and a well-lived life.

Surprising to Belinda, he had never married. As children, Bernard had insisted it was because Uncle John had lost his one true love. When pushed, Bernard would never put a name or face to his "true love" candidate, but Belinda thought it might be their deceased mother Linda Margaret. It was an innocent and romantic fantasy for the two children.

These days, many years from childhood, Belinda occasionally wondered if John might be gay. She doubted it; and it didn't matter to her anyway. She would love him no matter what.

"Want some water or coffee? I'll even make you tea if you invite me to dinner tonight."

"You know Bernie's the tea fanatic. But you're welcome to dinner any night." They never let him pay for meals; they emotionally owed him so much. He was however allowed to leave a tip for Patrick and MaryAnn, which the students had confided, were extremely generous. "Which reminds me," Belinda suddenly remembered. "We're having a little party tomorrow night around five or so. Janice Tanner's birthday. I think you've met her? The engineer?"

"Oh yeah." He winked. "The good looking one."

"You know there's nothing worse than an *old* lecher."

He laughed and leaned back in his chair, an ancient wooden swivel monstrosity that should have gone to charity eons ago. "Sounds like something Glory would have said."

Belinda smiled. "Does, doesn't it. But I made it up all by myself." She had plopped down in the armchair hidden in the corner behind the door. To her mind, it was the only decent chair in the place.

But enough chitchat, she was anxious to talk about Philly.

She asked, "How was Philly murdered?"

He shook his head, "Whoa. I don't remember anyone mentioning murder and Philly in the same sentence."

Suddenly, she was very tired. "So it was an accident?" She failed to keep the sarcasm out of her tone of voice. "He just happened to bash his head in...." She caught herself. "I don't remember any mention of him bashing his head in *The Dispatch* now that I think about it. How did Theresa Bacera know that?"

John ran his finger underneath his collar and took on a pained look. "Haven't a clue."

Belinda caught her breath and inwardly prayed Theresa had nothing to do with this. She could not, however, rule out that possibility; but in deference to John she moved on. "Okay, *I* think Philly was murdered and the murder was connected to Lana Norris's murder. So, are you going to tell me how Philly died or not?"

"A little testy, aren't you?"

He was right. She took a deep breath. "Okay. Could you just tell me what happened?"

"Don't see how that would hurt anything. Confidential you understand?"

Belinda nodded.

"Philly did have a horrendous gash on the back of his head and most probably that was the cause of death. We found him with his head up against a vicious looking rock protruding from the ground and it looks like he fell and hit his head."

"You think it was an accident?"

"What I think doesn't matter right now. I--"

"You guys are going for the easy mark? Right? Too much trouble trying to find out who *really* killed Philly and Lana." Anger heated the edges of her voice.

"*'You guys'* is unfair and you know it, Belinda. I haven't even given up on finding the woman who ran-down Junior and Linda Margaret, and that was what, thirty five, forty years ago? And I never will give up. So what makes you think I wouldn't take the Norris woman and Philly's deaths seriously?"

Ashamed, she squirmed in her chair. "I know, Uncle John," she said. "I'm really sorry. That ass, Calvin Pope, has sent me spiraling into some kind of awful frame of mind. Now I'm sounding even more rude and arrogant than he is. Please forgive me."

"Ah, the Senator. Know him too well."

"Really?" Belinda raised inquiring eyebrows.

He shook his head. "Afraid you're going to have to discover the Senator on your own. Wouldn't want to pre-load you."

"Hmm." She was tired of thinking about Calvin anyway. It was Philly she wanted to know more about. "Is there *anything* more you can tell me?"

"Well," he leaned back in his chair and looked up at the ceiling, a smile Belinda couldn't see but knew was there, creasing the corners of his mouth. "The ME, without any direction from me, will of course explore that wound to make sure Philly wasn't brought down with a blow, and I've asked for some specific tox screens."

"Because?"

"You shouldn't be surprised to know Philly was on several antidepressants. Alcohol, and or Librium could at the minimum really slow Philly down, and at the worse, actually kill him."

"Librium." Belinda rolled the word around while she thought. "Librium, as in *Librium* found in Lana's system."

"Yep."

"Philly was a nice man."

"Yep."

"I'm not sure if I like working on a murder investigation."

"Who's paying you? Olive Norris?"

It was her turn for a monosyllabic response, "Yep."

John sat up straight and caught Belinda in one of the steely stares he was famous for. "You're all that woman has between her son and the electric chair, or if he's lucky, life in prison."

"Or, if Calvin has his way, life in a nut house." Belinda dropped back against her chair and next spoke through a sigh. "Liking it or not...I think I *do* want this to be who I am."

"A detective, you mean?"

"Yep."

John kept his counsel and waited.

After a few seconds, Belinda looked at her watch. "I've got to get back. Adam Mason-Martin said he'd try to get there around noon and I don't want to miss grilling him about his boss. Are you coming over for lunch, or sticking with DQ?"

"DQ. But maybe I'll see you at dinner. Not promising though. And who is Adam Mason-Martin?"

"Calvin Pope's assistant. Have you met him?" She almost added that she liked him, but she didn't want her uncle to get the wrong impression. It was just in comparison to Calvin that Adam seemed to shine.

He walked Belinda to the door, "Maybe, can't quite remember." Then John put his arm around Belinda's shoulders. "You're tougher than you think, Belinda. You'll figure this out."

She certainly hoped so. "Anybody in town you can think of that had it in for both Lana and Philly?"

"Yep. Jake West. Owns land along the trail. Vehemently against the trail going in and thought Philly was a nuisance and a blight on the neighborhood." John scoffed at his own words. "Jake's place is a pigsty. How he has the nerve to criticize Philly..." He sighed wearily and shook his head. "People."

It was a little after noon and Belinda was leaving the

kitchen when Adam arrived. She stepped to the side of the kitchen's swinging double doors for a moment and watched as Mary Ann greeted and seated the young lawyer. She recognized her hesitation as odd--and wondered for a second why she had stopped and stared.

"Smells good in here," Adam said, taking a seat at the table offered him. Mary Ann was seating him at one of their best tables facing the front windows.

Belinda couldn't help smiling as Mary Ann hovered over Adam.

Indeed, Adam was a good looking and well dressed young man--well, not so young compared to Mary Ann--but a baby compared to most of the men who ate at the residence.

Belinda didn't move, but continued to watch and listen.

"It always smells good...it's one of the things I like about working here," Mary Ann said as she handed Adam a menu. "Chef Jones and Chef Milton are great cooks. The two luncheon specials are spinach ravioli with gorgonzola cheese sauce, and stuffed Portobello mushrooms and garden salad."

Still smiling, Mary Ann waited for his response, and even from across the dining room, Belinda could see the young woman's interest in the stranger.

Belinda liked MaryAnn. She was a clean-faced math student studying to become a biomedical researcher. She wore large black-rimmed glasses that were always sliding down her nose and detracted from her pleasant features. Nonetheless, Belinda was sure Mary Ann's career choice and intellectual proclivities, did not blind her to the allure of the opposite sex.

Adam smiled and said, "I've never been here before. It'll take me a few minutes to look over the menu."

MaryAnn blushed. "Oh yeah, of course. Take your time." Obviously flustered, she rushed off past Belinda into the kitchen.

"Seems you've made a new friend," Belinda said, finally coming up to Adam's table. "May I join you?"

With an olden-style smoothness lacking in self-conceit, Adam stood and pulled out the chair next to him. "Please, be my guest."

"Thank you." Belinda sat down. "I'm impressed with

your gentlemanly manners. Unusual for..."

"Someone my age?"

"Well," Belinda wasn't sure how to get out of this one without patronizing his youth or making herself sound old as dirt. She turned her head to look outside. What had begun as a bright sunny day in Cedar Valley was turning overcast.

He laughed pleasantly and sat back down himself. "It's okay. Actually I look younger than I really am and I owe any good behavior on my part to my grandmother."

His voice had a nice sound to it. *Much too young for you, Belinda,* she chastised herself before turning back to Adam and the business at hand. "Thanks for bringing the pictures." Belinda hadn't failed to notice a manila envelope laying on the table across from her. "I know I was asking for an awfully quick turnaround."

Adam pulled his chair in closer to the table, leaned in, and lowered his voice. "Actually, we already had copies made. I wanted a chance to talk to you alone."

Belinda thought he might have winked mischievously, but wasn't sure. Well, *she* was certainly going to keep this on a business level. "I also wanted to talk to you about Kirby. Away from Calvin." She hoped her tone was neutral and business-like.

Mary Ann returned with goblets of water, their rims adorned with slices of lemon. "Hello Ms. Jones." She repeated the specials for Belinda as if she wouldn't know what they were, then asked, "Are you both ready to order?"

Belinda ordered the ravioli, and without looking at the menu Adam chose the mushrooms.

After Mary Ann left, Adam said, "I'm not much of a cook--eat out a lot. I've never been here though. But what I've seen so far, I like."

"Thanks, we like compliments. You're single then?" Belinda surprised herself asking such a personal question.

"Yeah, easier to eat out than go through all the trouble just for one. I do cook wonderful scrambled eggs."

Belinda had to smile. She had few memories of her mother and father, but one she did retain was of her father Bertram, stirring scrambled eggs on the stove, smiling at her, asking her to get a plate. "That takes some skill, Adam. Good scrambled eggs."

He sat back in his chair, seemingly at ease in his surroundings, and relaxed in talking with Belinda. "These are comfortable chairs for a restaurant. So, what would you like to know first? Why I work for such a jackass? Or do I think Kirby is innocent?"

"Jeez! You do get to the point fast, don't you?"

"So do you."

She smiled; Adam was easy to like. "Fair enough. So what's the story with Calvin? Why is he caving in?"

He lowered his voice again, "You know, he only takes high exposure cases and people remember him as one who defends the defenseless."

She nodded.

He continued in an even lower voice, "In truth he's not a very smart or good lawyer. He does package himself well though, and it's paid off in the past. Still does."

"But," Belinda leaned forward herself. "He's not giving Kirby a very good defense. I gather he hasn't hired out any detective work himself?"

"Anything that's gotten done, I've done. And that's very little."

"Adam, is there any other evidence I don't know about? You know--forensics kind of stuff, hair fibers, gun powder residue, blood splatter analysis..."

He smiled at her expense. "You've been watching too many of those CSI and ME type TV shows."

She wasn't amused, but didn't take offense. "I'm just trying to figure out where best to start. I'm planning on talking to Walter and Melissa Norris this afternoon, then the housekeeper. Then Jake West as soon as I can. But after that..."

"You're right to hit up Kirby's brother and sister-in-law first off. Neither the police nor Calvin are pursuing investigating them."

"Why do you think that is?"

"Kirby is easy. Husband with the gun and panties in his car. Rocky marriage and a big life insurance policy."

"My thoughts exactly. No wonder poor Olive hired me."

The two fell silent.

"Hi." A melodic allegro voice at Belinda's rear interrupted their reveries. "Do you have a moment, Belinda?" Janice Tanner. Belinda didn't need to turn and look--Janice's scent, Tresor, albeit lightly applied, was the giveaway. Janice's aura projected alacrity, intelligence, and composure. Approaching forty and highly attractive, her chestnut hair (professionally streaked, Belinda guessed) and cut stylishly short, complimented a nicely proportioned and symmetrical face. Janice was a relatively new resident, having moved to Puget Sound from San Jose. She had easily fit into life at Cedar Valley Residence.

"Of course." Since Janice seldom came to meals at the residence, Belinda was surprised to see her, and slow to make introductions.

Clearly not one to wait, Janice extended her hand to Adam. "Hello, my name's Janice. Do you mind if I just have a quick moment with Ms. Jones?" She walked around the table, heading toward the chair next to Adam.

He stood, almost colliding with her. "Adam Mason-Martin. Please, let me help you..."

But Janice already had the chair out and was starting the process of sitting.

Adam sat back down, smiling slightly, as if amused at Janice and his slapstick maneuver.

Belinda was by now used to Janice and her ways, and knew the engineer's impatience was sparked by a quick intellect and a continually forward moving stream of thought.

In fact, during several introspective moments Belinda had wished for some of Janice's drive--and on one occasion, confided that wish to Janice. Janice had responded cryptically, "Oh, Belinda, how does that old saying go, *'Be careful what you wish for.'*"

"What can I help you with?" Belinda was not overly joyed with the interruption, but residents came first. Besides, Adam and Janice were both single, attractive, and close in age; although she guessed Adam to be a smidgen younger than Janice. Maybe they would hit it off, not that she had ever tried matchmaking before, but why not? It was a much more pleasant thought than Lana and Philly's murders.

"I'm off today. I've been working a lot of overtime and have tons of comp time to use as I please. *So*, I decided to stay home today and do some cleaning and organizing." She smiled. "By the way, I'm looking forward to the party tomorrow tonight. I just can't believe you guys do that for all the residents on their birthdays."

"It's our pleasure."

"Maybe I should sign up for that cleaning service you mentioned. My suite was sort of a mess. I'm finished now, and I'm off to the Bellevue Art Museum for the afternoon, but I wanted to mention to you before I forget that I can't find my backup watch." She looked down at her wrist where she wore an inexpensive Minnie Mouse watch. "It's an antique my mother left me so I don't wear it much. I'm too careless with putting things down. Anyway, Belinda, if you happen to see it around, you'll know who it belongs to."

"I'll keep a lookout." Belinda's heart raced anxiously and she felt her cheeks warm. *Not another theft.*

Her priority task now evidently completed, Janice turned her attention to Adam. "Are you a new resident?"

Belinda thought Adam had been intently watching her and Janice's conversation; nonetheless, he appeared caught off guard.

"Ah, ah, no," he responded clumsily.

Belinda was surprised by Janice's boldness and Adam's temporary distress. *Interesting*, she thought, and felt a fleeting inkling to know more about him. *But why?*

Janice said, "I know I'm being nosey and it's none of my business, but if you were considering moving in I just wanted to put in a good word. It's very nice here. You'll like it." She smiled broadly and comfortably. "The building's architectural features, as you can see, have really been enhanced by Belinda and Bernard's improvements. And even though my work hours keep me from eating here often, the food is great."

Belinda was taken aback and embarrassingly pleased with Janice's positive review. "Thanks, Janice. I'm glad you like it here," was all she managed to sputter.

"Oh, more than *like*. For me it's been perfect." She

lowered her voice, "Lana Norris's murder is a terrible thing and I sure hope it doesn't change things here in Cedar Valley. You know I go to the same gym in Issaquah Lana went to. It's just too terrible to think about it a lot." She shook her head as if that simple act would make it all go away. "Well, won't keep you, just wanted to let you know about the watch. Ta!" With that she was gone as seamlessly as she had arrived.

Adam exhaled, "Whew." His sharp dark eyes, however, betrayed a composure his words contradicted.

Playing a part for me, Belinda wondered?

Quite possibly. A lawyer good enough to be the Senator's right-hand man shouldn't be as easily swayed by Janice's femininity--as enticing as it was.

But then again, maybe he found Janice attractive, and all bets were off. Belinda was painfully aware that when sex was involved, anything was possible.

After a lunch of portobello mushroom caps sautéed in extra dry sherry and filled with an Italian sausage stuffing for Adam, and delicately light raviolis swimming in herbed olive oil accompanied with fresh baguettes for Belinda, Adam asked for a tour of the residence.

"Besides," he said, at the front entry glass doors, "I think I need to walk off some of that lunch. But look, it's starting to rain. Again."

Something in the way he emphasized *again* prompted Belinda to ask, "I gather you don't like the Pacific Northwest that much?"

He dodged her question with, "It's alright."

She let it drop and readily agreed to a tour.

Anything but deal with Lana and Philly's murders and the thefts at the residence.

Naja also evidently agreed, and insisted on accompanying them.

In the parlor Adam surprised Belinda yet again by commenting on the feeling of warmth and comfortableness the mauve color pallet they used for the walls and carpet imbued.

"You haven't been to the Norris house yet, right?" Adam asked.

She shook her head.

"They have nice things. But for some reason it's not warm. Not like your..."

"Parlor," Belinda provided.

He smiled (boyishly she thought). "Yes, Parlor it would be. An old-fashioned word for an old-fashioned feel."

As they moved on into the Activity Room, she noticed Adam's height, about 5'9" or a little less she guessed. Not too tall, but tall enough to look good with Janice. Indeed, maybe with Martha too.

He continued, "Do you know Kirby and Lana didn't have children?"

"Yeah, I do. You think maybe a possible point of conflict?" Motivation for Kirby could go either way--because he wanted children, or because he didn't. "Did Lana's autopsy include a check for pregnancy?" Belinda figured it must have.

"Yes. And no, she wasn't pregnant. Walter and Melissa are childless too." Looking around, he said, "You've got appeal here for a lot of interests." He took a number-three red ball out of a pocket of the pool table that dominated the Activity Room and rolled it across the table. "Level," he said, almost in a mutter.

Belinda remembered Uncle John had done the same thing.

"I think I mentioned I'm planning on going to the Norris house this afternoon," she said.

"I'll be interested in your opinion."

She sensed Adam hadn't taken to Walter and Melissa. "Anything I should know up front?"

"Nope. Don't want to set you up. Does my tour include upstairs?"

"Sure." Belinda was surprised by her desire for Adam to see and approve of Cedar Valley Residence. *Who cared if he liked the place or not?* She barely knew the man--for goodness sakes.

*   *   *   *   *

Finally back at the front entrance and trying to leave, Adam was accosted by a stern-faced young woman, her jet black hair pulled back in a tight ponytail and wearing a black rain-slicker and heavy duty walking boots. She had a clipboard protected with plastic clutched in one hand, and the expression of a warrior ready for battle engraved on her face. "Is this your place?" she demanded.

Adam met his challenger head-on, amused eye to hostile eye, Gucci loafer encased toe to L.L. Bean take-no-prisoners reinforced toe. "No, I'm afraid not." Then he stepped aside, revealing Belinda to his rear. "But I'm sure Ms. Jones can help you."

What now! Belinda groaned internally as she watched Adam leave, seemingly unfazed and unconcerned. "Can I help you?" She however, instinctively knew this was trouble--but unfortunately felt helpless to avoid whatever was about to unfold.

Naja, who had come out of the dining room to inspect the stranger, also recognized the scent of an enemy and scurried off into the parlor.

Morris and Anna, having just finished a rather late and lengthy lunch were also passing through the foyer, and of course stopped to view the unfolding drama.

The woman jerked a business card off her clipboard and handed it to Belinda. "Lois Michael, King County Land Development. You have to replant those raspberry bushes and you have forty-eight hours to do it in."

Belinda was astonished, confused, and instantly angry. "What are you talking about?"

"Do you not know that this place," she looked around derisively, "is in a critical area and covered under The Critical Area Ordinances for clearing and grading?" A sense of superiority and condescension controlled her tone and delivery. Lois whipped a pamphlet off her clipboard and handed it to Belinda.

Belinda didn't take the offered pamphlet and instead asked, "What clearing and grading?"

"Suit yourself." Lois sighed and reclaimed her handout. "You cannot trim or remove raspberry bushes on your property without a permit. You do not have one and are consequently in violation. You will receive a citation in the mail within forty-eight hours. If you've remedied the situation, you will only have to pay a fine. Otherwise we will put a lien on your title."

Belinda was outraged. Clearly this woman must be acting outside the limits of her authority. "Are you talking about Jorge trimming the bushes out back?"

"Yes."

"You do know there's been a murder on that trail, don't you? And I asked Jorge to trim and take out some bushes for safety and security reasons."

"Not my problem." Lois turned to go.

"Why would you care about my little raspberry bushes? And, this is my property."

"Somebody complained."

"Who?"

Lois reopened the entry door and stepped across the threshold The skies were darkening further and thunder rumbled in the distance.

"Confidential information," Lois answered smugly. "By the way, did I see a dog coming out of the dining room? Good day." With that, Lois Michael stomped down the porch stairs and headed to a midnight-blue Volvo wagon parked in front of a silver BMW with steam coming out of its tail pipe. Belinda guessed the Beamer belonged to Adam, and figured he had been watching the show after all. *From the comfortable safety of his luxury car.*

"Government tyranny! That's what it is!" Morris said, seemingly as outraged as Belinda. Maybe more. His whole body was puffed up in anger and his eyes were shooting daggers. "City folk trying to tell rural folk what to do with property they spent their hard earned money on buying."

Yeah, Belinda thought.

"They've lost complete sight of property rights."

Bernard, with Martha to his rear, appeared at the dining room entrance. "What's going on? We could hear your voices all the way back in the kitchen. Is everyone okay?"

Morris and Anna started explaining to Bernard what had just occurred while Belinda took a step back, and a deep breath.

This Lois Michael County thing could end up being a huge expense and another distraction from her finding out who killed Lana and Philly.

Something would have to be removed from her plate, and in an instant she knew what, and to whom.

"Oh, Bernard," Belinda said pleasantly, hoping there wasn't any coyness in her tone. "This raspberry bush thing is something only you can handle." If she could dump Lois and King County on Bernard, maybe, just maybe she could continue to pursue Lana's murderer.

Within her peripheral vision, through the entry doors, Belinda could see Theresa standing outside by the raspberry hedge in question talking to Jorge Villareal, who in Belinda's opinion was the best darned gardener ever.

However, she put on mental blinders and ignored what her eyes were catching. Whatever she was witnessing between Theresa and Jorge could be yet another complication she might have to deal with.

Besides, it would probably start raining any second.

No, not today. Questions about Theresa would just have to wait.

Now that the "law" had left, Naja protruded her nose around the parlor arch looking for her mistress. Then Buster appeared from her rear, and she growled a "get-back" directive.

Buster, however, was not deterred. He moved forward and licked Naja on the snout. He and Naja shared a secret and needed to be buddies; and that was that.

Olive visited Kirby Tuesday morning as she had done every morning since his detainment.

The judge should have granted Kirby bail, but Olive

knew the woman had been blinded by the prosecutor's arguments.

Silly judge, where would Kirby flee to anyway? His home was here in Cedar Valley, here with his mother. Well, no matter, she would be here for him in his time of need, rain or shine, no matter the cost. Monetary or personal.

After Olive left her son, she drove her sparkling 1967 purple Caddy directly home and cleaned house. Housecleaning was an activity she considered therapeutic and saintly. God, she knew, did indeed prefer cleanliness over slovenliness.

Around noon Olive went to Cedar Valley's St. Francis church as she did every Tuesday and Thursday.

St. Francis Church, a little south of Cedar Valley Residence, also sat on the Snoqualmie trail. It was a modest church in comparison to older and grander city structures of worship; but unimposing as it might be, inside there were still pews, a pulpit, and altars (main and side), that required vigilant upkeep and adornment.

Olive and several other ladies had taken on the task of cleaning and preparing the church for mass several years previous. Olive was in charge and also responsible for managing the gardener. She believed God's house, just like her own, should be clean and beautiful inside and outside.

Sure, she knew in earlier days, eager and willing nuns lived in the attached convent and performed those duties. Times had changed, however, and the convent part of St. Francis was now the refurbished home for food distribution to the needy, and weekly Bingo.

This Tuesday, before she started her duties at the church, and while Adam and Belinda supped on mushrooms and ravioli in the comfort of Cedar Valley Residence's Dining room, Olive Norris knelt on the hard tile slab at the altar of The Blessed Virgin.

"Dear Mother Mary," she prayed in a low and devout voice to the Holy Virgin. "Please let the Jones woman figure out a way to get Kirby out of this horrible mess. I've done my part as you well know."

Senator should have figured out that her Kirby was being framed. What was wrong with the man? Well, Belinda

Jones didn't seem that bright either, but Olive figured she was smart enough at least to realize Kirby wasn't stupid enough to stuff the murder weapon and his own wife's panties in the trunk of his car. And Kirby's alibi was ironclad. Were they all blind?

The church was cold, and she could hear rain starting to tap dance on the high roof above the altars. It had been that way all morning, rain, then sun, rain, then sun. Olive was glad she'd worn a heavy sweater--a dark purple cable knit Lana had given her, and her bright purple rain-slicker.

And for the first time since Kirby's incarceration, Olive entertained the thought that maybe her humble prayers were inadequate. Maybe she just wasn't praying long or hard enough?

The thought that she might lose this battle scared Olive, and caused her hands to tremble as she fumbled through her gargantuan purse to eventually pull out a velvet pouch. It contained her cherished rosary, the one she had gotten at the Vatican in 1960 and had had blessed by Pope John the XXIII in St. Peter's Basilica Square. The rosary beads were brown in color, the cross modest.

She hadn't been a Catholic then, but buying the rosary and having it blessed had seemed the thing to do at the time. Her Reverend had been non-denominational Christian, embracing all; and she, of course, had followed her husband's lead.

Olive didn't really miss her deceased husband, the Reverend William Norris. Near the end he had even become an obstacle in her relationship with Kirby. But now, praying alone in this silent church, she thought it would be easier if she had someone to help and support her in her struggle to free Kirby. For a fleeting moment she wished William was still alive.

But he wasn't, and that was that.

Olive did miss not having grandchildren. Both her daughters-in-law--barren. She tried to remember, wasn't there something in the Bible about that?

All she had now was Kirby. Walter didn't count, he'd married that horrid Melissa woman.

Solemnly Olive touched the crucifix on her rosary and began, "In the name of the Father, the Son, and the Holy Ghost."

She would say the rosary before starting to clean.
Olive hadn't completely given up on The Blessed Virgin.
She just had to pray harder.

After a quick visit to the kitchen where she extracted
solemn promises from Bernard and Martha to handle what they
now dubbed "The County Incident," Belinda grabbed a rain-
slicker, just in case, and headed to Covington to tackle Walter
and Melissa Norris.

Maybe this afternoon she would get the lead she needed.
If anyone could give her the inside scoop on Lana and Kirby, it
should be Kirby's brother and sister-in-law.

Not that she wasn't apprehensive. Belinda needed to get
this interview right. If she screwed up and turned Walter and
Melissa off, she wasn't sure who to turn to next for information
on the couple.

By the time Belinda reached I-90 it was raining. On
weekday afternoons Puget Sound freeways started piling up
around 2:00 P.M. and remained that way until after rush-hour.
She figured with rain thrown into the mix, her drive could turn
into a nightmare. To avoid a possible standstill on I-405, she cut
off I-90 onto Highway 18, notorious for accidents, but a quick
shortcut to the southern part of Puget Sound.

It was a smart move. Within half an hour Belinda was
standing on the covered front stoop of a newer and expansive
custom home sitting on a couple of nicely-treed acres. And it
wasn't raining on that particular spot in Covington.

After a deep breath followed by a nervous jab at their
doorbell, Belinda heard Westminster chimes within the Norris
home. She could also hear dogs barking--somewhere from the
rear--but she wasn't sure how many or whether they were inside
or out.

Involuntarily, a smile passed her lips and Belinda
felt her jaw and shoulders relax a bit. The thought of canines
soothed her edginess--the Norris couple couldn't be that bad,
now could they?

Walter and Melissa, accompanied by a jet black German

Shepherd and a Golden Retriever, arrived together at the front
door to meet Belinda.

The expressions on the couple's faces were clear--they
had been waiting for her arrival, and seemed glad she had come.
Belinda hadn't needed to worry.

After hellos were exchanged and iced tea and cake were
served, Commander, their German Shepherd, and Max, Lana
and Kirby's Golden Retriever, had to be appreciated and petted.
Then there was the rose garden rimming the back patio to be
pointed out and admired.

Their home was furnished in moderately priced Early
American with warm blues and deep greens. Some pieces were
clearly antiques and heirlooms. Adam, Belinda now thought,
had been overly harsh in his assessment of the "warm feel" of
the Norris home.

On top of that, Belinda found Melissa a gracious and
practiced hostess.

Melissa was petite in height and build, with a narrow
pinched face that wasn't helped by thin lips and unusually
violet-colored squinty eyes. Her makeup however was applied
expertly, did wonders to enhance her features, and spoke
of a woman who cared about her appearance and spent the
appropriate money necessary to put her best face forward.

She was dressed casually and tastefully in what Belinda
recognized as a Nordstrom outfit, and a gold chain supporting a
sizable ruby hung from a thin and model-long neck.

Walter on the other hand, was dressed in worn jeans and
a well washed Hendley shirt. He had one of those mouths that
seemed to be perpetually smiling and was touched with a hint
of sensuality. His eyes were dark brown, deep set, and alert.
Unfortunately, like his brother Kirby, and despite his appealing
mouth and eyes, Walter was also not a handsome man. In
fact, his head was too large, his nose too big, his lips too thick,
his neck too short, his torso too long, and his ears protruded
inordinately from his head.

Consequently, Belinda found the Norris brothers
amazing and inexplicable; and she couldn't help but wonder
what the Reverend William Norris had looked like.

Had the Reverend been homely, but with the same

come-hither eyes? If he had, what an effect that must have had on his female parishioners.

Belinda also noticed Walter seemed content to let Melissa do the introductions, serve refreshments, and carry the initial chitchat.

The three of them eventually settled in on the patio, sipped tea, munched carrot cake, and talked. Commander and Max were more interested in sniffing around in the bushes along the back fence.

"It's about time Olive realized the great Calvin Pope is all show and not worth the thousands she's shelling out." Melissa's voice was deep in resonance, cultured, clear and concise--quite fitting with her personality. "I must say, though, you're not at all what I expected when she told us she'd hired a detective." Mildly implied in her tone was a question of Belinda's *bona fides*.

Belinda was unapologetic. "Books and their covers, as the cliché goes. My success in clearing Kirby I believe will have a lot to do with the information I get from people like you. I believe the motive for killing Lana is hidden somewhere in the details of her life."

"Oh, be assured, we'll help you in anyway we can." She looked to Walter. "Right, honey?"

"Absolutely. What do you want to know?" He drained his glass and looked at Belinda eagerly. "Kirby didn't kill Lana. I know that for a fact. It's not in his personality."

Melissa agreed. "Honestly, Kirby wouldn't even kill spiders in his own house. He'd scoop them up in an envelope and release them outside." She refilled Belinda's glass. "Do you want to ask us specific questions, or should we just let it flow?"

"Why don't you start by telling me what Lana was like? You know, her personality, what she did, who were her friends? How she and Kirby got along."

Walter and Melissa exchanged a glance, then Walter finally took the lead. "I don't think either of us can say we really knew Lana. But I can give you my opinion." He smiled indulgently at his wife. "Which I don't think is as harsh as Melly's."

Belinda nodded her head encouragingly.

"My sister-in-law," Walter continued, "was a rather self absorbed person. I'm not sure what Kirby or Mother have told you...." Again a quick exchange of looks with Melissa. "But she wasn't a generous person. Lana didn't exactly control their money, but she did pay the bills and had a large say in how their money was spent."

Melissa added, "How she looked and how her house looked were more important to her than Kirby."

It was clear from her tone, Melissa had not liked her sister-in-law.

"How Kirby let her get away with some of the things she did--he's such a sweet guy." She reached across the table and squeezed Walter's hand. "A lot like Walter. Funny how Olive could raise such sweet boys and be such a b--." Melissa caught herself with a nervous little laugh.

Commander came over to Belinda and sat directly in front of her and stared--the canine's eyes quizzical and intelligent. Belinda figured he was trying to determine if she was friend or foe. She held her hand out to him, palm up; which he sniffed, and then nodded his approval.

Belinda restarted their conversation. "Walter and Melissa," she said, leaning forward. "I'm not here to judge, just collect information. Anything negative you have to say about anyone stays with me. I don't think Kirby killed Lana and I want to find out who did. None of us are perfect and if Kirby or Olive or Lana have character flaws, so be it. We all do."

Belinda straightened up and smiled, earnestly, she hoped. She needed to come across as competent and sincere. "But those kind of things are important because they could lead to someone who had it in for Lana or Kirby. Or even Olive, just for those 'personality' reasons. Believe me, I won't hold anything you say against you. I just want to know how you saw things."

"I think Kirby still loved Lana," Walter admitted. "But I don't think there was much of a relationship left between the two."

"Do you think your brother was having an affair?"

He laughed, "I hope so!" Then apologized, "Poor joke. Sorry. To be honest, I don't really know. Kirby and I didn't share that kind of information. Maybe with Mother..." His voice trailed off, other thoughts evidently taking over. Thoughts Walter was appeared reluctant to share.

Belinda however rushed to press the point, "I don't want to sound insensitive, but so far it seems like Olive..." She had started but was now stuck and at a loss for the appropriate words. How the heck do you ask a person why their mother doesn't like them as much as their sibling?

Melissa followed Belinda's line of thought and wasn't shy about addressing the mother-son issue. "Olive has always favored Kirby." she said. "Kirby this, Kirby that. The only time she called or came over was to tell us something about Kirby and Lana."

"You're being a bit unfair, Melly," Walter countered mildly. "Mother has always paid more attention to Kirby, even when we were kids. Lana didn't change anything in that respect." His tone of voice and body language indicated this wasn't such a big deal.

No repressed sibling rivalry? Belinda doubted that, despite his verbal and body language.

Walter continued, "Kirby and I have talked about it actually. Ironic thing, he wished she'd just leave him alone. Always felt smothered."

"Well," Melissa insisted. "It just isn't right."

Had it ever occurred to Melissa that sibling jealousy was a darned good motive for murder? Belinda wondered. More likely, Melissa was one smart cookie and was playing the innocent as a reverse psychology ploy.

"What about Lana?" Belinda asked. "Did Olive like Lana?"

"I don't think she disliked her," Walter equivocated.

"Oh Walter, why don't you just tell Belinda the truth? This isn't the time for nicey-nicey." The exasperation Belinda heard in Melissa's voice made her think Walter's "hear no evil, see no evil" perspective was a personality constant.

A small breeze stirred from nowhere and rustled the branches of the old-growth cedars surrounding the Norris' patio. The movement caught Commander's attention, drawing him away from his sit-in inquisition of Belinda. Max also appeared from somewhere else on the property and joined the hunt for the source of the wind. They seemed happy together.

"Nice of you to take Max in," Belinda mused, off track. "I had wondered where he was."

"Sure thing Olive wasn't going to take care of him," Melissa said, anger sharpening her words.

Walter sighed. "Okay Ms. Jones, Melissa is right," he acknowledged. "You should get the truth. It's just that it doesn't seem right talking badly about one's mother." He paused for a moment. "Or about the dead. But if it will help you, Mother didn't like Lana, and for that matter, she doesn't like Melly." He scoffed sardonically and squirmed a bit in his arm chair. "In fact, Mother didn't take to anyone Kirby or I liked, male or female." Then less critically, he added, "Maybe that's the way it is with all mothers. I don't know. And to your question about Max, Mother's not a dog fancier like Melly and me. Not that she dislikes them--but, you know, some people are dog people and some aren't. And to be honest, even though Lana took Max for a walk every morning, Max is really Kirby's dog. Not Mother's or Lana's."

"Your mother seemed nice when we met," Belinda offered as she tried to reconcile the distraught purple vision she'd met the day before with the Norris' portrayal of Olive.

"My mother *is* nice. She goes to mass almost everyday, cleans St. Francis church, volunteers at the free-meals-program. It's just that she's protective when it comes to her sons. Prime example--she hired you to help Kirby." Walter stood up and walked over to the edge of their flagstone patio and looked out into an extensive rhododendron garden.

Melissa refrained from further comment on Olive, but returned to Lana. "Whether Olive liked Lana or not is probably not relevant, don't you think?" She leaned across the table toward Belinda. "You really want to know about Lana. Her character, things she did, right?"

"Right."

Apropos to Belinda's earlier question, Walter turned back to the two women and said, "You know, I think Kirby might have actually been having an affair."

"Why do you think that?"

"Don't know, just a feeling." He shrugged.. "Like I said earlier, Kirby didn't confide in me, but I got the idea the last couple of times we saw each other that he wanted to tell me something. And now that I really think about it, Kirby has always been Mr. Goody-Goody to Mother. An affair probably isn't something he'd confide to her." He shook his head sagely. "But my brother isn't a saint by any stretch of the imagination." Then he turned back to contemplating their garden

"Do you have a woman's name for me?"

"Nope. Sorry," he answered over his shoulder.

Belinda straightened herself against her chair back and sighed. "Well, it's a place to start. I plan on seeing Kirby in the morning. I'll press him on the point. And," she added to forestall any objection from Walter, "rest assured, I won't divulge the source of my information." She was thoughtful for a few seconds, then said, "I still don't have a picture of Kirby and Lana as a couple. Can either of you tell me anything more about their relationship?"

"I think they both had their separate lives." Walter turned back to look at Belinda. "I know Kirby spent a lot of time at work, often going in early and staying late. Working weekends kind of thing. My brother is fairly ambitious. Lana was sort of a joiner--you know--book club meetings, bridge group, athletic club."

Melissa interjected, "Lana and I both went to the same health club in Issaquah. We both have the same trainer."

"Have you ever met a Janice Tanner there?" It didn't seem relevant, but Belinda asked anyway.

"Sure, Janice and I often have a drink together after we work out. Seems like we're often there at the same time." Acknowledging Belinda's raised eyebrow, Melissa added, "Health drinks. There's a juice bar at the club."

"Anyone at the club Lana seemed tight with?"

"Well, I don't really know. Lana had a different start time. And usually when I did see her there, she was exercising and we'd just exchange a little wave. Lana was big on little waves and pecks on the cheek."

"Do you know her trainer's name?"

"Todd Johnson."

Walter perked up. "You think he might have something to do with it?"

"Too early to tell, Walter, but it's another lead."

Both Walter and Melissa smiled, and Melissa spoke for the both of them. "You know we both really like Kirby. And we both know he couldn't have killed Lana, no matter what she was like. I certainly hope we've told you something."

They talked another ten or fifteen minutes, Melissa giving Belinda the name and address of their athletic club, and Walter filling in more detail on Olive's motherly intentions. "When all is said and done, Mother took good care of us. Father too, though he spent so much of his time at church or with parishioners."

A memory surfaced for Belinda. "Isn't St. Francis a Catholic church? And I thought Olive referred to your father as 'Reverend.'" There was also the little matter of Catholic priests not marrying.

"Quite true. Father led several Protestant congregations, then we became Episcopalian for some reason. Then right after Father passed away, Mother became a Catholic."

Melissa tsked out the side of her mouth and shook her head. "Walter says his father was seldom called 'Reverend' at anytime, anyway. As to why Olive left the last church, all she would say was there weren't so many hypocrites at St. Francis."

"We don't know specifics on what Mother was talking about," Walter added.

He said his good-byes at the door so as to keep the dogs in while Melissa walked Belinda to her car. Once out of Walter's earshot, Melissa said, "I do know Olive 'converted' to Catholic because she didn't want to be in the same church with Maggie Muldune. She's the one Olive tried to get run out of the congregation because..."

"Because?"

Melissa sighed. "Well, because Maggie, I guess there's no way of getting around it--Maggie slept around. *Slut* was Olive's word for Maggie. I don't think this has anything to do with your investigation, but I thought I'd better fill you in. I still go to St. Hilary's."

Olive evidently was not a tolerant woman when it came

to morality. If Kirby was having an affair, Walter was probably right, he wouldn't have confided in Olive. But maybe this thing with Maggie went deeper? Revenge toward an overly zealous Olive through her son and daughter-in-law? Belinda doubted it. Melissa snatched a quick look back at the house. Walter was nowhere in sight. She leaned in closer and furtively touched Belinda's arm. "But what I really wanted to tell you, Belinda, is I *know* Lana was fooling around. You know, having an affair."

Belinda's mind immediately jumped to Todd Johnson, but Melissa said, "I think his name is Jerry. I heard Lana on the phone once; she didn't know I was close enough to hear. And, this was recent, right before she died. I'm thinking maybe he killed her."

"Jerry," Belinda rolled the name over her tongue and in her mind. "Thanks, Melissa, I'll see what I can dig up."

Thunder clapped and both women jumped. "Funny day, huh?" Melissa mused. "Rain, then sun, on and off, all day." For a moment, she chewed on her lip thoughtfully. "I wasn't that close to Lana, but I'm guessing her housekeeper, Mrs. Keyes, would know the most about Lana and Kirby's relationship. You should give her a try."

Belinda expected tomorrow to be another busy day, but maybe she should fit Mrs. Keyes in. Melissa was right, who better than the housekeeper to know what was going on between husband and wife?

Once back in town, her brain still playing with the information she'd gotten from Walter and Melissa, Belinda almost whizzed right past the Snoqualmie Valley Credit Union without dropping off the deposit she had prepared earlier in the day.

The credit union wasn't large or fancy, but the building was fairly new, and the parking lot was large with roomy parking spaces. Most importantly to Belinda, the people were old-fashioned nice.

She pulled into a space near the front door between a vacant handicapped spot and a lilac '67 Cadillac.

"Perfect car for Olive Norris," she told her dashboard. Then before she could gather her purse, keys, and deposit, Olive Norris in person came out of the credit union and started digging into her gigantic O. N.-emblazoned bag, probably looking for her car keys.

"It just can't be." Belinda again informed her dashboard. "A purple car too. That's really just too much."

Then she smiled to herself, after all, there was actually something endearing about an old lady who not only bedecked and be-dangled herself in shades of purple, but who also extended the theme to her mode of transportation.

Truly amazing.

Olive was so intent on retrieving her keys and getting in her car that she didn't notice Belinda as the occupant of the car right next to her. A frown creased her forehead and she seemed preoccupied.

Belinda decided to remain incognito and slid down low in her seat. A drizzle had started and was spotting her windshield, helping her hide.

She really didn't want to face Olive yet. She didn't have anything to tell her except her other son and daughter-in-law had just trashed her. So Belinda waited discreetly until she could see Olive's Caddy pull out of the parking lot in her rearview mirror.

After a quick dash through light rain, and once inside, the credit union was toasty and dry. Laura, a young teller Belinda recognized was on duty and free.

Laura greeted Belinda with her usual large smile. "Hello, Ms. Jones, what can I do for you today?"

"How do you remember customer's names like that?" Belinda shot a quick glance at the young woman's name tag to make sure *she* was remembering correctly. "Laura, do you have a trick up your sleeve?"

"Oh, you give me too much credit. I don't remember everyone, just some, like you. You're distinctive looking and I've been to your place for dinner with my Mom. You weren't around, but I met your brother. He came around to the tables to ask if we were enjoying our food. It was great."

Well! She would have to tell Bernie his dining room

schmoozing was paying off. "Mrs. Norris is *distinctive.*"

"Wow, you can say that again!"

Belinda handed Laura her deposit envelope. "I'll wait for my receipt if you don't mind." She smiled at the teller, nodded toward the exit, and hoped she sounded like a close and long time friend of Olive's. "In fact, is Olive okay? She seemed upset. I tried getting her attention," she lied. "But she seemed preoccupied."

"It's terrible what happened." Expertly, Laura counted the deposit, stowed the money, checks, and credit card reconciliation in their proper places. Then as they waited for Belinda's receipt to pop out of her machine, Laura said quietly, "I'd be upset too."

"Yes, losing your daughter-in-law, especially to murder, is a terrible thing." So Olive was visibly wearing her grief. Not exactly the she-devil Melissa would have her believe.

Laura took a quick look around, then leaned forward confidentially. "Sometimes it just seems so unfair. You know, bad things happening to such nice people. Mrs. Norris is such a good person, you know. We used to go to the same church, you know. My Mom just loves Mrs. Norris." The young woman lowered her voice almost to a whisper. "There was a very wicked couple," she blushed, "wife swapping."

Belinda made an appropriate whispery reply, "Oh my."

"Yep. Mrs. Norris had them drummed right out. Wish she was still there. And Mr. Norris, he was such a kind man."

Belinda shook her head, took her receipt, and headed out back into the afternoon. The sun was now out, and the air was sparkling clear.

She took a thoughtful deep breath of refreshing rain-washed air before getting back into her car and heading home.

"So what's the scoop? Do we really only have forty-eight hours to get new raspberry bushes back in? How can they do this? Can we complain to anyone?" Belinda asked in rapid succession.

The defeated look on Bernard's face told Belinda

answers she would not like to hear were forthcoming.

"Since you asked me to handle this," he said. "I'll spare you the details and jump to the bottom line of what I think we should do." They were in the office, Bernard behind the desk and Belinda with her knees pulled up to her chest in one armchair. Naja, eyes closed, occupied the other.

Bernard said, "I made a quick dash to the County Offices in Issaquah this afternoon while Martha prepped dinner."

"You missed your nap." Belinda thought her dear brother must be extremely tired; he certainly looked it.

In truth, so was she.

"Yeah, well, we sort of have an emergency, right?"

"Right." Emergency, yes that was precisely the word she had used earlier in the afternoon when persuading Bernard to deal with "The County Incident."

"As best I can tell, Bella, and I haven't had time to read the whole code or talk to more than a couple people in her department, is Lois Michael was definitely out of line in her manner and demands. I guess she's not a 'people person,' even though she considers herself as protecting 'the people's' interest. Basically, though, cutting down raspberries does fall under their purview, and we do have a very short turn around on bringing that stretch back to the way it was. We have no property rights in these matters under the code."

Belinda still wanted to believe reason should prevail. "But it's flat out there, Bernie, you know that. We only took out a few bushes. We've always been concerned about the environment, there's nothing eroding, no species being harmed...."

Bernard sighed heavily, "Listen, I know this sounds harsh, but we don't have any recourse unless we want to pay a lot of money to some lawyers and take the county to court. We don't have any power or political influence. So we do what they say, or move. Actually we'd have to do what they say before we could actually sell and move anyway."

Belinda wanted to scream and collapse, simultaneously. But compelling as it was, that was the stuff of childhood.

"You'll have to grow up sometime, Bella dear." Grandma Glory's words still rang clearly. "How much for Jorge to

replant? It's only a few bushes."

"Well, that's another bad part. They're claiming all our bushes are too close to the trail and have to be moved back."

"How much will it cost?"

Defeat.

"Eleven hundred dollars."

"No choice, have we? Damn, Bernie. Who the hell called up and complained? And what could they be complaining about?"

Cedar Valley Residence sat on three acres, with a trail and then open farmland to its rear, and at least an acre between the residence and its neighbors to the North and South, one of which was a church for goodness sake.

Out front, a row of five or six 1940s era bungalows sat across the street from them, but Cedar Valley Residence didn't obstruct their view or impact their access to the trail.

Belinda just couldn't imagine why anyone around would give a damn.

"I'll get Jorge started first thing in the morning," Bernard assured her. He reached out and took Belinda's hands. "You look so down." He then patted her hands comfortingly, but with resolve. "I think I'll go to the kitchen and bring you up a piece of chocolate and raspberry cheesecake Martha made for dinner. And maybe a cup of tea, with lemon?"

Bless Bernie! Food made everything better. Well almost everything. *He* was successfully dealing with Lois Michael, but *she* didn't have a clue who had murdered Lana Norris.

The cheesecake turned out to be marvelously rich and creamy, but later, around nine in the evening, Belinda was hungry again. And tired. Almost too tired to bother with food.

Hunger eventually won out and she made a call to the kitchen and Martha obliged by whipping together a BLT pilled high with bacon and slathered with mayonnaise.

When Belinda came down to the kitchen to collect her prize, Martha issued a caution. "This is not something you should eat this late," she said. "You'll have nightmares. Count on it."

Belinda of course ignored Martha's warning, and while watching a pre-recorded episode of *House* and eating from atop a TV tray, Belinda savored every bite, let no stray morsel escape, and licked every drop of mayonnaise off her fingers and plate.

Luckily, neither Naja nor Buster were around to insist on their cut.

Her tummy satisfied, she got into bed, propped herself up with pillows, and stared at the boob-tube for a couple more shows.

In between the late-night news and a later-night talk show, Buster joined her in bed, and pushed himself contentedly against her side like a sack of potatoes. Naja's whereabouts were still unknown.

Sometime after the talk-show host's monologue and the special guest's appearance, Belinda fell asleep, dirty dishes still on the stand, and the TV on.

At one in the morning, as forewarned by Martha, grease-and-fat provoked dreams found Belinda on a viewer's ledge at the eastern end of the Grand Canyon. It was dusk and everyone else had left the park except for her, Lana, and Olive Norris. Lana stood at Belinda's right side. And Olive to Belinda's left.

So vividly real was her dream state, Belinda's mind could feel a gentle dry canyon wind caress her cheeks, and a whiff of pine and juniper entice her nostrils.

Indeed, she was also dreaming in color. The scenery was spectacular and overwhelmingly beautiful, the canyon's rugged and vivid grandeur magnified and enhanced by evening light and attendant shadows.

Yet, she felt herself trembling with apprehension and fear.

Then incomprehensibly and quite suddenly as it often is in dreams--Lana, her figure outlined in dusk light and wearing an Ester Williams-style swimsuit, took a swan-dive out into the great expanse. A spectacular dive it was, part flight and part free fall, head back, lower back arched, and toes pointed.

It was then that Belinda's conscious mind managed to re-assert itself, and she awoke groggy, sweaty, and scared--Lana's eventual fate unknown.

Had Lana morphed into a graceful bird of flight, gliding on Grand Canyon wind eddies, or...?

"Darn," she said, sitting up. She hated ridiculous dreams that defied commonly accepted principles of physics, yet still managed to feel so real.

Buster was gone and Naja was in his place. Dogs.

But then Belinda caught a wonderful aroma--and her involuntarily response was to smile dreamily. It was commonly known and accepted among Cedar Valley residents that Martha baked whenever she damn well felt like it. Tonight was evidently one of those times.

So under wafts of lusciousness, and with the help of several deep yoga breaths and an old mantra she still retained from way-back-when, Belinda finally fell back asleep--time unknown--with her last waking thoughts formed by the faint and very real smell of cinnamon-pecan coffeecake spiked with Contreau. Belinda was sure the lovely aroma teasing her nostrils would lead to better and sweeter dreams.

PART TWO

In for a Dime, in for a Dollar

CHAPTER THREE

Wednesday

No matter Belinda had eaten late the previous night, no matter the disconcerting Grand Canyon dream she'd had, and no matter it was only around 5:30 A.M Wednesday morning, she woke up ravenous--and after brushing her teeth and throwing on jeans and a T-shirt, she headed straight for the kitchen and was on her second piece of coffeecake and third cup of tea when Martha joined her to prep for breakfast.

Martha, upon seeing the gaping hole in one of her coffeecakes and the crumbs surrounding Belinda, smiled and teased, "You look like the little mouse who found the cracker barrel."

"It's your fault, you know. I think I smelled this stuff all night. Don't you ever sleep?" She finished off her second piece and licked her fingers--each one individually--savoring every last smidgen of icing. "Actually, when *do* you leave your suite or this kitchen? I really don't think you take enough time off."

For morning-loving Belinda, even after a rough night, this was a wonderful time of day.

The Residence was cool and quiet. What better time to pig-out on coffeecake and ponder the way of the world in general, and the ways of Martha in particular?

"You sound just like your brother," Martha answered. "And haven't we had this conversation before?" She was in freshly laundered chef-whites--looking and sounding in fine fettle for someone who had probably been up baking most of the night.

Belinda didn't immediately counter. Instead, she reached down and patted Buster. He had reappeared and was now laying at her feet hoping for the miracle of stray crumbs. But Belinda was still thinking about Martha, and considering if she had any right to stick her nose into her affairs.

Easier to pry into Martha's life than figure out who killed Lana.

She figured Martha, like everyone else in the world, had her own secrets. But it didn't seem natural for a woman her age to be such a recluse. And Belinda fancied Martha's secrets might involve demons--demons fierce enough to run away from and stay hidden among pots and pans, knives, and kitchen chrome. Had Martha had her own "The Bum" to deal with? Heck, maybe she was in a witness protection program for all she knew. Her references had seemed valid enough, but those things could be easily fabricated.

On the other hand, Bernard hardly ever ventured out either; and for herself, she certainly didn't have much of a social life.

"Yeah, I guess we have talked about this before," Belinda eventually answered. "Bernard doesn't take enough time off either." She glanced around the kitchen, "By the way, have you seen Naja?"

"Neither do you--take enough time off that is. And Naja's in my suite. For some reason she wanted to sleep with me last night. I figured it was because Buster was upstairs with you. I've been keeping a close eye on him since I freaked the other day. He seems okay, not inclined to leave at all like I thought. But Naja is acting weird. Jealous would be my guess."

Belinda nodded in knowing agreement and snagged another wedge of coffeecake. "Yeah, you're right about Naja, *and* about the time off. Maybe when things settle down around here...."

"Don't kid yourself. There's always reasons why you can't 'get away.' I know. All those years when I had my own business, I always had an excuse. Thought the damn place would fall apart without me." She chuckled. "Truth was quite different. The guys I sold it to are making a lot more money than I ever did."

Belinda also knew first hand the truth of what Martha said. Sound advice--hard to follow.

Martha opened the refrigerator door and pulled out a watermelon. "Which reminds me, since you mentioned making money, *I* ran some figures the other night and I think we need to talk." Martha's tone turned careful, neutral.

"About what?" Belinda asked absently while

considering having another cup of tea.

"Money. And the lack of."

That got Belinda's attention. "Uh oh. If this is about raising your salary...." She certainly would like to pay Martha more, but that certainly would move them into the red. Maybe they should just tell Martha the truth about their trust fund money and raise her salary?

"It's not about my salary." She put the watermelon down on the island counter and pulled up a stool so she was facing Belinda. "It's about the Residence."

Martha looked away for a second; and when she returned her gaze to Belinda, her expression and tone reflected determination. "I know this is none of my business. I'm butting in, but hell, Belinda, after these last four years, Cedar Valley Residence has become my home." She took a deep breath. "And you and Bernard have become like family." Only a tiny glistening in the corners of her eyes betrayed her emotions. "So what happens here is important to me."

Belinda carefully poured herself another cup of tea and with a pantomime gesture offered to pour Martha a cup. She needed a couple seconds, since she didn't consider herself good at handling moments like this. "I know how much you care. Otherwise you wouldn't work your butt off like you do. You want lemon and sugar?"

Martha nodded.

Belinda chose her next words carefully, she didn't want to mess up this moment with Martha. She was not prone to what she considered schmaltzy sentiment but at the same time Belinda felt she owed Martha an in-kind response. "We feel the same about you."

"*Sometimes simple statements are the best statements, Bella Dear.*"

Belinda took her own fortifying deep breath. "And I want to hear what you have to say."

Encouraged, Martha continued, "So I ran some numbers, nothing like the stuff you do, and a lot were guesses. But Belinda, I don't see how you're keeping this place going. You can't possibly be making any money."

"Well." Again she considered, *maybe we should tell*

Martha the truth.

"So I'm guessing you're 'deficit spending' as the politicians would say. Probably using up savings from your last business. Up to now though, I wasn't worried, I figured this place would start turning a profit in a couple years. Now though, well, I'm worried."

Belinda acknowledged Martha's words with a slight nod.

"These thefts are going to lose you some loyal residents. Suppose we don't figure out who's doing it? Can't you just tell Vera that Kaitlin has to go back home?"

"So you think it's Kaitlin?"

Martha sighed. "Oh, I just don't know, Belinda. Things didn't start disappearing until she came here and her attitude toward adults is horrendous. But..."

"But what?"

"Well you know Bernard and I have been keeping an eye on her. And well, the girl is listening to French tapes on that stupid headset most of the time. I thought it was loud music destroying her brain and eardrums. And," Martha leaned across the table conspiratorially, "a lot of the time when we think she's in Vera's suite sulking, she's actually reading."

"So, if you're smart you can't also be a thief? Is that what you're saying?"

"Of course not! What I'm saying is, it isn't as clear cut as we might hope."

"You actually catch her doing anything suspicious?"

"Not really."

This time, Belinda sighed. "Well, you're right as usual Martha--these thefts aren't good for us. And if everyone moves we're definitely screwed. And this damn raspberry inspector, she's costing us more money that we can't afford to spend."

"Is Olive Norris paying you?"

"Yeah." Belinda didn't confide that the flat two-thousand dollar fee she had asked for wouldn't make a dent in next month's bills if all the residents left. "But don't worry, something will come up."

Then she decided to tell Martha about her Grand Canyon dream.

After the telling, Martha asked, "And when you went back to sleep you didn't finish the dream?"

Belinda scoffed, "Never happens."

"Does to me, all the time."

"Not to me. My new dream went in a completely different direction." A direction she was surprised still pulled at her unconscious; and hated that it did.

"Ah," Martha intuitively said. "Back to dreaming about 'The Bum?'"

Indeed, contrary to her hopes last night, Belinda's subsequent dreams had not been sweeter. "Yep, sadly so," she answered while helping herself to another small sliver of coffeecake.

By 8:00 A.M. Belinda had balanced the previous days receipts, made up another deposit; and because Martha's comments were still nagging at her brain, run another break-even analysis. Her results weren't encouraging.

By 9:00 A. M. she had showered, dressed anew in a going-outside outfit, and started her drive into Seattle.

And by 9:30 A.M. she was sitting across the table from Kirby Norris in the King County Jail--the same guard as before vigilant at the door.

"Why didn't you tell me about having an affair?" Belinda knew she had to win Kirby's trust, and control him at the same time. "I'm trying to help you. And I can't do that without you telling me the truth. No secrets, Kirby, or I'm out of here."

Everyone has secrets, Bella Dear, everyone has secrets.

"If you knew I was having an affair would you have started helping me?"

"Of course." Belinda shot back, knowing she was telling a lie.

He tsked and snorted, but without much animosity. "You can try lying to me, Belinda Jones. But I know you would have written me off as a philandering, murdering, scumbag if I'd told you about Moira." He sighed and looked at the guard.

"Okay if I go over to the window, Mack?"

The guard nodded a solemn affirmative, and Kirby got up, stretched, and walked over to the Lilliputian-sized barred window looking out onto the tops of downtown Seattle buildings. For a long moment his back was to Belinda and Mack. Finally when Kirby did turn around his demeanor was calm and resigned.

Belinda was again surprised at his physique-- even shorter, more stout, and more asymmetrical than she remembered from her first visit. However, his look of remembered affection and longing metamorphosed Kirby-the-frog into Sir-Kirby-the-Prince.

"Moira Stephens used to be my boss," he explained. "And this is going to sound like forties pulp fiction, but Moira is a real 'looker.' She has bright shiny auburn hair, come to bed eyes, curves in the right places--all wrapped-up in a business suit." He chuckled self-mockingly. "Cliché ridden, I know. But damnit, Moira is a vision."

Belinda had seen several pictures of Lana. "Kirby," she said trying to keep her tone neutral despite her accusing words. "Your wife was *beautiful.*"

He sat back down across the table from her and smiled wryly. "You're right there. But there's more to it than just looks. I can't really explain it though. Just the first time I met Moira it was *kismet.*"

Kismet, of all things. Moira must indeed be something special. "Is Moira married?"

"No!" he answered emphatically. "Moira would never cheat on *her* husband."

"But, Lana would?"

"We've had that discussion already."

"You're right. Let's drop Lana. Fill me in on your relationship with Moira."

"In what way? And why?"

"Look, Kirby, I really don't care who you sleep with." She needed to manage this conversation better if she was going to find Lana's murderer. "But we're looking for someone besides you who had a motive to kill your wife." Belinda leaned forward, holding Kirby's eyes in a firm gaze. "Now I know you're not as dense as you're putting on. Either you want me to help you, or you don't. What's it going to be?" She was pleased with the firmness she heard in her voice.

"Moira wouldn't kill Lana," Kirby countered. "Besides, she couldn't have."

"You know that for a fact?"

"Yes."

She waited.

Kirby thought for a bit then sighed. "I guess I better tell you the whole story, huh?"

"I guess you better." Why was he making this so hard? It was like pulling teeth.

He leaned back in his chair and dropped his head back slightly, evidently remembering. "Like I said before, and no, it isn't justification, but Lana and I pretty much had gone our separate ways these latter years. I wasn't planning on having an affair, but there Moira was. It just happened."

He cleared his throat, sat back up straight, and continued, "Moira couldn't have killed Lana because at the time of the murder she was with me."

"Go on, " Belinda said flatly.

"Everything I've told you so far is true except the part about being at the meeting the whole time. After the breakfast part, and after the slides had started, I got up like I was going for a coffee refill but I slipped out the back instead. I think the waiter, I don't remember his name, saw me, but I'm not sure. Moira was waiting for me in a room we'd reserved, and well..." he spread his hands and gave Belinda a knowing look.

"And you reappeared around...?" *Sex with his wife the night before, then sex with his paramour the next morning--amazing.*

"Oh, I don't know, around nine or so because I remember getting back to work around 9:30 A.M. and calling Mother to see how she was. You know she lives on our property, in a separate studio apartment?"

There was something very screwy about a man slipping out of a meeting to have a morning tryst with a colleague a few floors below, then popping back to his office and calling his mother to see how she's doing. Kirby, Lana, and Olive's relationships were definitely unusual.

"You can check with the hotel if you want," he continued. "We registered as Mr. and Mrs. Smith."

Belinda raised a sarcastic eyebrow at his hackneyed use of "Smith." She would have wished him more creative. "I assume you haven't told Senator about this."

"Hell, no. He's already trying to hang me out to dry. Mother has almost fired him several times." Kirby made a noise with his mouth that sounded like a large balloon suddenly deflating. "But he's gotten so many people off. We're scared to try anyone else."

It was a good alibi. But not good enough. He certainly could have killed Lana before the meeting.

After he gave her Moira's phone number, Belinda asked, "Is there anything else you haven't told me?"

He shook his head.

"Kirby, I also want to know about the gun." From the beginning Kirby had not seemed to her the gun-toting type. And how could he be so stupid as to leave it in the trunk of his car?

"There's nothing really to tell you except I didn't even know how to load the damn thing." He shook his head in apparent amazement. "Lana and Mother said we needed them for protection, one for our house, one for Mother's apartment. Wish I'd never listened to them." His expression spoke, *"Wish I'd never listened to them about a lot of things."*

"By the way, how did Calvin Pope arrange this private meeting room?"

Kirby shrugged. "Beats the heck out of me."

Belinda's mind was clicking off the items she didn't want to miss. "Any ideas on the ring? Special meaning for anyone?" She was thinking Moira. The hated wife as motive for murder?

"No one would want the damn thing," he said. "Wasn't worth even worrying about. I can't imagine who would want it. It isn't valuable at all."

Belinda doubted that. Some antique jewelry was quite valuable. Theft could not be ruled out.

"Have you told your mother about Moira?"

"No. But she's coming by this morning." Kirby's face

clearly registered discomfort and displeasure at the thought of informing Olive that he had been a very bad boy. "I guess I'd better tell her."

.

After Belinda, and then Olive's departures, and once back in his dank and depressing cell, Kirby flopped on his bed, face toward the ceiling, staring at the crack that zigzagged out from the door. "Maybe I shouldn't have told her everything," he said to the plasterwork.

It was early for lunch when Belinda arrived back in Cedar Valley, so she decided to see if she could catch Sheriff John Thomas in his office.

Weather-wise, the morning had turned out wonderfully. The skies still remained clear blue and cloudless despite forecasted thundershowers again.

She drove from Seattle to Cedar Valley on I-90 and the sight of evergreen laden hillsides and Cascade outcroppings temporarily overshadowed her thoughts of Lana Norris and problems at the Residence.

In fact, by the time she pulled up in front of the Sheriff's office, she was almost in good humor.

Belinda found John in his office, leaning back in his oversized swivel chair, legs crossed at the ankles and propped up on his desk, reading some kind of report.

"Hello, Bella," John said, through an amused smile. "I was just thinking about you guys. Thinking I might come over for lunch today. Do you know what Martha and Bernie are dishing up?" He was able to use "Bernie" because Bernard hadn't yet found the nerve to challenge him.

Belinda smiled in return. "You make it sound like we're running a hash-joint."

"You know," he reminisced. "Sometimes you sound just like your grandmother. 'Hash-joint' isn't exactly in the current vernacular."

She dragged a wooden slat-backed chair from against the wall to the front of his desk. "These things weigh a ton. Mind if I sit for a couple secs?" She didn't wait for a reply. "And if you think *I'm* out of date, this morning Kirby Norris called his paramour a 'looker.'"

"Whoa! You saw Norris today and he said he had a girlfriend?" John tossed his reading material on the desk and snapped upright--alert and listening. Belinda had his full attention.

She leaned forward, childlike in his presence, eager to tell him about her visit with Kirby.

When Belinda finished, and after a low whistle, John said, "I'll be damned, Bella. That gives him a pretty good alibi, now doesn't it? What was her name again, Moira something?"

"Moira Stephens. And well, yes, I guess that does give Kirby a good alibi. What *I* was thinking was *now* I have a new suspect with a motive."

"Who also has an alibi. How convenient they alibi each other." A wistful look passed fleetingly across his face. "This isn't really an open case, you know that, right? Kirby's going to trial--"

"I wish it were still an open case. *Your* case, Uncle John."

"Don't know about that. Would be interesting to solve, though, and I sure would be following up on other suspects." He looked up at the ceiling for a couple seconds, then back to her. "Kirby is too easy. But, I have my hands full with figuring out who bashed poor Philly on the head." He spread his hands, "And high profile cases like Kirby's, if you screw up..."

"So I've got two people who have motives but they also have alibis--each other. The prosecutor will easily make both their statements suspect."

"Maybe somebody saw them going in or out of their hotel room? Maybe somebody heard something? Maybe a bellman?"

She wasn't comforted. "Would the times have worked out for either of them to have sneaked back to Cedar Valley and kill Lana? Or done it before the meeting?"

He retrieved a file from a lower desk drawer. After a

couple minutes flipping papers, he said, "Well, let's see here.
Coroner says she was killed sometime between seven and ten
in the morning. The Puget Power line workers claim she didn't
pass them after nine." He dropped the folder on his desk with
the rest of the clutter. "I'd say our window is between seven and
nine A.M."

"Interesting. Not an open case, and not your case, but
you have a folder?"

He shrugged.

Belinda moved on. "Eye witnesses are notoriously
wrong."

"True enough."

"But still, I think you're right. Somebody attacked
Lana on that trail between seven and nine." She leaned down
and fumbled through her canvas carryall bag, spilling several
items in the process. "Good grief. What a mess I have in here.
Worse than Olive Norris." Finally she found her notebook.
"Okay, what I've got here is that Kirby's movements can be
independently verified until around eight. After that, it's his
word."

"Or Moira's word."

"They could have been in it together." Next she told
him what Kirby had said about the gun.

He shook his head in disbelief. "Doesn't know anything
about guns? Not even how to load the thing?"

She smiled indulgently at her lifelong friend. "Not
everyone is as comfortable with a gun as you or I, Uncle John.
But what he said reminded me of something. If Kirby was
telling me the truth about not even knowing how to load their
gun, maybe somebody else put the bullets in."

"Fingerprints. I'm guessing the lab..." he stopped, mid-
sentence. "Tell you what, Bella, I'm going to make a call and
make sure there're no prints on the bullets left in Kirby's thirty-
eight."

"It was Lana's thirty-eight too," Belinda reflected.

"Meaning?"

"I don't know."

They sighed in unison, then John donned his avuncular
look and voice. "I don't want you to be discouraged. You're

doing a good job."

"Now you're patronizing me," she said. "Will you always see me as 'little' Bella?"

"Yep."

She had to smile. Then they both got up and headed toward the door.

Belinda said, "I just can't see Kirby getting someone to kill Philly. He couldn't have done it personally. He's in jail. And why, for Christ's sake?"

"Just maybe," he said and held up a hand to ward off Belinda's objections. "Just maybe the two aren't connected. And don't curse, it's not becoming."

"Huh!"

"Okay, okay. For the time being we'll continue to assume Philly's death is somehow connected to Lana's, and I'll also concede you're grown enough to be a potty-mouth if you want. In the meantime, how about lunch?"

"Did we tell you Cousin Tessa's flying in today?"

"Tessa Harrington? Your Uncle Bernie and Aunt Cloris's kid?"

"One and the same."

He stopped for a moment and instructed Frieda, his latest temp, to forward any calls to his cell, and if she couldn't get hold of him, to call the Sheriff's office in North Bend. Then to Belinda, he said, "I'll be. Haven't seen Tessa in what, three or four years?"

"Yep."

When they arrived at the front door, he held it open for her. "Well, that'll be nice, now won't it?"

"If you say so."

He chuckled, "Come on, lets go get some chow. You can fill me in on anything else our boy Kirby had to say over lunch."

Lunch was a New Mexican-inspired quesadilla swimming in green-chili salsa for Belinda, and Yankee pot-roast and cornbread for John. After eating and a quick visit with Bernard, John headed back to his office to make some calls; and

Belinda, tired and "after-eating-sleepy", grabbed the keys to the minivan--she knew Tessa traveled with a substantial amount of luggage--and headed out for the long drive down to SeaTac Airport. It was time to pick up Cousin Tessa.
Oddly, and happily in Belinda's opinion, the topic of Kirby and Lana Norris did not resurface during lunch.

"I remember your place well," Tessa Harrington said in her distinctively petulant tone of voice. "You've made your own little world, warm and cozy, afghans on the couches, doilies in the parlor, vases always full of flowers. Must have cost you a fortune." Tessa's eyes were turned away from Belinda, looking out the passenger-side window.

Belinda was driving, keeping her eyes on the road in the heavy traffic surrounding SeaTac Airport. She wished she could see Tessa's face, however, to help judge her cousin's immediate intent.

Tessa continued, "No wonder Bernard never wants to leave. So safe." She turned her gaze to Belinda. "But don't worry, your precious Residence will survive, and you'll figure out who killed this Lana woman."

Despite the positive spin Tessa's words could have imparted, the way Tessa stressed *precious* left no doubt in Belinda's mind--even without actually turning to see her cousin's face--that nothing had changed in their relationship since their last meeting--three years ago for a family Thanksgiving in LA.

Not a big surprise, for even as children, Belinda and Bernard had dubbed her Tessa "the terrible."

Belinda forced herself to gloss over Tessa's jab and chanced a quick look for a second to catch her eye. "You give me too much credit."

Why had she mentioned the murder to Tessa anyway? As an ice breaker, the information had obviously failed.

This morning, Belinda was trying her best to start things off on the right note; and to that end, had arrived at SeaTac on time, early in fact, and waited at the crowded baggage carousel for Tessa.

However, the moment she caught sight of her cousin's slim and stylishly adorned figure coming down the escalator, Belinda knew this visit would again be a bumpy ride. For Tessa's features (refined to classical perfection by her plastic surgeon husband Gavin), were set in her characteristic disagreeable scowl.

From the airport, to the parking garage, to the car-- Tessa's animosity became more obvious; and by the time Belinda started the drive back home, the tension in the car between the two women was unavoidable.

Through the years, Belinda had never been able to figure out the source of Tessa's continued anger; and up to now, familial survival in dealing with her had evolved into a barely manageable tolerance. Which meant, she usually tried not to rise to Tessa's red flags.

"You're *just* so perfect, Belinda." Tessa went on. "Of course you had Grandma Glory and Grandpa Bert to pamper you. And you never had children. Care free and fancy free." Tessa hissed derisively as punctuation before her next jibe. "You even managed to get rid of Clive."

This was too far, even for Tessa. Her cousin had always been snide, but not this hurtful.

What the hell was going on?

Belinda had chosen to exit the airport onto Highway 99, then hop onto the freeway at the 509. But in response to this last salvo from Tessa, she abruptly pulled over into a car rental parking lot and stopped more suddenly than she would have wished.

"Look, Tessa," Belinda said through clenched teeth. She was finding it decidedly hard to keep herself, and her tone of voice in control. "I'm glad to see you. But that doesn't mean I'll put up with more than your usual nastiness. Why the hell did you come up here if you don't like Bernard and me?"

For several long moments they sat in silence, Belinda staring at Tessa's expertly made up profile, and her cousin staring straight ahead. Belinda was about to turn around and take her right back to the airport when she saw tears rolling down Tessa's cheeks.

Belinda had never seen her cry before, even as children; and now, was at a complete loss as to what to do or say.

Eventually, Tessa broke the silence. "You think I'm a crazy mean woman, I know. Maybe even stupid. But..."

"But what?" Belinda asked in a gentler tone than she felt.

Tessa sucked in a breath, then hiccuped. "I can't tell you yet. But I need a place to stay. And well, you and Bernard are my cousins. I didn't know where else to go." Finally she turned and met Belinda's eyes. "I'm sorry for being such a bitch. Sometimes I just can't help..." Again she didn't finish her thought.

"Be nice, Bella dear. You never know what it's like to walk in other people's shoes." Belinda did as Glory Jones bid. "Well," she said, "I think I better get you to Cedar Valley Residence so you can eat or nap or whatever. Don't worry, whatever it is, it'll be fine."

Who would have thought Tessa would have secrets of any kind? Tessa's seemingly glitzy LA life had always been an open book.

"Thank you, Belinda," Tessa said, then meekly changed the subject. "How is Bernard doing?"

Tessa sounded genuinely interested and concerned. Still, she didn't answer immediately.

"I mean," Tessa continued, "does he leave the residence much these days?"

"Yes. All the time," Belinda lied.

"And the dreams, visions I think he called them, right? Is he still having them?"

"No," Belinda lied again.

Once they arrived at the Residence, Tessa, still subdued and apologetic, explained she wanted to get settled in before greeting Bernard and Martha. "I'd like to project a better face than I did with you."

Belinda thought that an excellent idea and quickly shepherded Tessa and her luggage upstairs to the vacant double-suite next to the common room. Then she came back downstairs to see how lunch had gone and how Janice Tanner's dinner-party preparations were progressing. Mostly, she was eager to tell Bernard about their cousin's odd behavior. The dining room was empty as she passed through--restaurant twilight time between lunch and dinner. She found Bernard and Martha on stools at the main prep table looking at some papers. Buster was snoozing in the doorway to Martha's suite, and Naja, for some odd reason, was stretched out guarding the pantry door.

"Did I tell you," Belinda said by way of announcing her presence, "that the Lois woman mentioned a 'dog' in the Residence. I think she was hinting we better not give her any trouble, or else."

"Or else she turns us in?" Martha didn't sound happy. "We've spent over an hour here," she said tapping her finger menacingly on the papers in front of them on the table, "making out a new planting diagram for her approval. These county people."

"I think it's more *her* personality and the *power* she's been given than anything," Bernard interrupted. "After all Uncle John is a county employee, and the ladies at the library, and--"

"Alright," Martha conceded irritably. "I won't defame all county employees. I sure would like to know though *who* called her and complained."

"Me too," Belinda agreed. "I just can't believe anybody out here would do that." She pulled up a stool. "But I didn't come down to talk about the raspberries, I'm sure you guys will sort it out."

She said the words easily, and it sounded good, but she knew dealing with government bureaucrats was never easy. She did think, however, that Bernard and Martha were better suited to the task than she.

"Well, what did you want to talk about?" Martha sounded eager to know what was up.

"Tessa. I've just brought her from the airport and gotten her settled in the vacant suite."

"Okay."

Not a peep from Bernard who had earlier been so excited about Tessa's visit.

Belinda continued, "She's upset. And I don't think it has to do with us. No--something at home."

"You don't think she's getting a divorce, do you?" Martha's tone was ripe with speculation.

"I can't imagine that," Belinda answered considering. "But she did say she didn't have anyplace to go. That's why she came here."

Finally, Bernard re-entered the conversation. "Sure sounds like a divorce to me," he said. "Surprised she stayed married to him this long. And just what we need. Another complication in our lives."

Visitors usually excited and energized Bernard, even Tessa. Belinda knew this was not like him.

"Are you okay?" she asked.

Inside Martha's suite the phone rang and she went to answer.

"I've had another dream," Bernard confided once Martha was out of earshot. "This afternoon during my nap."

"You think..."

"I don't know."

"What was it?"

Martha returned before he could elaborate. "That was Mr. Maher. He's personally bringing over the case of *Blanc de Blancs*--you know--that champagne I like from Gruet Winery in New Mexico. He said he's stored the case in his walk-in, so it's already cool. He's also bringing a big tub they use for displays filled with ice." She turned to Belinda. "We're setting up a special table just for the drinks. Did you notice when you came through?"

"No," Belinda answered. "Are we getting low on bubbly?"

"Yeah, only a couple bottles left. But Maher--he's the grocery store wine manager. You know him right?"

Belinda nodded. She had a vague memory of a rotund man with a dour face and a vast knowledge of "spirits" of all kinds.

"Well, he said he could buy all our wines at wholesale."

Martha's smile was self-congratulatory.

"No table-service tonight." Bernard looked a bit more animated now that they were talking about Janice Tanner's birthday party. "Anybody showing up can participate in the party's buffet for a mere five bucks. I'm guessing we should get at least thirty or so diners. And of course it's complementary for all our residents." He winked. "Didn't you see the sign out front?"

"I didn't." Belinda shook her head in wonderment. Her mind must have been a thousand miles away. *So much to figure out, and it just keeps piling up.*

Martha looked at her with concern, "We used the folding sign. It's huge. I can't believe you didn't see it."

"Tessa." Easy to blame it on the latest predicament.

"Ah, yes," Martha said. "I can see how she can distract a person."

Belinda remembered Martha had been with them during a previous Tessa visit. At that time, she had confided to Belinda that she thought Tessa was definitely not an easy person to get along with, much less like.

"You know she cried in the car," Belinda said feeling she was betraying a confidence, an intimate moment Tessa would not like the whole world to know about. But they needed to be aware. Tessa might need some delicate handling.

"Did you tell her about Lana and Philly's murders?" Bernard asked.

"Yes, unfortunately. And you know the police haven't said Philly's death was murder."

"They will," Bernard declared. "I'm sure the ME is going to find something. Which reminds me, Olive Norris called you twice. I'm supposed to tell you to call her back."

"Okay, I'll call her when I go upstairs. Anything from Uncle John?"

Bernard perked up even more. "Why? What are you expecting?"

She quickly filled them in on the Moira Stephens' affair and John's promise to check for fingerprints on the bullets in the Norris' .38.

From the dining room they heard the sound of clanking

dishes and silverware.

"Must be Patrick and Mary Ann back to set up," Bernard said. "I'll go make sure they do it right."

Both women smiled at his departing back.

Martha said, "He's such a darn perfectionist. Those kids know perfectly well how to set up a buffet." Then in a lowered and softer voice, "Bernard's had another dream. I can tell by that soppy look on his face."

"Yeah." Belinda sighed. "I don't know what it was though. What, by the way are you and Bernard serving the birthday girl?"

"Well, it was hard deciding what she might like. I really don't know much about her. Like what she likes to eat or…" Martha shrugged. "Well, anything actually. She's definitely an unknown culinary quantity as far as I'm concerned."

Belinda got up, "Mind if I make myself a pot of tea to take upstairs?" Fifty small white porcelain teapots had been an addition Martha had strongly recommended--and Belinda had readily embraced. Reminiscent in style and size of their stainless-steel restaurant brethren, in porcelain they were far more elegant. Thea James (the mailman Gordy's wife) had made miniature cozies for them. Belinda loved them--made her feel quite British.

"Be my guest. Everything is already prepped for the party. I just have to put the steam tables out."

"You are an amazing woman."

Her out of nowhere compliment caused Martha to blush. "Thanks."

Belinda put the kettle on a front burner. "I just can't believe you're sitting here calmly talking to me with party and dinner guests just an hour away. I know you're well--organized and I know you prep way ahead of time, but this is…" Belinda shook her head in amazement. "Well, unbelievable."

Martha laughed heartily. "It's all in the menu I make, Belinda."

"Meaning?"

"When I've got a big bash, *and* I've got control over the menu, and I'm not out to impress with fancy stuff, I pick things I can make ahead, or at least have all the ingredients assembled ahead of time."

Belinda looked over Martha's shoulder at a piece of paper she pulled from under the raspberry planning pile. It was a handwritten menu.

Southwest theme...individual size three-cheese enchiladas... chili relleno casserole...Spanish rice...black bean and chipotle dips with chips...Luvenia's Mexican corn-mush casserole...taco shells and fixings. For desert, use frozen petit fours in the back freezer and Apricot Birthday sheet cake in the fridge.

When Belinda looked up, Martha was pointing to several rolling carts behind her. "The enchiladas are rolled and in those steam tables," Martha said. "The *relleno* casseroles are made and in the refrigerator. Just have to pop them in to cook for twenty minutes, rice and dips are already made, taco fixings are sliced and in bowls." She wrinkled her forehead for second. "Oh yeah, the corn-mush is made and cooked, and the cakes are defrosting."

Belinda smiled. "Well, I still say you're amazing and I'm glad you're here." She then cleared her throat--moving them through the moment. "Does your choice of menu mean you think Janice might like Mexican food?"

"It's a wild guess. I think I remember you saying she moved here from Albuquerque? Well, I'm thinking if she doesn't like it, she should at least be used to it."

"Pretty hot, as in pepper hot?" Belinda inclined her head toward the prep tables.

"Yep."

"Mmm."

"Don't worry," Martha assured her. "I also made a pile of ham, salami, and Swiss cheese sandwiches for our milder palette guests. They're in the refrigerator too. I used tortillas for the bread, you know, to keep with the theme."

Their menu discussion started Belinda thinking, and speculating. How well *did* she know Janice Tanner? In fact did she know her at all? Janice's residence application form was in the office file cabinet, maybe she should give it a second look.

*   *   *   *   *

Bernard had known Patrick and Mary Ann didn't require his assistance to set up the buffet and tables. He wanted the time to be alone with his thoughts.

So after a few perfunctory and unnecessary comments on table cloths and glasses, Bernard sat down at his and Belinda's table by the door--ostensibly to make up Thursday's dairy order.

He would, of course, eventually tell Belinda about his dream. But first, he wanted to make sure he had it right in his own mind.

It was so bizarre, even he wasn't sure he was remembering correctly.

Then there was the not so small matter of Tessa. His cousin always put Belinda out of sorts.

Jeez, why did Tessa have to visit now, of all times? They had enough on their hands with murders, thefts, and county raspberry enforcers.

Tessa looked out her suite's window at the bungalows across the street. They were all modest two-story wooden structures--several painted white, several blue, and all with porches and cupolas--and one with a widow's-walk.

For landscaping, their generously-sized properties were crowded with old-growth evergreens, mature people-sized rhododendrons and azaleas, and ubiquitous native undergrowth such as raspberry and blackberry bushes.

Tessa knew that all in all, she was looking at a picturesquely old fashioned postcard view.

She was also aware that on such a sunny afternoon, with puffy white smidgens of clouds accentuating an otherwise clear blue sky, and towering cedars leading the eye to ragged mountain outcroppings in the rear--the sight alone should stir within her heart, or in the heart of any relatively normal human being, a pleasurable sensation akin to joy, inner peace, or at the very least, an esthetic appreciation of Western Washington scenery.

But she would have none of it. She might as well have been looking down into ooze at La Brea Tar Pits in LA.

Her mind and heart, indeed her soul, refused to enjoy the scene before her.

Instead, the idyllic view from her suite was just another cause to increase her ire. Look what her cousins had--while her life was in shambles.

Tessa sighed with disgust--partly at Belinda and Bernard's bounty--but mostly at her own current predicament. *Damn Gavin.* How could he put her in this position?

She couldn't deny her suite was nice. Obviously, it didn't compare to her and Gavin's lovely ocean-view estate on the Palos Verdes Peninsula. But to her cousins' credit, Belinda and Bernard had done a good job with this place.

Then, again, with the advantages they had, why shouldn't they? What with Glory and Bertram to raise them, and each other to lean on.

She walked over to the queen-sized bed to start unpacking. If her own parents, Cloris and Bernard, hadn't been so damn selfish. They could have had a second child if they had wanted to. But they hadn't. Tessa knew that for a fact--heard them talking about it--one never to be forgotten afternoon--when her mother was still alive.

Carefully, Tessa started laying her clothes out on the bed, deciding what to hang in the antique wardrobe that dominated one bedroom wall. Well, at least her taste in clothes was excellent. Belinda and Bernard went around in stuff that looked like it had come from The Salvation Army, for Christ's sake.

There was an antique Victorian mirror angled next to a French Provincial dresser on the other side of the bedroom. She unfolded a faux-suede pantsuit and held it up in front of herself.

A fleeting glimmer of a smile passed across her perfectly made-up face. "Not bad," she informed the mirror. The outfit had been a last minute purchase at an LAX shop. Tessa prided herself on being a savvy shopper.

Still gazing into the mirror, and remembering the pictures she had found in her father's attic after her mother's death, Tessa was struck by how much she favored her father. Favored all the Jones male lineage, in fact.

So did Bernard.

Belinda though, was different. Thin and willowy in face and body.

Those pictures had led Tessa to an interest in the Jones family-tree, and genealogy in general. Maybe she'd tell Belinda about her research, maybe not. Would be nice for *someone* to appreciate all the work she'd done.

Tessa took the suit over to the wardrobe and hung it up.

Might be even more interesting to tell Belinda about how her *saintly* parents had almost split up? How, if it weren't for John Thomas getting them back together Belinda and Bernard would have been products of divorced parents, and their lives could have been quite different.

Not so privileged.

Sure, as it turned out, they were successful little entrepreneurs, making plenty of money. But she also knew their little secret--all about their trust fund.

"Hah," she scoffed. How saintly of them to say they won't touch it. Oh, they'd touch it alright--if they had to.

Tessa had actually worried a bit before leaving LA about the expense she would cause her cousins. But now, "They can afford it," she said out loud. "Don't think I'll be in a hurry to leave, either."

What are relatives for, anyway?

In the meantime, she had better start acting nicer. For despite her entrenched resentment, Tessa was painfully aware how much she needed Belinda and Bernard right now.

To antagonize them would *not* be a smart thing to do.

And what was this latest silliness of Belinda's? Catching murderers--of all things.

On her way back upstairs Belinda passed Bernard who looked fully engrossed in making some sort of list. So she didn't stop to talk--just a quick little wave which he acknowledged with a perfunctory return wave. He had his own ways, and she loved him dearly, for and in spite of his peculiarities.

She also successfully returned to her office without bumping into any residents (with more tales of missing items), or Tessa. And once in their office, Belinda did the unthinkable. She closed the door.

She was tired, but she needed to get some phone calls completed. So after making a quick list, she started dialing.

Mrs. Geri Keyes, the Norris' housekeeper was first. The woman answered after only two rings and agreed to see her.

Good. Belinda hoped to get a better feel for Lana, the woman, and just maybe, a clue as to who would want her dead. They agreed to meet around noon the next day at Mrs. Keyes' condo in Kirkland.

Jake West was next on Belinda's list. His wife, Faith, answered the phone. Faith assumed Belinda had called to remind them about Janice Tanner's birthday party--they were planning on coming--but, did they still have to pay since they knew Janice? After Belinda assured her the buffet would be complementary (she would have to tell Bernard), Faith called Jake to the phone.

"Listen, Ms. Jones, I don't want to be rude 'cause I understand we're eating at your place tonight, but I've been through all this with the police and that lawyer guy, Senator something." He sounded tired, irritated, and hard.

Belinda guessed that despite his protestation to the opposite, Jake would have been even ruder if his wife hadn't been standing nearby. "I certainly understand you must be tired of all the questions, but if I could just have a few moments of your time tomorrow?" She sweetened the pot. "If we could meet around one or so for a late lunch, oh, say, at Salish Lodge, *my treat*, it would be great."

"We'll see." He hung up before Belinda could say more.

She had to leave answering machine messages for both Bull Morton and Pete Naldeen, the Puget Sound employees who had been working on the Snoqualmie trail the morning of Lana's murder.

Moira Stephens, Kirby's paramour, was also a message left.

Olive was at home, and seemingly eager to talk to

Belinda. "You saw Kirby this morning, right?"

"Yes, Mrs. Norris, I did." Belinda wasn't going to be the one to tell Olive about Moira if Kirby hadn't. "He seemed in pretty good spirits."

"He told you about that Stephens woman, didn't he?"

"Yes he did," she admitted. So, Kirby had been true to his word--but Belinda wasn't sure where Olive was going with this. She certainly didn't sound happy. So Belinda tried putting a positive spin on Kirby's affair. "It could strengthen his alibi."

"You think so?" Olive sounded doubtful.

"Well, yes, if the jury believes her testimony, there's no way Kirby could have had time to kill Lana."

"If they believe her *and* Kirby's testimony."

Belinda was suddenly overcome with weariness. "Don't worry, Mrs. Norris, I'm still talking to people and doing my best to find out who killed your daughter-in-law." Belinda just wanted to hang up and take a nap.

"Thank you, Ms. Jones. Thank you."

Poor woman, Belinda thought after hanging up. She's worried sick her son is going to be convicted, and all I want to do is sleep.

Olive was deeply disappointed with the lack of progress Belinda Jones was making. She was probably wasting her money on the stupid woman. Especially because what Belinda *should* be doing was not only obvious, but relatively simple.

Find all the other people who had motives to kill Lana.

Then, point the DA in their direction. At a minimum, dig up enough information to raise reasonable doubt.

Indeed, it had been a disappointing day all around-- starting with Kirby's bombshell this morning.

Shame, shame! What Kirby had been doing with that Moira Stephens slut was a mortal sin. And he could go straight to hell if he didn't confess his sinfulness immediately. She had told him that this very morning. She had even checked that there was a priest available at the jail.

Maybe she was old-school in some of her beliefs, but the

ten commandments, in her opinion, couldn't just be whisked away because cultural attitudes change. God's law was God's law.

Olive did, however, understand why her son would *want* to have an affair. Especially with Lana's lack of interest there at the end.

But in bed with an adulteress hussy on the very morning he needed an alibi?

What a horrible stroke of bad luck. Any jury would figure he and this Stephens woman had killed Lana together.

But Kirby was *innocent*.

Unfortunately, though, all she could do now was trust in God and continue to follow the adage: *"Those are helped who help themselves."* She had lived her whole life based on that premise. Now was *not* the time to change.

Maybe she should go over to St. Francis and do some yard work. She needed to keep the place up even if others didn't care. And it wasn't dark yet. It would give her some time to think and plan, and she would be doing God's good work at the same time.

Yes, she needed to figure a way to help Belinda. To be fair, she had asked the wannabe detective to accomplish a lot in a very short time.

CHAPTER FOUR

Wednesday Evening--Party Time

Moira Stephens loved her Reading Group meetings. They called themselves "Books and Cooks". The name was easily chosen in that it reflected their triple joys of gourmet cooking, eating good food, *and* reading.

They met Wednesday evenings, once a month, at each other's homes. Tonight was Book Club Wednesday and they were meeting at Kathie's in Renton. Moira lived in North Bend, so it was a bit of a drive, and it had started raining, so she left early, not wanting to be late, or, heaven forbid, miss their get-together entirely.

She needed the break.

Her mind had been churning relentlessly all day with work hassles (endless computer network problems)--and Kirby. *What to do about Kirby?*

She had visited him only once since his incarceration; but what a visit it had been. Kirby had stated quite emphatically that he was in love with her. *"The real thing,"* he had proclaimed. And yes, he wanted to marry her.

It didn't matter he was in prison awaiting trial for murder.

Moira sighed. It wasn't that this was her first marriage proposal. Indeed, at 5'7", 120 pounds thin, but with Ava Gardner proportioned curves, Moira was physically attractive. She had also been told by several suitors her mannerisms were most appealing. Add to that her thick short cropped brown hair, brown eyes, and expansive smile--all she thought enhanced and intensified her femininity and personality.

She smiled to herself now, remembering that Kirby once called her a "looker."

This evening, beginning her drive down to Renton, Moira had some time to *really* think about what marriage to Kirby would *really* entail.

And though the skies were turning nasty, it was still

nice to have no interruptions. Just her and her thoughts.

Gordy and Dorothea James were the first outside
guests to arrive for Janice Tanner's party; and from their intent
expressions and purposeful movements, the couple was of one
mind, and on a mission.

They quickly located Belinda in the dining room and
corralled her in a corner by the front windows.

"Belinda." Gordy lowered his voice to a near whisper
and grabbed Belinda by the hand, pulling her even closer into
him and Thea. "We've got to know what you think? Do you
believe Philly was actually *murdered?*"

Thea put her arm around Belinda's shoulder and
nudged her in even closer. "We just can't understand anyone
wanting to murder poor, poor Philly."

Belinda was now so close to Thea, she could smell her
breath (sweet like cinnamon), and see the tears welling in Thea's
eyes.

Belinda gave Thea a hug and said, "I'm so sorry. Did
you know Philly well?"

"A lot of years." Thea took a deep breath and reined
in her grief. "We helped him a lot, in the early days when he
first came to Cedar Valley. As it turned out, Philly liked living
rough. Why would anyone want to kill him?"

"So you think it was murder too?"

"Of course," Gordy answered for them both. "And
you've answered our question. You think Philly was
murdered." He was now almost whispering directly into
Belinda's ear. "We also think it's connected to that Lana
woman's death."

"It sounds like you didn't like Lana Norris?" Belinda
cautiously proposed. She had seldom heard Gordy make
derogative remarks about locals, but something in his
phraseology and word-emphasis made her think Gordy hadn't
been that fond of Lana Norris.

"Snooty." He said it like that one word encompassed it
all. No need to elaborate.

Thea pursed her lips primly and nodded as punctuation for her husband's statement.

"Can you think of any connection between the two?" Belinda asked. "Lana and Philly, that is?" That was still a real puzzler in her mind, how the two victim's paths crossed.

"I'm in five charitable organizations in and around Cedar Valley," Thea explained. "And, Philly was helped by most of them. Never ever saw Lana participate in any of them. I'm darned sure she had the money to help. Just not that kind of person."

"Mmm."

"And," Gordy took up the thread, "I never ran into either of them, Kirby or Lana at the Safeway or TrueValue."

"Video store or church either," Thea added.

Where did the Norris' do their shopping, Belinda wondered? And did it matter? Probably Issaquah. Definitely more upscale than Cedar Valley. And she wasn't surprised Kirby and Lana weren't church-goers. Olive was probably the praying one in the family.

"Olive Norris, now," Thea continued in a decidedly more complementary tone, "goes to my church and contributes her time to a lot of charities."

"You don't think Kirby did it?" Gordy pressed Belinda. "Do you?"

"No, I don't."

He grabbed her hand again, squeezing it surprisingly tightly. "You are going to figure out who killed Philly, aren't you, Belinda?" he asked in a pleading whisper.

How could she answer such a question, posed by such a decent man, asked so sincerely, and at the start of a birthday celebration?

"Yes, Gordy. Yes I am." *There.* Belinda made her commitment quite real and immediate.

"What are you guys doing over here in the corner? Plotting? Planning? Scrutinizing the rest of us?" Tessa's tone was light and teasing--cheerful almost. She was carrying a champagne flute, and judging by the blush to her cheeks, Belinda guessed it was not her first. And, though she wasn't exactly smiling, Tessa was clearly trying for civility.

Belinda made the necessary introductions, and in the spirit of the moment, bestowed a generous smile Tessa's way. "Still early, but our party seems to be picking up and going well." Her cousin was certainly experiencing an epiphany of some sort--why not see how far and how long her goodwill was going to last. "Yes, seems to be. Do you always give your residents a birthday party?" "Actually, yes. And even though it's raining tonight, we'll still probably get a lot of locals here for the buffet. We're used to rain."

Gordy and Thea made some agreeing comments, bestowed pointed and knowing looks Belinda's way, then headed toward the birthday buffet.

Belinda was pleased with how Bernard and Martha had set up the buffet *entrée* and drink tables along the back wall in front of the kitchen. For dessert, Mary Ann had been assigned the task of rolling a *petit four* cart to the different tables as needed, and Janice's birthday cake sat on its own table, intact and its icing birthday message readable, but already sliced and available for self serve.

Even though they had hated doing it, Buster had been banished to Martha's suite for the night, and Naja to Belinda's. They didn't need any more trouble with King County.

Tessa drained her glass and looked around for Patrick who was performing waiter duties for the evening. On catching his eye across the dining room, she held up her glass, and he headed her way. "Your young man looks good in a waiter's outfit."

Belinda gave her cousin a reflective look. "The outfit is rented." Maybe she could risk a joke with the liquored-up and apparently transformed Tessa "the terrible." "He's only twenty-one. Don't tell me you're turning into a lecherous middle-aged woman?"

Tessa actually laughed. "Just looking--not to worry. And yes, it is turning into a good party. As always Bernard's cooking is great and the birthday lady--Janice, right?--seems genuinely pleased. And those folks over there," she pointed to a group seated at a long table by the window, "they have nothing but good stuff to say about you and Bernard. Residents?"

"Yes, they're residents. Actually, some of my favorite people." Belinda was pleased. Not only was Tessa being civil and complementary, but the kind words, true or not, from the table (Anna, Morris, Phoebe, Vera, Kaitlin, and Miss Shirley) warmed her heart. *Maybe* she could relax a bit? At least for the night. *Maybe* even forget about murderers, bills, raspberries, and items gone missing.

"That Kaitlin kid reminds me of Gillian at that age." Tessa shook her head. "I thought she'd never come out of her craziness. Of course her thing was *Punk*, I think that's what it was called. Whatever, it stunk."

"How is she now?"

"Fine."

Tessa's tone was hesitant, and Belinda took it to mean she didn't want to elaborate. However, Belinda was not going to drop everything. "Tessa," she said, knowing she would, though, have to step gingerly, "you and I should talk, don't you think?"

Her cousin's voice, again unusual for her, turned weak and tiny. "Tomorrow, okay?"

"Sure, tomorrow is fine."

Two clean-shaven forty-something men, one tall, one short, dressed in freshly pressed off-the-rack suits, blinding white shirts, and subdued ties, entered the dining room, stopped, and took a moment to look around. In their individual ways, each was on the good-looking side, and gushed health and vigor.

"Who are *they*?" Tessa asked provocatively.

Has Tessa completely flipped? She would have to ask Martha the name of tonight's champagne again. "I don't know."

Moira considered the stretch of I-90 between North Bend and Snoqualmie incredibly beautiful.

When driving through it, she invariably felt as if she'd entered another place. A mini-universe of quiet, peace, and beauty.

Such a change from work.

She loved the way the evergreens, alders, ferns, mosses, lichen, even the weeds, all harmoniously hugged ragged rock-face through a stretch of rolling curves. Wherever greenery could get a toehold, it did; and the result was truly unique. This evening, though it was raining and getting dark, it was still nice.

Equally amazing to her as its beauty, was I-90's final completion along this stretch. Man-created--with dynamite used for blasting through existing hard rock foothills she was told--to finish up this last cross-country section of the interstate.

Moira noticed a car behind her, so she slowed down a bit to let the car pass and to be alone on *her* section of highway. Sometimes it happened that way--if it wasn't rush hour or a holiday. Drivers seemed to spread out between Fall City and North Bend. She didn't have a theory why, just knew that it happened.

When she next looked in her rearview mirror the car behind her had disappeared. Odd; she hadn't seen it pass, and there weren't any turnoffs. Maybe the driver, like herself, had slowed down to feel the solitude.

She let her mind float to thoughts of what marriage to Kirby would be like.

Did she actually love him?

Belinda felt dwarfish next to Bull Morton, and cyclopean next to Pete Naldeen. She had walked over to welcome them and invite them to dine. There was plenty of food, and her early residents, meals now finished, were just beginning to mingle.

In return, the two men congenially introduced themselves with hearty handshakes.

"We both got your messages," Bull explained. Everything about him was either big, booming, or both--his height, his weight, his voice. "We knew about the party and thought we'd save you the time of making two trips to interview us." He smiled at his companion, "Right, Pete?"

Belinda thought she recognized that smile--the smile of lovers?

"Right," Pete cheerfully agreed. He surveyed the dining

room. "Should we talk before eating? The food here is great by the way." In contrast to Bull, Pete's voice was mellow and smooth, but equally hearty.

"Why don't we go in the parlor and talk," Belinda suggested. She didn't want to miss this opportunity to gather information. "You've eaten here before?" She didn't remember seeing either man at the Residence before.

"Oh, yeah," Bull answered as they followed her. "Met your brother, Bernie right? Real friendly, told us all about the difference between sauces and gravies, and about making roux, and..." He looked to Pete for help in remembering. "And making stock from scratch. Right?"

"Right."

Bernie?

As they passed through the foyer, Belinda noticed the sound of rain was more insistent, and darkness was now decidedly upon them.

"Been here several times," Bull continued. "But I guess you weren't around. Mostly we come around noon, right, Pete?"

"Right."

They're good friends at a minimum, Belinda thought. Seem nice. "My brother prefers, 'Bernard.'" She led them to a settee in the parlor's back corner. "I really appreciate you guys talking to me. You know I don't have an official position--"

Pete said, "But Mrs. Norris hired you."

They sat down, and Belinda sat down in a chair facing them. "You know Olive Norris?"

Bull dropped back comfortably into settee cushions and spread his arm across the settee's back. "Used to go to her husband's church."

"And now?"

"Things change."

In contrasting style, Pete leaned forward, eager. "Norris was a nice man. Tolerant. When he died, well, as Bull said, things changed. His death was sudden, a surprise." Pete rubbed his chin, then leaned-in even closer to Belinda, as if to ensure she didn't miss a word. "Then after church political maneuverings, moving pastors around and crap, well, we were left with someone neither Bull nor I liked. Even Mrs. Norris left and she was one of the most... What's the word I'm looking for, Bull?"

"Devout." He said it with distaste.

"Yes, that's it, *devout* members." Pete, like Bull, now relaxed back into the settee cushions.

Belinda wasn't sure exactly how they would help her investigation, but she needed to ask the right questions. "I understand you two were working together on the trail the morning of Lana's murder."

They looked at each other for a second as if to decide who would do the talking. Bull shrugged and nodded toward Pete, who answered, "Yes. Bull and I are both bachelors and we hang around together a lot. You know, pool, Seahawk games, stuff like that." Pete again leaned forward, evidently eager to explain. "So we try to get matching shifts when we can. Can't count on it, you know, when lines go down, we go to work no matter the time." He smiled. "But our supervisor is pretty cool. If it's not emergency duty, he usually assigns us out together."

"Was it emergency duty that Monday morning?"

"Nope. Like I told the police, Meadow Street crossing was routine maintenance."

A clap of thunder sounding close caused all three to pause and look out the parlor windows. Out into the dark.

"I didn't see the lightning," Pete mumbled to himself. He looked back to Belinda. "The box we were working on is right there on the corner of the trail. You know there's fiber optics and cable coming through there?"

Belinda smiled and nodded. She really didn't care about the specifics of their work, but wisely figured it best to let him tell his tale the way he wanted.

"We were checking on some already laid cable and laying some new at the Meadow Street crossing. You know where that is?"

Again she nodded.

"Well, we got there at nine. And I'm sure of that Ms. Jones."

"*Belinda*, please."

Pete continued his tale. "You see, I'm in charge of calling-in when we're on site. Right, Bull?"

"Yep."

"So, I checked my watch. Then at noon when we headed off to lunch, I called in again." His tone turned conspiratorial. "And, I'll tell you something I didn't tell the cops or that snooty lawyer." He rolled his eyes, evidently at the thought of Senator. "We actually left the site at one minute *before* noon and I called in while we were moving. But from nine until eleven-fifty-nine, Lana Norris and her dog did not come through there."

The three of them fell silent for a moment.

Then Bull said, "The way we figure it, whoever killed her started out in Cedar Valley heading to North Bend just like she did, then backtracked the same way after he.. " Bull cleared his throat. "Well, after he killed her."

"Is there anyplace the killer could have cut off the trail out to North Bend Way?"

Pete was back as spokesman for the two. "Sure, several spots. Mostly though through other folks property."

Or, Belinda conjectured, maybe the murderer is someone already living on the trail. "Like across Jake West's property?"

"Yep." Pete's tone and facial expression made it clear Jake West was not a friend. "I'm also going to tell you something else, Belinda." He gave his friend a look. "Bull and I talked about it on our way over here. We never told anybody else this either. I don't know why, guess we kinda didn't want folks poking in *our* business. We didn't know Lana Norris, but we had seen her before. A couple times."

Something new. Belinda held her breath.

"We've seen her a couple times in Pioneer Square."

"Doing what?"

"Well," he said, again looking to Bull for confirmation, "we don't really know. Both times it seemed she was waiting for someone."

"You don't mean, like…" It took her a second to decide on the right word. "Soliciting?"

Both men laughed. Then Pete answered, "No, more like waiting to meet someone. There's a couple specialty bars around, and we figured she was waiting to go have a drink. Like after work or something. Or maybe a party."

"Or maybe an assignation," Belinda mumbled.

"A what?"

"A *tryst*?" Surely Pete must of heard of that.

Still Pete frowned.

"Good grief, Pete," Bull said in a friendly tease. "Meeting a guy? You know, as in having an affair."

"Oh, yeah," Pete agreed once he understood. "That's what we thought too."

Belinda sat back for a moment. She found the interaction between these two men interesting. Surely, more than work acquaintances. Lovers? No, she wasn't prepared to go that far. But they certainly seemed at ease with each other.

"Did either of you know Phillip Towers?"

"What? Philly?" This time Bull wanted to talk. "Sure, everybody knew Philly. Damn shame him dying like that. And I don't believe it was an accident. Some asshole holier-than-thou type smashed him over the head 'cause he wasn't 'regular,' if you know what I mean."

Pete added, "Or some kids, just for the hell of it, or high on meth or whatever the latest is." He shook his head sadly. "Ain't being raised right these days, if you ask me. Can't tell who's the parent and who's the kid. Parents have forgotten what their job is supposed to be. And give me a good joint over any of this synthetic crap. These new drugs are nasty."

Bull rolled his eyes and indulged in a weak and chiding sigh. "If we've finished with Pete's parenting and drug harangues, I have a question for *you*, Belinda." Bull switched to an engaging and broad smile. "Is your cook, Martha, married?"

There goes my gay lifestyle conjecture. She returned the smile. "No, Martha isn't married. But actually she's a *chef*, not a cook, and I know she'd prefer you used that title."

He winked. "Got your drift, Belinda. I'll be sure not to make that mistake, again." Implied was his intent to ask her out.

That pleased Belinda. Martha needed a life outside of Cedar Valley Residence.

"As if you don't, Bella Dear!" Glory Jones scolded.

It was raining harder and I-90 was becoming slick, but

still driveable. Thunder could be heard in the distance and occasionally flashes of lightening cut through the blackness.

Moira was entering the last set of curves before a flat suburbia-beleaguered stretch of I-90 took over. Once in Issaquah proper it would not be the same--cars, construction, lights--all snatching her serenity. She would no longer be able to think about Kirby; all her mental faculties would be needed to focus on driving.

On the matter of Kirby, she was now leaning toward caution. An affair was one thing, marriage another. Not that Kirby wasn't sexy or nice or reliable or all those good things.

But marriage was a gigantic step.

Then there was Lana's death.

In her mind she knew Kirby hadn't killed his wife. *He couldn't have, he was with me.* But in her heart, well, in truth, there was a speck of doubt. And Moira was self-aware enough to recognize she could overcome mental doubts, but in the heart? No, her heart had to *know* Kirby had not killed Lana.

There was that car again in her rearview mirror, surprisingly close. Too close. Where the hell had it come from?

Moira slowed, the car behind her slowed.

Moira sped up, the car behind her sped up.

The car started to pass, then slowed once beside her, but she couldn't see who was driving. Too dark, too much rain.

Her instincts compelled her to speed up and pull ahead. She felt her wheels hydroplane, but was able to keep control of her Maxima. Once back in front of the other car she fumbled for her cell phone. It flew from her hand and dropped to the floor on the passenger side of the car.

"Damn!"

She needed to get into Issaquah where there were lights and people and phones.

For the moment, she managed to stay rational and calm; but she couldn't stop her hands from trembling.

Belinda decided to remain hidden back in the parlor corner for a bit after Bull and Pete headed to the dining room. A couple moments to think.

From the dining room she could hear sounds of merriment--good sounds. Bernard and Martha would be pleased, and hopefully, so would Janice.

Before she could snatch her couple of moments, a man she had never seen before came marching into the parlor. It was clear he was a man on a mission.

Before he reached what Glory Jones would have considered polite speaking distance, he called out, "You Belinda Jones?"

Belinda sighed and muttered *sotto voce*, "What now?" To the stranger, she answered through a smile and in a pleasant voice, "Yes, I am. What can I do for you?"

The man was tight looking, short and wiry, with unusually straight posture and a precise stride. Ex-military, Belinda wondered? He was balding in front but had swept longer hair from the back up and around on top to give the appearance of what everyone seeing him knew was not the case. Comb-over, she'd heard it called.

Something about him made her anxious.

Behind him, at the parlor entrance, a woman stood. Evidently, she had followed him to the parlor door, but then chosen to stop there. She was large and loose, with a round face, round body, and sour smile. His wife, Belinda figured, and their physical contrast put her in mind of *"Jack Sprat could eat no fat, his wife could eat no lean,..."*

"I'm here 'cause my wife dragged me. Could have eaten at home happier, 'specially for what you charge here."

"For Christ's sake," Belinda's brain talked back, *"It's only five dollars for a gourmet buffet."*

"Not costing us a dime," the woman from the door yelled out. "I told you that."

Belinda had first sought out the parlor for a quiet talk with Bull and Pete, then as a refuge for a few moments of solitude. These two, the man strident and rude, the woman loud and shrewish, did not fit.

Spoilers--she wanted them gone.

Nonetheless, she held her role as gracious proprietress. "I'm sure you'll enjoy the buffet, Mr..." She paused and waited.

He took a few seconds before begrudgingly admitting, "West. Jake West."

So this was Jake West--one of her prime suspects-- and the woman at the door must be Faith. She had definitely sounded more refined on the phone.

"And your dinners are complementary, Mr. West. It's Janice Tanner's birthday, whom, I gather, you know."

"You said you wanted to talk to me. Well, I hear things, Missy, and I know you're sticking your nose into this Lana Norris thing. I didn't kill the woman, and I don't know a damn thing about it. And," he came closer to Belinda and wagged his finger at her, "I'm not surprised she was murdered. Nosey bitch like her. No surprise to me."

Belinda stood up. "Could we just meet tomorrow, Mr. West? Lunch maybe? As I offered before, my treat?" She could hear pleading in her tone and didn't like the sound of it.

An almost imperceptible smirk twitched the corner of his mouth. "Where?"

"Like I offered earlier, the Salish?"

"When?"

"One."

"Don't be late, *Ms.* Jones."

The driver of the other car did not try to move next to her again, but Moira sensed it was not over--and before she realized what was actually happening she felt and heard her car being slammed from behind--the sound of slammed and grating metal piercing her emotional defenses.

Again she hydroplaned, this time almost losing control.

"I've got to get into Issaquah, I've got to get to Issaquah..."

Her heart was pounding, her mind racing. "I've got to get to Issaquah..."

The rain seemed to be coming down harder. And again the car behind slammed into her rear bumper.

"Dear God, dear God..."

She didn't know what to do.

Again, the sound and feel of metal slamming against metal. She started to cry, then she lost control; and through her tears and rain soaked windshield, Moira couldn't believe how fast she was careening into a solid face of rock.

"I saw you talking to Jake West." Sheriff John Thomas was standing right inside Cedar Valley Residence dining room entrance, holding a plate of goodies--and still in uniform.

"And you didn't come to rescue me?" Belinda demanded. "What an ass."

He chuckled. "Him or me? I had my eye on you all the time, you know. Good party, by the way." He inclined his head toward Janice who was standing talking with a small group of people across the room. "Tanner seems to be enjoying herself."

"I think she is. I sure don't recognize any of those people she's talking to." Curious. Or was it? There was no reason she should know Janice's friends. Heck, she barely knew the woman herself. "Janice is sort of an enigma, you know."

"Really?" He sounded only slightly interested. "In what way?" He jabbed his fork at some food on his plate. "What is this stuff, anyway?"

"Chili-Relleno casserole," Belinda answered. "She seldom takes her meals here, I've had very few conversations with her, and it certainly is funny why a woman like her would isolate herself way out here."

"It's great, this relleno thing. Bernie and Martha make a good team, huh?"

"Too good," she agreed, patting her stomach. "As I was saying about Janice..."

"You want me to see what I can find out? Is that what you're hinting at?"

"Well..." she let her voice fade into a question mark.

His cellphone rang and after a couple quick who, what, and wheres, he ended the conversation with a disappointed sigh. "Got to go." He put his half full plate on the reception desk. "Okay if I leave this here?"

Belinda didn't miss the concern in his eyes. "Everything okay?"

"Oh," he blew out a breath, "just some damn fool's gone and crashed right before you come into Issaquah. Every time it rains..." He shook his head and spoke in a road-weary tone heavy with amazement and disappointment, "You'd think they'd learn."

"And you're on call," she said, stating the obvious. "It's a bad night to be out, it's raining harder."

"Yep, I'm on call." He gave her a hug, "And don't worry, Bella, I'm a cop. Remember? I get paid to go out on nights like this."

"Sorry." Before she could finish saying goodbye, the residence phone rang.

As she picked up the phone call at the reception desk, John gave her a quick peck on the cheek and an equally quick goodbye wave.

On the phone was Adam Mason-Martin asking if it was too late to come over.

Belinda wanted to say yes, indeed it was, but remembering his possible interest in Martha, decided to play cupid--not a role she often ventured into. "No, come on out, Adam. We're still in the thick of things and there's plenty of food left."

He seemed quite pleased.

Good. Two men interested in Martha, even better.

"Oh, Adam," she added before he hung up. "I understand the roads are pretty wet. Are you coming from Issaquah?"

"Yeah."

"Drive carefully." Once said, she felt like an old mother hen.

Interestingly, she didn't detect any pique in Adam's voice when he responded, "Will do."

In fact, she thought he sounded quite pleased she cared.

Moira was terrified she was going to die.

She couldn't speak.

She couldn't move.

She couldn't open her eyes. She could, though, hear the paramedics, and her brain registered the words "airlift"--"Harborview"--"trauma."' How many times had she seen this very scene on TV--injured and bloody bodies strapped on gurneys, helicopters, police cars? Now it was her.

She wondered if there really was a heaven. Then she was overcome by a blinding white light--so, so bright.

It was after 10 P.M. and still raining, a consistent patter against the front windows, almost comforting, now that the thunder and lightening had passed on eastward toward Snoqualmie Pass. All non-residents, seemingly satiated and happy, had departed--except for Adam.

Patrick and Mary Ann had done well tip-wise and had headed home smiling a few minutes earlier.

About half-an-hour earlier Janice had thanked everyone profusely, made her apologies for cutting out, and retired to her suite--also seemingly quite pleased.

Kaitlin, ubiquitous headphones in place, had made her escape hours earlier at the first possible moment after eating birthday cake. And Tessa retired upstairs a few minutes later.

Theresa had not appeared all evening.

Now, the four of them, Belinda, Adam, Bernard and Martha were comfortably ensconced in the parlor enjoying a final cordial.

"My compliments to the chefs," Adam offered as he raised his brandy snifter first to Martha, then to Bernard. His voice was mellow and a charmingly boyish smile encompassed his face--his entire demeanor seemingly at ease.

Belinda was smiling too--partly the effect of several glasses of *Blanc de Blancs* during the evening, now followed by a generous pouring of B&B. For the first time in several days she felt relaxed.

Bernard and Martha, sitting in wing-chairs facing

Belinda and Adam, were also smiling with alcohol-induced warmth, and acknowledged his complement with return raisings of their glasses.

Buster and Naja, now released from jail, had chosen sides: Naja sprawled on her back at Bernard's feet, and Buster, splayed on his tummy, long legs pointing in all directions, was at Martha's feet, staring at her adoringly.

In the dining room, still at their table, Miss Shirley, Vera, Phoebe, Morris, and Anna lingered over empty coffee cups and tales of past accomplishments and regrets. As Belinda caught the whispery edges of their voices, she imagined their memories brought much happiness.

Probably some sadness too.

And in the thinking about them, Belinda's smile faded and her eyes misted over for a second. In such a short time she had become quite fond of her residents.

"Did I say there was a bad accident on I-90 headed West?" Adam asked. Then changing the subject before Belinda could answer, "And did you talk to Olive Norris today?"

Both his questions brought Belinda back from her oddly-timed flight of emotion.

She found a Kleenex in her jacket pocket, blew her nose and unobtrusively dabbed the corners of her eyes. "I think our uncle, Sheriff Thomas was headed to that accident. And yes, I talked to Olive, but I'm afraid I didn't give her much to be optimistic about."

"Mmm."

"Adam, you can say anything you'd say to me in front of Bernard and Martha. What are you thinking?"

Martha assured, "We know all about what Belinda's doing."

He laughed lightly. "No, it's not that," he explained. "Besides, this B&B has already loosened my lips." Again he raised his glass appreciatively.

And Belinda thought he might have blushed, but she couldn't be sure. For certain he was looking directly at her as if she would understand not only his words, but also his feelings.

"What I'm trying to get at is, it's Olive I feel particularly sorry for."

"Because?" Martha challenged. "She's not the one sitting in jail."

"But she so desperately wants to get her son out. She truly believes he's innocent and Calvin..." he caught himself, further comment *would* be talking "out of school".

"He *is* innocent," Bernard insisted. "I know he is."

"Well of course," Adam said. "But did you know Olive is very religious? She told Calvin she prays every night for her son. And, she volunteers at St. Francis Church, just down the street from you, you know." His voice took on a slight tone of awe. "Arranges flowers, even does yard work. Lights tons of vigil candles. She's moralistic too, in a biblical sense that is. Quoted from the bible on justice to Calvin." He chuckled lightly. "That put him back a tad."

"She's also very determined," Belinda added. "But all that good stuff doesn't make her son not guilty of murder, even though I do believe Kirby is innocent."

"Well, then," Adam pushed. "How are you going to prove it?"

"Whatever I do, it won't include advising him to plead insanity."

Adam interrupted her by loudly clearing his throat.

Belinda took his meaning and amended, "Not that I know Calvin is thinking of doing that."

"Well I should hope not," Martha said.

Belinda looked back and forth between the two of them, Adam and Martha, both young, vibrant, passionate. Could something actually develop, or was she just hoping for Martha's sake?

And there's still Bull waiting in the wings. Belinda covered a hiccup with her hand.

"I did some digging today," Adam offered.

"About what?" Belinda asked. He had a lot more resources than she did. And if he was willing to pass some information on to her, so much the better.

"More like, *who.* Or is it whom?" He laughed sillily--then stopped abruptly--the emotion reflected in his eyes morphing from eager to mortified.

Belinda took Adam's actions to mean he'd put his foot

in it, and wasn't pleased that he had. Quite clearly to her, too much booze for the sharp up-and-coming young lawyer. She put her own glass down--wisely she thought.

Martha stood up. "You know what, Adam? I think I need a pot of tea. Too much alcohol for me tonight. Are you a tea drinker, or would you like some coffee?"

"Coffee," he answered. "I have to drive back to Issaquah."

"You'll have to follow me to the kitchen first."

"Right behind you." He got up, bowed sloppily to Belinda, saluted Bernard, and followed Martha to the kitchen.

As soon as they were out of earshot, Bernard leaned forward. "Bella, I need to talk to you, alone. Tonight. I want to tell you about my dream."

"I'll wait up for you."

"Great." He took in a deep fortifying breath. "And I need to tell you about Lois."

"The county inspection woman?" *Oh dear.*

"I called up the County today after Martha and I had so much trouble with the map." His tone was apologetic--but minimizing his news was impossible. "And now she's coming back here Friday morning."

Belinda groaned loudly, then flopped back against the settee, grabbed a cushion, and hugged it to her stomach.

"Are you alright?"

"I don't feel too well, Bernie." She had been doing okay just a few moments ago. Now she felt dizzy. "Does this mean we have to have the raspberry work done by then?"

He hung his head, reminiscent of a naughty school boy, and the act sent a comforting wave of fondness through Belinda for her brother, and his ways.

"I'm afraid it does," he answered through a sad little sigh.

She tsked out the side of her mouth and said with champagne and *liqueur* induced bravado, "Don't worry about it." Then she finished in one gulp the remainder of her drink--the same drink she had so rashly given up just moments previous.

Bernard leaned forward and continued in a solemn

and hushed voice, "And right now, I have this horrible, horrible feeling something terrible is happening. Or maybe just happened."

She was glowing warmly from drink and brotherly love, but still, she shivered. "Premonition?"

He nodded. "Yes."

Then in the blink of an eye, something similar she guessed, but not the same, engulfed her. It hit, with a brilliant clarity, almost like a blinding flash of bright white light. If she didn't find out who killed Lana Norris real, real, soon--someone else was going to die. Whatever was going on, it was not over.

She hugged the cushion closer. "Have you seen Theresa tonight?"

He shook his head.

PART THREE

Wheat from the Chaff

CHAPTER FIVE

Thursday

Despite everything that happened the day before, Belinda woke up Thursday morning at her regular 6:00 A.M., surprisingly eager and energetic. Her head did hurt a bit, and though her stomach was slightly queasy, it certainly could have been worse.

For sure, she didn't just hop up and go for a swim or take a shower. No, this morning she needed time to think before rushing full-steam ahead into her day

The "feeling," or whatever she had experienced last night, had shaken Belinda and left a driving sense of urgency in its wake. She had to move fast, but first, at a minimum, she needed to think out and plan who to see, when, and where. Jake West was already scheduled; she would work everything else around him.

Then there was Bernard's dream.

Last night after retiring, and as planned, he had come to her room. It had only taken him a couple moments to relate it, but the meaning imbedded in his dream, if any, was illusive and bizarre--adding to her current apprehension.

In the past, his dreams, or night-visions as he sometimes called them, had always been symbolic and required a fair bit of analysis. But this one was weirder than most. What Belinda remembered most vividly, was the size of the lizard. Bernard had described it as being broader and taller than Cedar Valley Residence.

He had been very serious in the telling, but at first, she had found it difficult not to smile. The immediate pictures her brain had conjured up were from fifties Japanese movies-- Godzilla and his relatives.

But as Bernard continued his tale--which involved the lizard's color being blood-red, that it had sucked in and swallowed her, Bernard, and Kirby in one greedy act, and then it had stomped Cedar Valley Residence into the ground in a fit of inexplicable rage--Belinda's emotional state quickly moved from amusement to apprehension bordering on fear.

She felt certain Bernard's giant lizard was symbolic of someone she had yet to identify. *Hiding out in his psyche as a Technicolor giant lizard, for goodness sakes.*

"Over here, Belinda!" Phoebe was sitting at her regular window table with Vera, and waving a white embroidered handkerchief Belinda's way. Miss Shirley, Morris, and his wife Anna were also sitting with at the two ladies. Spent breakfast dishes were piled neatly waiting for Patrick, or was it Mary Ann this morning? She couldn't remember.

As bid, Belinda went over to their table. "Didn't you guys go to bed last night?"

Morris stood and flashed her a smile. "My dear Belinda, what a lovely time we had last night. I think Janice was duly impressed." He cleared his throat. "And touched. Hard to know for sure, don't really know her, if you know what I mean."

"It sure was a wonderful party," Anna agreed with her husband. "The food was great. I told Bernard and Martha just that last night."

"I'm so glad you enjoyed it." In fact--Belinda did a quick table survey--there were smiles all around, including staid and proper Vera. The champagne Martha bought was definitely a keeper.

Kaitlin, not surprisingly, wasn't with the group.

Vera read Belinda's mind. "My great-granddaughter is still upstairs. Studying actually. I think we've come to the point where she rather do most things without me breathing down her neck."

"Understandable at her age," Miss Shirley reassured. "Teenagers. And we're probably not that much fun to a youngster like her."

"And," Vera said, "that's why I asked dear Phoebe to hail you."

"Ah..." Belinda wasn't sure where Vera was headed, nor did she have a clue to the "that" Vera was talking about.

"We wanted to talk to you while my Kaitlin wasn't around," Vera attempted to clarify.

Still confused, Belinda waited patiently while Vera framed her next sentence.

"We've all talked it out, you see." Vera waved her hand, to indicate she meant those at the table. "And we want you to understand that we aren't concerned about the items gone missing. You do understand what I'm saying?"

Belinda wasn't sure she did. "You mean you don't care if we find them? Or catch the thief?" Puzzled, she looked at Phoebe. "What about your brooch?"

Phoebe, fiddling nervously with the edges of her handkerchief, blushed, then dropped her head.

"Darn it, Belinda," Morris puffed up his chest. "You're making this awfully difficult." This morning, the smell of Mixture 79 was particularly strong.

Belinda was standing behind Anna, who after her husband spoke, turned slightly and took Belinda's hands in hers. "We're trying to tell you in our disjointed way, that we don't want you to worry about our 'stuff.' It's just *things*, Belinda. We're old, all of us." Anna looked around the table at her friends. "And we know that *things* are just *things*. There are so many more important aspects to life than possessions."

Evidently emboldened by Anna's words, Miss Shirley took up the chorus, "Like friendship, and love, and health…"

They all stared intently at Belinda, seemingly trying to will her to understand the emotion they were attempting to convey.

Belinda almost broke into tears on the spot. "No," she demanded, more for her own benefit. "I appreciate the sentiment, dear friends." *Yes, they have become our friends.* "But I *will* find out who stole your possessions." *And I'll wring whose ever thieving neck it is when I find them. Even if it's Kaitlin's skinny little neck I wrap my hands around.*

Belinda then turned away from her boarders and headed toward the kitchen. She couldn't look at their kind and earnest faces any longer; her emotions were too close to the surface. Especially knowing Miss Shirley, Morris, and Anna would most probably be leaving soon. She just didn't want to think about it.

Once safely through the kitchen swinging doors, she was met with another surprise. Adam was sitting at the table closest to Martha's suite, drinking a cup of coffee and eating an English muffin.

Mary Ann was on her way out to the dining room with a cleanup tray; and on passing Belinda, smiled mischievously before the swinging door closed behind her.

Belinda thought she also knew what was up the moment she saw him. He'd stayed the night.

The signs? Adam looked like he had just taken a shower, his hair didn't look quite right, his clothes, which she recognized from last night, had that "I wore these yesterday' crumple", and the look on his face was childishly sheepish for a grown man his age.

He'd be a lousy poker player.

"It's not what you think." His tone of voice was somber, bordering on dismal. "That stuff you made me drink last night was deadly."

Could he possibly think it was her fault?

Belinda pulled up a stool opposite him. "*I* made you drink?" It was clear Martha was pampering him, having laid out tea service as well as coffee, and a couple slices of Kringle.

"I couldn't be this stupid on my own, now could I?"

"Actually you don't look that bad." She waited to hear the rest, if he was so inclined to spill the beans.

"I slept on your cot back there." He inclined his head toward the pantry entrance, "Martha made me."

Belinda wasn't sure if he was telling the truth or not; for sure he *had* looked rather wiped out last night. Part of her hoped he was lying. She could see them as a couple--almost. He was a little young. But who cared nowadays?

"I'm glad she did. If you'd had an accident in the condition you were in--"

"I know! I know!" He propped up his head in his hands. "I'm a lawyer, remember?"

Belinda found his woebegone tone of voice and the sorry look on his face so pathetic, she wanted to laugh outright. She didn't. Instead, she asked casually, "Martha around?"

"She's out back with that big black dog of hers. Buster,

right?"

Belinda nodded. Adam was rather charming, especially when he smiled. Martha could do worse. There was a boyish twinkle in his eye, and a curl in the corner of his mouth. She wondered what he was like in court? Was his style to influence with facts, reason, and logic? Or, to charm their socks off!?

"She and Buster," he continued, "are picking herbs." He leaned forward, and looked at her closely. "Listen, Belinda, I'm really glad you came down. I mean, I am…well, I'm personally very happy to see you again."

Belinda swallowed, speechless.

Adam straightened up, chagrined boyish demeanor now gone, concerned defense attorney taking the lead. "Actually, I really need to talk to you about something. I was going to last night, but it just didn't work out."

Belinda took a breath, and said, "Okay. Mind if I grab a cup of tea first?"

Adam pushed the pot towards her and waited until she poured, doctored up, and tested her tea.

After a couple well needed sips, Belinda asked, "What's on your mind?"

He looked her straight on now. "Like I said last night, I really do feel sorry for Olive." He took in a deep breath. "And, what I didn't want to say last night was…" He looked a way for only a second, then turned back. "I'm concerned Calvin may not be giving her his best shot."

Belinda was pleased Adam felt he could talk to her in confidence, but was surprised that such a level of trust on his part had developed so quickly. However, she was not about to question, caution, or object. "Why not?"

"I'm not sure he can."

She leaned forward herself and lowered her tone. "You mean, what? He's not smart enough, or…?" She hoped Martha wouldn't return for a few more minutes. She wasn't sure Adam would talk so freely in front of her, or Bernard for that matter.

He rubbed his forehead. "His forgetfulness, his poor defense attorney tactics…heck, I'm not sure what I mean. But I'm damn well going to find out. Today."

"Find out what? And how?"

"Calvin is out of town." He looked past her, thoughtful. "I'll call you later today." He rubbed his head again. "I'll never drink that much again."

"Listen, Adam," Belinda said, suddenly angry. "You brought this up and now you're clamming up on me?"

Sheepish boy with charming smile returned. "Sorry. I guess I'm just not myself this morning."

Jerk. Well, who needed him or his information anyway?

She had planned on telling him about Kirby's affair. But now, the heck with Adam Mason-Martin.

Within seconds after Belinda saw Adam off with an atypically ungracious goodbye, Sheriff John Thomas called.

She answered his call on the phone at the foyer reception desk.

"Yes," he informed her. "They had lifted a print off one of the bullets in Kirby and Lana's gun. And surprise, surprise, the print belonged to Todd Johnson."

"Todd Johnson?" She knew the name, but couldn't immediately bring him up.

"Lana's trainer at the Eastside Athletic club in Issaquah." Even over the phone he sounded excited. "The one Kirby's sister-in-law mentioned."

Janice Tanner knew him too. Belinda remembered her mentioning him when they were sitting with Adam in the dining room.

"But get this, Bella," John said. "Lieutenant Hurts in Seattle Crime Investigations doesn't think it's important enough to pull Johnson in ASAP. Says he'll go talk to him tomorrow."

"But..." Belinda was also incredulous. *Todd Johnson could be the murderer.*

"So I think we should get our butts out there right now." He didn't give Belinda time to produce excuses. "I know you've got stuff to do at the Residence, but do you or don't you want to solve this murder?"

"Technically," she said, having felt the needle in his nudge. "I'm trying to dredge up enough evidence to sustain a reasonable doubt. And can we just go barging in on *their* suspect like that?"

"Bella, Bella, Bella." His tone turned condescendingly tolerant. "You don't have to be there with me. I'm doing *you* the favor. I'm the cop, remember. Maybe not on the Seattle Police Department payroll, but a policeman is a policeman is a policeman. And you're the lay person getting a boon from your favorite Uncle." Then he sighed loud enough for Belinda to catch his impatience. "But if you're so concerned about the jurisdictional boundaries, I got the go ahead from Lieutenant Katheryne Colyer. You met her once. She's Hurt's boss on this one."

"You're right, as usual." *Again reduced to an apologetic little brat.*

"Sooo…you're saying you're going to talk to him this morning and you want me there?" His excitement had finally infected Belinda. "Maybe Todd actually did it."

"Maybe. Are you in or you out?"

"In of course."

"Okay, meet me in Issaquah at the Eastside Athletic Club in one hour. And Bella…"

"Yes?"

"Don't' go in without me. Understand?"

Adam was not happy with himself for several reasons.

First off, he shouldn't have drunk so much alcohol the night before. Then there was the matter of spending the night at Cedar Valley Residence. He should have gone to a motel--if there actually was a motel in Cedar Valley.

While sitting at Calvin "Senator" Pope's desk and waiting for the perfect opportunity to rummage through his office, Adam had had plenty of time to reflect and regret.

Now, he rubbed his forehead and eyes with both hands as if such a simple act would make his headache disappear--or change last night--or just make it all go away.

Some very poor choices on my part.

Belinda and Martha must think him an immature jerk.

Not the suave intelligent lawyer image he would have wanted to leave in his wake.

Especially Belinda. First, her meeting with Calvin and his ludicrous "insanity plea", and now this. Adam groaned and lifted his head from his hands.

"What the hell," he said to Calvin's empty office. "What do I care what they think anyway?"

But he did, and that irked him even more.

One good thing about this morning, if he overlooked his headache and his morning-after self evaluation, "Senator"--*god did he hate that moniker*--was out of town. Consequently Adam had free run of the office.

He had waited through several minor interruptions from junior staff, but at last, Adam had the time and place to himself. He was free to do all the digging he wanted to.

So why was he wasting time thinking about Cedar Valley Residence? Obviously because he had made of fool of himself. *Behaving like a first year law student for heaven's sake.*

Forcing his mind back on the task at hand, and without apology, Adam went through Calvin's locked desk drawers and file cabinet. Calvin thought he had the only keys with him, but Adam had made himself a set within weeks of starting work at the firm.

Notwithstanding his clandestine key copying actions, Adam considered himself an ethical and upright kind of guy; but, he also saw himself as intelligent, savvy, and ambitious. Adam was sure Calvin would screw right over him if he didn't stay a couple steps ahead.

Not something Adam was about to let happen.

Although, as he saw his hands shake while unlocking Calvin's file cabinet, he smiled bemusedly at his own inner-contradictions playing themselves out in the physical world.

Eventually, in Calvin's lower desk drawer, he found the folder that explained what was going on.

One typewritten white page of paper. Not fancy. But life-changing for Calvin.

Adam had expected something to the effect of what he read, but seeing the words in black and white, the facts were no longer theoretical in nature, but quietly disconcerting--and enormously sad.

Calvin Pope was in the early stages of dementia, Early Onset Alzheimer's disease, to put an exact name to it.

"Damn," Adam cursed. Then he dropped back into Calvin's inordinately comfortable swivel chair and stared at the ceiling.

Thinking. Wondering what to do next.

Calvin probably should not be practicing law any longer. But was that his call? The letter from Calvin's doctor hadn't included recommendations. Just the clinical facts.

God, he thought, *it must be horrible to realize you're losing your faculties.*

Adam let out a sigh of empathy on Calvin's behalf, pulled himself upright, and switched on Calvin's desktop computer.

He also wanted to see what he could find on Theresa Bacera and Janice Tanner. His boss had access to the best databases money could buy, and it would give Adam a real ego boost to actually help Belinda. After all, they *were* trying to establish Kirby's innocence. Time to get down to business.

Of course he could use his own computer.

But Calvin's chair felt like a comfortable old glove.

Ten minutes had passed since John's last call, and Belinda still sat in her Altima staring at the Eastside Athletic Club.

The sky was clear blue; last night's hellish storm had dissipated into nothing, and the air was freshly scrubbed and smelling the-day-after-a-storm sweet.

Sometimes she found her uncle's reluctance to alarm her infuriating. Something *else* happened last night and she wanted to know what it was. There was a paper stand at the gym entrance, maybe she should get one and find out for herself.

For now, however, John had said to wait, and she would. *Maybe.*

The front length of the gym was roof-to-foundation window glass, and Belinda could make out the outlines of hard-bodied men and women on treadmills, stair-steppers, and rowing machines inside.

Indeed, she could almost smell their sweat and hear their grunts.

Most were young, fit, and firm. Like-thinking comrades, eager to be seen, and equally eager to compete. They were a *group* to which she didn't belong, and Belinda childishly fancied the Eastside Athletic Club was their *clubhouse.*

She should wait for John.

Although, if Todd were at work today, all she needed to do was ask him about the bullets, and she certainly felt up to that confrontation. Besides, even though her uncle was a County Sheriff, this was a Seattle Police case, despite his assurances. *And*, the intimidation factor that came with his uniform could actually be a hindrance.

In truth, Belinda knew it wasn't John's admonishment to wait for him, or his uniform, or any self-doubt as to her interviewing competence--it was the Eastside Athletic Club itself that kept her glued to her car seat.

She turned the ignition key until the battery clicked on, then turned on the radio. Maybe XM classics could help her sort out whatever silliness was going on within.

Strains of Vivaldi's *Spring* filled her automobile sanctum.

A BMW driven by a business-attired thirty-something young man pulled in next to her. As he got out, tall and lean, gym bag in head, he gave Belinda a confident smile that said, *"I belong here, can't you tell?"*

Why was she making walking into Eastside Athletic Club such a big deal? Especially since confronting Todd was so important. Finding out why his fingerprints were on the remaining bullets in the Norris' .38 could be the key to solving this murder.

"It's just a building," she said, out loud.

Marveling at her immature indecision, Belinda closed her eyes and dropped her head back against her headrest. Evidently, a piece of her psyche was still in fifth grade.

Here she was, possibly on the verge of finding a murderer and getting an innocent man out of jail. Yet, she sat, pondering the psychological aspects of why she had so often felt like a misfit in the past, and was unable to act here in the present.

"You and Bernie are different, Bella Dear. Not to worry." Grandma Glory, always there to comfort--and advise. *"Groups can breed mediocrity. And if anything, Bella Dear, you and your brother are not mediocre."*

Her cellphone rang, probably Devlin. She ignored it.

A tap on her closed window. "Belinda, is that you?"

Startled, she jumped, then smiled. It was Janice Tanner smiling back at her and looking ebullient. Janice must have truly enjoyed last night's birthday party.

"I bet you're here to talk to Todd because he was Lana's trainer. Am I right?"

Belinda opened her window. "Yes, you're right." She would keep her own counsel regarding the bullets. "I did come to see Todd."

"Great." Janice grabbed Belinda's door handle. "Come on in with me. Your timing is perfect. I'll introduce you."

Belinda was rescued from her unpleasant and silly remnants of childhood. Janice would walk her into the *clubhouse* and introduce her into the *group*.

Inside, the Eastside Athletic Club was warm, odiferous, and noisy. Exactly what she expected, and dreaded.

All Belinda's senses were immediately assaulted by the unmistakable and universal smell of human sweat, the clanking of exercise machine metal being repeatedly and rhythmically challenged, and the grunts and groans of driven human beings battling to conquer and sculpt their recalcitrant flesh. And ironically, all this activity was back lit and framed by what Belinda considered architecturally stunning floor to ceiling glass.

"Amazing," Belinda whispered to herself.

She and Janice had to walk by the line of window exercise stations; and up close, the *group* were far less intimidating, albeit even more hard-bodied and youthful looking. Belinda envisioned Lana Norris among them, vigorous, athletic, and very much alive.

She couldn't, however, picture her savior Janice as one of the *group*--nor Melissa Norris, Lana's sister-in-law. Neither woman seemed to fit.

Reading Belinda's mind, Janice touched her arm, "I'm not one of them," she inclined her head slightly toward the *group.* "Neither was Lana or Melissa. There are several exercise areas." She leaned in closer to whisper, "They're sort of a *clique,* snobby actually. We call them *'the showoffs.'*" Janice laughed.

Belinda felt her shoulders relax. Evidently she wasn't the only one still in fifth grade. She said, "Thanks. I was feeling a lot old, out of shape, and immature."

Janice laughed again. They had survived the hard-bodied gauntlet and reached the front desk.

"You'll need to sign in, Belinda," Janice said. "Then I'll take you back to see Todd as my guest."

The Eastside Athletic Club turned out to be much more expansive than its glass façade suggested. Janice gave her a quick tour--lap pool--Jacuzzi--sauna--dance studio--racquet ball and tennis courts--and two more exercise rooms.

They found Todd Johnson standing right inside the door of a small glass fronted office connected to one of the back exercise rooms. A sparse space, metal desk, metal chair, metal file cabinet--Todd's office was clearly not designed for comfort or esthetic ambiance.

In addition, except for one floor-to-ceiling poster showing male and female bodies at a muscular level, the numerous posters wallpapering his space and proclaiming the benefits of various energy drinks, vitamin supplements, and exercise regimens, seemed to further dehumanize, rather than decorate his small space--or inform his clients.

The exercise room itself, however, was painted a relaxing blue, had several frosted skylights overhead, contained dark blue upholstered benches, and had a Swedish-finish hardwood floor. Dance bars, roll balls, wands, and exercise mats dotted the room.

"He does personal training back here," Janice explained. "You *know*, a lot of dance-routine kinds of things." Then after quick introductions while standing in Todd's office doorway, Janice was off to the locker room.

Belinda didn't *know* about dance routines, but she was truly grateful for Janice's help.

"Good timing," Todd said, extending his hand and

bestowing upon Belinda a broad smile. "I'm between clients. You looking to join? If you are, a personal trainer can help a lot." Belinda accepted Todd's weak handshake and stepped into his office.

Medium height, medium build, an average timbre to his voice, and nondescript features, Todd would easily fade into the background--except for the hair and the smile. Both big and cheeky. And his cologne, Belinda didn't know it's name, reminded her of Uncle Bernard's after-shave lotion. Intense and tangy.

Seeing, hearing, and smelling Todd in person, Belinda made a quick decision to use her slight advantage--the element of surprise--and go directly to the heart of the matter.

"My name's Belinda Jones, Mr. Johnson." She stepped farther forward into his office. "I've been hired by Olive Norris and Calvin Pope," *only a small lie* "to prove Kirby Norris innocent of killing his wife."

"What?"

Belinda heard confusion, and maybe a little fear in his voice. "And," she continued, "your prints have been found on the bullets in the murder weapon."

"What?" This time, with the utterance of the word, Todd's smile disappeared, and his eyes turned cautious.

Belinda pressed her advantage. "The Cedar Valley Sheriff will also be here soon, but I thought you might prefer talking to me first." Where the heck *was* Uncle John anyway?

Todd continued to stand, staring at Belinda with obvious disbelief.

"Mind if we sit, Mr. Johnson?" Not waiting for a reply, Belinda walked around Todd to the front of his desk and sat down in the one metal chair provided.

Todd finally spoke again, anger surfacing. "Who the hell do you think you are? Barging in here--"

"We don't have time to play games." Belinda hoped she was coming across tough--mean even. "Several people have implicated you--one of whom believes you were having an affair with Lana Norris."

"Now listen..."

Anger was still there in his voice, and fear had also

returned. Belinda could hear it and instinctively knew Todd was not only hiding something, but additionally felt himself at a disadvantage. Unfortunately Uncle John wasn't around to back her up, and Grandmother Glory Jones was curiously silent.

She would have to handle this on her own.

"I just want to know--"

Todd cut Belinda off. "I don't have to tell you anything," he said. Still, he moved to behind his desk.

"No you don't *have* to tell me anything. But I should tell you Calvin Pope is planning on issuing a subpoena for you as a trial witness." *Another lie, this time a little bigger.* "If I could persuade him that was unnecessary...." She backed off a little, not sure if it was the right move.

Todd stared at Belinda silently for what seemed a very long time. It almost felt like her heart stopped beating while she waited and watched. She even thought she could see in his eyes the weighing of his dilemma--throw this woman out, or play ball?

Then, evidently having made up his mind, yet still not ready to speak, Todd went over and closed his office door. He came back and dropped into his desk chair--an action punctuated with a long loud sigh.

"You know you've got balls, what was your name again?"

Belinda was not about to let Todd turn the tables on her. "Belinda Jones," she answered calmly. "It's not balls I have, Mr. Johnson, but evidence. Can you explain to me why your prints are on the bullets in Lana and Kirby's .38?"

"Easy," he said. "I taught Lana how to shoot. You've met Kirby, right?" The disdain in Todd's tone was palpable. "Didn't know squat about shooting. Desk-jockey, you know?"

"How did you end up giving shooting lessons to an exercise client?"

He opened his hands and shrugged. "Just happened, you know, *Belinda*."

"No, I don't know, *Todd*. Or do you consider marksmanship part of strength-training?" She had to keep control and keep pushing, no matter how ridiculous his flirting, and intense his stare.

"Alright, alright." He sat up straight and leaned forward across his desk top. "I liked Lana. You know? I guess she mentioned it one day and I offered."

In an instant, Belinda could see the truth in Todd's eyes and hear in the undertones of his voice. Todd Johnson had indeed had an affair with Lana. Belinda just needed him to say or confirm it outright.

"Were the shooting lessons before or after your affair with Lana?

"Just *who* told you that?" His eyes narrowed.

"Someone who knew Lana very well." *Three lies in one interview!*

"I'm married and have two kids. And I'm not about to admit any kind of affair with anyone at anytime. Especially not on the witness stand. But..." he lowered his voice substantially and nervously bit his lower lip. "If hypothetically, you know..."

Todd waited for Belinda to nod her head, and say, "Yes, hypothetically."

The corner of his mouth twitched--possibly an aborted smile--and his eyes betrayed a hint of relief and mischief. "Hypothetically, if one did have an affair with a woman, and just by way of example, let's call that woman Lana. And just suppose that woman was to call out, say another man's name in bed. Now, still hypothetically, do you think that man would continue an affair with this Lana woman?"

"What name?"

"Maybe Jerry. Yeah, Jerry."

"When did it end, Todd?" No more game. Belinda was tired of Todd.

"At least six months ago." He stood. "You happy?"

Belinda stood also. She didn't think she'd get anymore information--but she was mistaken.

"And, Belinda Jones, you might want to check with the Travelodge in Renton. Lana met a man there on several occasions."

"How do you know that?" Belinda demanded.

"Because I followed her. No one steps out on Todd Johnson. You know?" He scoffed derisively. "Don't remember what he looked like, I just hung around long enough to see she was meeting a man. That was enough for me."

Belinda left quickly and quietly--letting Todd's distasteful statements of spying and macho bravado remain with him--unanswered, unchallenged, and floating on the stale gym air in his unattractive cubicle kingdom.

Once back in the safety of her car, Belinda allowed herself a deep joyous sigh.

She'd done it. Moved forward on finding out who had killed Lana. And she'd done it on her own.

She didn't even bother calling her uncle. He hadn't shown up, so let him figure it out on his own.

Belinda was feeling darned sassy; and very much enjoying the rush accompanying the experience.

"Are you trying to tell me you don't believe Kirby did it?" Geri asked. The sarcasm in her voice and manner couldn't be missed.

Belinda returned tit-for-tat, "And you think he *did*?" She was angry and disappointed. Things had gone so well with Todd. "Walter and Melissa Norris thought it would be a good idea for me to talk to you. They thought you would be able to fill me in on Lana and Kirby's relationship."

"Gossip, you mean."

Compared to Lana's housekeeper, Todd had been a cakewalk.

Belinda had naively expected a personality closer to "Alice" in "The Brady Bunch," warm and comfortable, tucked away in a cozy little bungalow. Instead, here she was, dueling with the housekeeper from hell in what felt like a fancy million-dollar box.

Should have guessed, maybe even known.

The signs had been there for the noticing from the moment she had located Geri's condo in a toney part of Kirkland on the shore of Lake Washington, not very far north of Calvin Pope's office. The development was new and stylish--angular townhouses with balconies and patios and a central entrance for security monitors and buzzers.

Definitely upscale and pricey. Not your stereotypical housekeeper habitat and Belinda had immediately wondered how Geri could afford such a place. However, she had quickly pushed that concern aside when she remembered it was "Mrs."--two incomes no doubt--one possibly in the big-buck, high-tech range.

Even Mother Nature had warned her. The moment Belinda had pulled into the visitor parking area it started pouring rain from dark low-hanging clouds. If there was a sun still up there, it had vanished behind a thick greyness that had suddenly encapsulated the east side of Lake Washington.

No big deal, it always rains in Puget Sound somewhere, for goodness sake. At that point in time, despite the weather and any initial misgivings, she still felt optimistic and believed the housekeeper would provide her with *eyes* inside the Norris household.

"Actually, I don't think he did it either." Warmth was still absent in Geri's tone, but she was backing off her hostile stance a milli-inch.

Ironically, Belinda thought Geri could be a very attractive woman, if not for her icy demeanor. In her mid forties, her features were well proportioned and symmetrical, her hair glossy brown, her eyes intelligent, and her mouth generous.

"And that's why I wanted to talk to you, Mrs. Keyes. To find out what you thought." By this time, Belinda was no longer sure it *was* "Mrs." If Geri was married, where were the family photos? In fact, where were any signs of life? Like newspapers? Magazines? Tossed keys or change? Pets?

Not a speck of dust dared present itself.

The bedroom doors were closed--maybe that was where all the "stuff" and dirt were hiding.

True enough, she had initially found Geri's condo architecturally interesting in that the entry was on the second floor, the ceilings were cathedral, there were several skylights, floor to ceiling window banks covered the front wall, and there was a patio on the lower level and a balcony up top. Interior décor had seemed to fit--angular, modern, with lots of chrome, unadorned cream walls, and tile floors minimally accented with nondescript pastel Asian rugs.

But now, as they sat in cream leather armchairs, angled to have a window view *and* see each other, Lake Washington and Belinda's prospects for extracting information looked ominously bleak. And despite a healthy fire in the fireplace, Belinda felt overwhelmingly chilled--almost as if she were in an ice cave. She shivered and wondered what Geri would throw at her next.

Then Belinda noticed a large portrait above the fireplace. It had been there all along, but she was just now seeing it. It was a watercolor nude of a very pretty woman whom Belinda found vaguely familiar. *Did she favor Janice Tanner? Or maybe Theresa Bacera? Couldn't be. No, just a beautiful woman and a beautiful piece of art.*

Like the rest of the house it was done in pastels, but somehow the artist had unexpectedly and brilliantly coaxed warmth and sensuality out of an almost monochromatic palette. Such skill, Belinda thought, and instantly liked it--liked it a lot. Maybe because it was the only soft touch in the entire place--that singular gold framed picture--a flicker of warmth.

"Kirby wasn't a saint, I can tell you that--left his stuff all over the house like I'm a maid. Housekeepers aren't maids." Geri looked at Belinda as if she also was an offender in this area. "You do know that?"

"Yes," Belinda answered calmly. "At our residence a housekeeping service comes in to dust and vacuum and do the bathrooms. But we don't expect them to pick up after us or the residents." All Belinda now knew to do was try to ingratiate herself to this improbable and distasteful housekeeper. For some part of this woman had selected that painting; and that was the Geri Keyes she needed to draw out.

"Melissa expects me to tell you their bedroom-secrets?" Geri asked. "Or more like which one left their dirty underwear laying around? Like I said. Gossip."

"Well, yes, I guess. But at this point 'gossip' could turn into a lead. I'm looking for someone with a reason to kill Lana." Keeping the lovely picture hanging on the wall in her mind's eye, Belinda leaned forward earnestly and added, "I really am just trying to find out who disliked Lana enough to kill her."

"Besides Kirby."

"Yes, besides Kirby." Belinda wondered how Lana had

faired with this woman? Her cleaning expertise must have been outstanding, a thought which prompted her to add, "Are you still cleaning the house?"

"Heaven's no." Geri made an indignant face that bordered on comical in its intensity. "Right after Lana was killed, battle-axe Olive made it quite clear she would be taking over."

Belinda didn't find Geri's description of Olive a good fit and wondered at the source of her animosity. "You didn't care for Lana's mother-in-law, I gather."

"You like the whole bunch of them, don't you? Walter and Melissa and Kirby and Olive."

"Well," Belinda hesitated. It was such an odd question. "I guess you could say I like them okay. I don't really know them, just from my investigation."

Geri said, "You should have heard what Lana thought of them. How she talked about them."

Belinda waited expectantly.

"Lana disliked Olive the most." She looked to a distant point beyond Belinda. "I think Lana could have liked the old biddy, but Olive never really gave her the chance. No one could possibly be good enough for her precious Kirby." Her gaze returned to Belinda. "Lana did feel sorry for Kirby though, even though he was pretty much spineless."

"But yet they still made love together?"

Geri took in a long breath and let it out slowly. "Yes they did."

"Did Lana and Kirby fight?"

"Not really, they pretty much had a live and let live policy. Besides, they each had their own interests."

Something in the housekeeper's tone prompted Belinda to ask, "Interests as in 'lovers'?"

At last Geri smiled. "Don't miss a beat do you?" Then her smile turned to a mild laugh. "You're pretty good, Belinda Jones. Seems like I'm telling you more than I'd planned."

Belinda ignored her praise. "Who?"

"I don't really *know* about Kirby, but I'm pretty sure he was seeing someone at his job. And Lana," she looked away again. "Well, Lana told me she was having an affair." Her expression clouded over. "Like it was any of my business."

"You didn't approve of your employer's life styles? Kirby or Lana?"

"Not my place to approve or disapprove. I'm just the hired help."

There was bitterness in Geri's last statement, but not wanting to break the spell, Belinda didn't pursue its source.

Geri continued, "Olive is the holier-than-thou one. Not me."

Curious, Belinda thought, Geri's air of familiarity when talking about Lana's family. "Have you been working for Lana and Kirby a long time?"

"About five years."

Again Belinda leaned forward earnestly. "Is there anything you can tell me that might shed some light on who killed Lana?"

Geri didn't have to stop and think. "If I were Walter I would have killed Kirby a long time ago. But," she smirked. "Fratricide isn't looked upon very kindly."

"But killing your sister-in-law is okay?"

"Well somebody had to do it. And I certainly didn't. The way I see it, what better way to get back at your brother than to kill his wife?"

"It is a thought. Anything else you can tell me?"

"Don't think so."

Belinda wasn't sure why, but she said, "You and your husband have a nice place here, Geri. And you've decorated it very nicely."

"I guess it doesn't make a difference if you know, but I'm not married. I use the Mrs. as not to get hassled by frisky clients."

Belinda knew that was a lie, but wasn't sure if it was important or not. She couldn't imagine anyone hassling Geri Keyes.

Just another secret.

"*Someone* else must have had it in for Lana," Belinda said.

"Jake West hated her guts."

"Did Lana tell you who she was having an affair with?"

"Yep."

Again Belinda waited.

"And I bet you want me to tell you who?"

It was Belinda's turn to be monosyllabic. "Yep."

"Todd Johnson, the brainless Mr. Muscles at Lana's athletic club."

Nothing new there. "He claims that was over. He also claims she met another man at the Travelodge in Renton."

"Oh yeah. That would be Jake West."

Now that was new. "Jake West, the man who hated her?"

"Yep."

"Why?"

"I'm afraid you're going to have to ask him that."

"I'm seeing him at lunch…" Belinda let the rest of her sentence and thought go.

The two women sat for a couple moments in silence, and Belinda marveled at the fact they did. Especially since it wasn't uncomfortable.

By then Lake Washington was being pelted by heavy raindrops, and visibility was barely more than fifty feet. Somewhere out there across the lake, Belinda was sure the city of Seattle still stood, despite the surrealistic perspective from Geri's armchair.

Eventually Geri asked, "Could you wait a minute?" Her voice had transformed--now surprisingly somber and gentle.

"Sure," Belinda answered quietly. Intrigued, she watched as Geri went into what she guessed to be a bedroom, and return with a photo album and a large manila envelope.

Then together, for a surprisingly long time, Belinda and Geri looked through a photo album of Lana and Kirby's wedding pictures--Geri occasionally touching a particular photo with surprising fondness, and offering snippets of history or explanation.

"No one wanted the album," she explained. "Not even Kirby. So I took it."

After finishing with the album, they next looked at loose family photos.

Pictures of lives in process. Lana, Kirby, Melissa,

Walter, and Olive. Olive always in purple standing next to her son, and Lana always smiling.

When Belinda finally left, she stood outside on the entry to Geri's condo for a moment, waiting for she didn't know what. Within seconds, sound reached Belinda from inside Geri's condo; and at first, soft as a whisper--then deep heart wrenching sobs. Geri had seemed such an ice-maiden. And now?

Well, Belinda thought, *at least someone is mourning Lana.*

Belinda arrived early to choose her table.

Salish Lodge--on the precipice of Snoqualmie Falls-- had window tables with spectacular views, and she managed to claim (with the help of an agreeable *maitre d')* the last table in the window row where they would have both view and privacy. She took the seat facing the door.

It had stopped raining in Snoqualmie and a rainbow graced the horizon outside the restaurant. Perfect.

She would be ready for him this time, not like the surprise confrontation last night in the parlor.

The Lodge's Restaurant was a place you came to on special occasions, and the menu was sufficiently pricey and sophisticated that Jake should be impressed. At the same time, the setting was relaxed, non-threatening.

Noon diners were leaving and tables were being reset with fresh white linen, gold rimmed crystal glasses, bone white china, and heavy-weighted freshly polished silverware. The aromas of olive oil, garlic, wine--all teased her nostrils.

She needed to find Lana's murderer; and regardless of his disclaimer, Jake West knew something. The trail had led to the Travelodge and Jake West. Todd and then Geri had just told her as much.

This interview might be *it.*

Last night Belinda had been hospitable and kind; this morning she would be prepared for him--and consequently calm and cool. Hadn't she just survived Todd Johnson and Geri Keyes?

"You can win more battles with your brain and a dab of honey, Bella dear," Glory Jones advised, *"but don't forget the stick."* She sighed to relieve any remaining anxiety.

"If you think you can impress me with a fancy lunch, it's your dime, not mine." He came upon her from the rear, from the bar. "But like I told you last night," he stepped into her view, "there's nothing new I can tell you."

Jake West had surprised her again.

"You can still sit and enjoy lunch anyway," she managed, her voice under control despite his ambush tactic. "Can't you?"

"Guess I could." He pulled out the chair across from Belinda and sat. "View's not bad," he said, his eyes glued to Belinda's.

She ignored the sexual undertone of his remark and held his stare. Last night, against the soft congenial parlor lighting, he had seemed sharply angular, hard, and scary. This afternoon, sunlight streaming through the windows, Jake West looked far less intimidating--even with his swaggering smirk. Maybe it was the eyes, not as piercingly black and hostile; and oddly enough, his "comb-over" didn't seem quite as ridiculous, rather almost endearing.

Belinda smiled. "You're right, Mr. West. You probably can't tell me anything new. It's just I want to hear *your* story from *you*, not filtered by some idiot cop." She closed her eyes for a second and asked Uncle John to forgive her slander. When she reopened them, Belinda noticed Jake was still watching her, but with renewed interest. "What do you think? Can we start over?"

After another moment of scrutiny, he laughed, revealing a not so great set of teeth. "Okay, okay. I'll go through it all again." He looked around at their surroundings, "At least this time I'll get a decent meal for the telling."

As if you didn't get a darned good meal last night.

Belinda waited while the busboy filled their water glasses, then their waiter, a young man in crisp black-and-whites and a deferring manner, took their drink order. Jake insisted on wine, and of course Belinda had to agree, but she in turn insisted their waiter take their luncheon order at the same time. She wanted a block of interrupted time with Jake.

Ordering accomplished, Belinda didn't waste any further time getting down to business. She felt certain she needed to keep the advantage if she wanted to get anything out of the man.

"I know you were meeting Lana Norris at the Travelodge in Renton."

As Belinda watched anger visibly rise through Jake's face she was no longer sure of the wisdom of her tactic. Much too late, she contemplated the possibility Jake might throw an awful scene right there in Salish Lodge's fancy dining room.

He didn't say anything for what felt to Belinda like an eternity. When he did finally speak, she was again surprised. "I have a problem. Faith calls it anger management. Claims I get PO'd too easy, say things I shouldn't."

And maybe do things you shouldn't?

"And she's going to leave me," he continued, "if I don't get it together." His tone was solemn, even sad. "I underestimated you. Didn't figure there was anything you could do to piss me off." He blew out air in a half-sigh, half-chuckle. "Guess I was wrong."

Belinda instinctively felt sorry for him, but knew she couldn't show it. "All I want to do is find out who murdered Lana Norris," she said. "I believe Kirby didn't do it, and if you didn't, you don't have anything to lose by telling me what you know."

Their waiter appeared with the wine. Jake waved his hand for Belinda to do the sniffing routine. Evidently he knew what was required but didn't want to bother.

Wine accepted, glasses filled, and waiter gone, Jake finally said, "Looks like I'm going to have to tell you the whole damn thing." He took a walloping good swallow of wine, just about draining his glass. "Lana Norris was a snooty nosed bitch," he said, evidently now alcohol fortified and more inclined to talk. "Thought she knew what was good for everybody. We didn't need a new trail and still don't. Doesn't do anything but attract yuppies from the city and the Eastside. Think this is their playground, you know." He refilled his glass and read the label. "Not bad for a local wine."

Belinda hoped she wouldn't have to drive Jake home. Another twist she hadn't anticipated, Jake getting drunk. "So you had words with her a couple times about the trail, right?" "More than words." He first scoffed, then chuckled remembering. "Had a real doozy at one town meeting. Haughty when she got mad. You ever meet her?"

She shook her head.

"You ever see my place?" He drank the remainder of his wine and immediately refilled his glass.

"No, I haven't."

"Isn't much. But it's mine. Needed even more work back then."

Belinda smiled encouragingly.

He emptied his glass again. "She paid me a hundred grand to back her in the trail fight--or at least shut up."

"Lana Norris bribed you to get the trail in?" Jake's information was so unexpected Belinda was unable to keep the incredulity out of her voice. She leaned forward and stared straight into Jake West's beady eyes. "Are you telling me you were at the Travelodge collecting money from Lana Norris?"

"Yes, Ma'am, that's exactly what I'm telling you." Bomb dropped, Jake leaned back in his chair and watched her.

This time Belinda saw past his trademark smirk--to the relief from the telling in his eyes. "Another glass of wine?" she offered. So what if she had to drive the jerk home, she was finally getting somewhere.

Even though Belinda was bone-tired--she'd hung around with Jake until she was sure he could drive--she couldn't wait to get back to Cedar Valley and tell her uncle and Bernard about her morning. She had uncovered quite a bit of information--on her own.

She had faced Todd Johnson, Geri Keyes, and Jake West. And to her way of thinking, come out the winner.

First, she would try to catch John at his office, then go home and update Bernard.

When Belinda pulled up in front of the Sheriff's office in

Cedar Valley, she noticed John's cruiser parked in the small side lot. An unmarked police vehicle was parked next to it.

Hastily she grabbed her canvas bag and headed inside. She was smiling, knowing John, like Bernard, would be proud. She had long been aware their praise and encouragement were vital to her well being, but Belinda didn't consider her dependency a bad thing. Besides, it was reciprocal. Hadn't she in return always been there for them? Especially Bernard?

She was only slightly surprised there wasn't a receptionist at the front counter. Evidently his latest temp hadn't lasted. She would never understand that phenomena. Didn't they realize he was one of the good guys?

She could see the door to his office was pulled closed, but not quite shut. She went straight back.

After a perfunctory knock, and while pushing open his office door, Belinda announced, "Uncle John, you're not going to believe what Jake West told me--"

Without ceremony, John interrupted her. "Belinda, you know Lieutenant Colyer? You've met a couple times." He was sitting rather stiffly at his desk, not exuding his regular relaxed aura, and looking surprised and undoubtedly irritated.

Then he cleared his throat, quickly averted his eyes, and brought his hand to his face in a clumsy and ineffectual attempt to mask a schoolboy-intensity blush.

Katheryne Colyer was standing to John's side, a little to his rear. Short, bobbed reddish-brown hair, eternal cheerleader face, Katheryne was not your typical looking law-enforcement type. But her hair was neat and professionally shaped, and she was wearing a black no-nonsense businesslike pantsuit that didn't quite hide her shoulder holstered Colt .38 snub-nose. There was no mistaking Katheryne Colyer as a cop.

But tough cop or not, when Belinda turned to look at Katheryne, she again saw a blush--hers less intense than John's--but a blush nonetheless: and that touch of redness in Katheryne's cheeks coupled with a quickly passing chagrined look hit Belinda as incongruous and cartoonishly intense. Up to this moment, Belinda had only thought of her as a no-nonsense, take-no-prisoners kind of policewoman.

Behind the cop was evidently a *woman*.

It took Belinda a few seconds to further interpret the scene she had just interrupted, but in the end, quickly realized she had barged in during a very personal moment between John and his lady-friend.

Lady-friend? This was her *Uncle John*, her mentor, her parent and grandparent substitute--her sexually neutral confidant.

Not a *man*. She was, however, not an idiot. It was blazingly clear to Belinda that her John and Katheryne were lovers.

"Hi, Lieutenant," Belinda said while covertly continuing her reappraisal of Katheryne and trying to accept this new revelation. Even though she had met the Lieutenant before, she had not given her much thought beyond her general looks and cop persona. Not that she disliked Katheryne, or knew any reason why she should--she just hadn't really paid attention.

"Ms. Jones. Nice to see you again." Any residual embarrassment evidently vanquished, Katheryne delivered Belinda's greeting with a pleasant and engaging smile.

Belinda also caught a faint whiff of amusement edging Katheryne's tone of voice.

Intuitively, though, Belinda knew she couldn't let whatever was going on within herself show. "Sorry I just barged in," Belinda said apologetically. "It's just I have news about our case." She looked to John for guidance. Could she freely discuss *their* case in front of *this woman?*

"Lieutenant Colyer has graciously supplied us with all the lab information I've passed on to you." The Sheriff, seemingly now more himself, relaxed and in control of the situation again, smiled wryly. He was looking directly and intensely at Katheryne. "The Lieutenant is a co-conspirator."

Katheryne let the amusement Belinda had sensed show through, touching one hand to her lips and speaking directly to John with her eyes.

And the faces of Belinda's own emotions became crystal clear.

And distasteful.

She was angry, jealous, and a bit chagrined. Most of all, she felt betrayed and rather foolish. For in a blink, her world had irrevocably changed.

And within another blink, and astonishing to Belinda, she was able to continue even though an integral piece of her life had flip-flopped. "Jake West told me Lana paid him to shut up about the trail." Her voice sounded steady and neutral to her own ear. Good. And amazing.

"I'll be damned," John said. All his attention was suddenly refocused on Belinda and catching a killer. "I'm really sorry I got called away, Belinda. I tried calling you. Overturned big-rig at Edgewick Rd." Then with a nod and a hand gesture, he indicated she should sit down.

Belinda continued to stand.

Katheryne politely cleared her throat and said, "The ADA heard about your little request on the fingerprints, John. So, he's now considering taking a closer look at Todd. My guess is Mr. Johnson is going to have some company today. Not that our dear ADA has backed away from Kirby yet. Still..." She let her thought fade with a speculative turn of her head.

"Which means," Belinda said. "Jake West will also be getting some visitors." A realization that almost made Belinda smile. But not really.

At the end of their lunch, she had come to feel some sympathy for the blowhard; besides, she doubted Jake actually had the nerve to kill Lana. Not unless he'd done it in the throes of one of his anger attacks? That was still a possibility.

"Well, Bella," John half-mused, half-postulated, "your suspects are beginning to line up."

Belinda heard praise in his voice. Happily, and reasonably so. She knew just because John had a girlfriend didn't mean he didn't care about her. It just felt darned strange.

"By the way," he added. "I did some quick searches, and can't find anything on Janice Tanner. Also checked Albuquerque and New Mexico criminal databases using her name. And nothing in DMV here or New Mexico."

"Do you have her social?" Belinda asked.

"No reason to."

Katheryne took in a breath as to speak, then quickly clamped her mouth shut.

Belinda didn't feel she had the authority or gumption

to press Katheryne, but she saw John give Katheryne a curious look. But he didn't press her either.

Instead, he asked Belinda, "Have you seen the paper today?"

Belinda shook her head and caught her breath; she could tell from John's change of tone he was about to tell her what happened last night.

"Moira Stephens. You know who I'm talking about?"

"Yeah…"

"Remember last night when I was called away from your party?"

"Oh no."

"Well, she was involved in a bad single-car rollover last night."

Belinda's mind rushed ahead. "Was it an accident?"

"The Washington State Patrol doesn't think so. But," the Sheriff bestowed a quick appreciative look Katheryne's way, "from what I've been told, no police jurisdiction is rushing in to link up Lana, Philly, and Moira. The Seattle Police department," again a quick look at Katheryne, "is *officially* still considering each an isolated incident. *And,* I still can't get anyone in the Sheriff's department or the Washington State Patrol to invest resources into Philly's death. *And,* it's been pointed out to me several times this morning that coincidences do happen, no matter what they claim on cop shows."

"Jeez," was all Belinda could say. But inside her stomach flopped. Finally, after a couple of seconds she managed to ask, "Is Moira dead?"

"No, but it's serious. We need to go see her this afternoon. After lunch." Again, he looked to Katheryne. "Want to tag along?"

"Got to get back," Katheryne answered. "Keep me posted, John?"

"Will do."

Belinda barely noticed Katheryne's departure.

She was feeling overwhelmed. Maybe this investigation was bigger than she could handle; and more people could die if she didn't stop Lana's murderer. She knew it.

But how was she going to catch this murderer? So far

she had nothing, nada, zilch. Just a lot of suspects and motives. Belinda heard herself say, "Uncle John, I'm running out of time, aren't I?" She could hear the despair in her voice. How quickly her morning accomplishments and accompanying elation had turned to dust.

When Belinda arrived back at Cedar Valley Residence, she stole a few moments just to sit in her car and think. She wanted to write everything down for Olive and Calvin, but she first needed to get her emotions under control and her thoughts in order.

Then there was the residence. Who knew what had happened since she left? What had been stolen now? How often had Devlin their architect called?

Unlike Kirkland, in Cedar Valley the sun was still shining, the sky still summer blue. Belinda's emotions and thoughts, however, were in turmoil--while the world around her was quiet. Peaceful.

Then, out of that serenity, a bit of understanding popped into Belinda's consciousness, a minor flash of intelligent and intuitive enlightenment amongst all the bits and pieces of information crashing around helter-skelter in her brain.

The "Jerry" Lana Norris was supposedly having an affair with was "Geri Keyes"--her housekeeper. The "specialty bars" in Pioneer Square Pete and Bull had eluded to now made sense.

However, she had no real evidence, just the tenor of Geri's eavesdropped sobs, and her sudden and intuitive retrospect awareness that the lovely portrait so prominently displayed in Geri's condo was of Lana.

By the time Sheriff John Thomas came by Thursday afternoon to pick up Belinda to go see Moira, she was mentally and emotionally grateful he was letting her tag along. In fact,

he had boosted her ego with his insistence she do the interview.
"Woman to woman," had been his words.

At the same time, she was also illogically angry he
wasn't handling it himself. He knew how much she hated and
feared hospitals. He also must realize what she went through
those long bedside days and nights in her grandmother Glory's
sick room.

Consequently, Belinda anticipated getting to Moira's
bedside would be a gut-wrenching experience. No way around
it. But then, what kind of a detective would she be if unable to
interview a victim because they were in the hospital?

A rotten one.

"I need to do this, I have to do this," she had repeatedly
whispered to herself as John dragged her through Emergency
into the bowels of Harborview Hospital on Ninth Avenue.

"This is where they airlift the really bad ones," John had
explained. "And it's quicker going through Emergency rather
than Admitting. Back door, front door kind of thing."

Belinda successfully beat-down her hospital phobia and
resurfacing pain from those miserable days way-back-when. It
had been a different time, and of course a different hospital, but
as she expected, her memories and accompanying grief had not
blurred with time; and for a second, tears wanted to surface.

She refused to let them.

The worst, however, was navigating those endless
corridors painted "hospital-cream" to calm anxiety, yet never
quite accomplishing that mission. Then going up, around,
and about via double-door elevators, and through a myriad of
overcrowded wards--never really looking--too afraid of what she
might see.

Nonetheless, despite her apprehensiveness and
resurfacing grief, Belinda survived the ordeal--arriving quite
safely in Moira's private room.

Once there, she found Kirby's coworker and paramour
easy to talk to. In fact, even though the room was sweltering,
and machine-made hospital-air burned her eyes and nose,
Belinda found herself after only a couple bits of conversation
holding Moira's hand.

Moira, an attractive woman in the photo Lieutenant

Katheryne Colyer had provided, was not recognizable; and though able to talk in a weak and thin voice, she looked and sounded pathetically vulnerable and uncomfortable.

Her face was swollen and blue-black from bruising, most of her body was wrapped in white gauze, one leg was in traction, one arm was in a cast, and her other arm was connected to several intravenous tubes leading to hanging plastic bags of God-only-knew-what.

Belinda's couldn't ignore the obvious. Her own psychological distress--partly real and partly imagined--was minor compared to Moira's very real pain and suffering. Consequently, after introductions and a couple explanatory comments, she had reached out and taken the poor woman's hand on impulse.

John hung back, standing in the room's open doorway, while a short and sturdy looking young State patrolman was stationed outside Moira's door.

Belinda could feel if not see John behind her, waiting and watching as she made herself look at Moira's battered face.

One part of Belinda knew it wasn't kind to further distress the injured woman, but she had paid her dues this afternoon: enduring an emergency room overwhelmed with blood and guts trauma, while simultaneously having her senses assaulted and permeated with the universal hospital odor of death and disease mixed with disinfectant.

As a reward, hopefully Moira would be able and willing to answer a few straightforward questions.

"Kirby told us about your affair." Why waste time with unnecessary niceties?

Moira managed to nod her head.

"Moira," Belinda leaned in closer. "I figure you're in a helluva lot of pain. So I'm not going to beat around the bush, just ask you some direct questions about your relationship. Okay?" She kept her voice soft and low as she could. She thought Moira's head must be aching horribly.

Moira tried to speak, her words coming slowly in obviously painful gulps, "Kirby's... such a kid... sometimes." She wheezed as she tried to pull herself up a bit to more directly look at her visitor. She failed and winced. "He just couldn't

keep our affair...to himself I guess. It was stupid...and mean...
for me to fool around with a married man. But...you've met,
Kirby,... right?"

Yes indeed, Belinda had met Kirby. She nodded, and
after a little squeeze of encouragement, let Moira's hand go.
"He was...just so sexy," Moira continued. "And smart.
Even witty...sometimes."

How inexplicable, Belinda mused, Lana and Moira--two
princesses in love with a frog.

Belinda asked, "Do you have any enemies? Anyone
who would want to run you off the road?"

Moira's eyelids were starting to droop, almost closing,
but she did manage to answer Belinda's last question before
dropping back into a morphine induced sleep.

"The only thing...that I can think...someone wants to
get back at Kirby for something." Even though she could barely
move, and obviously in a lot of pain, Moira seemed to shiver.
"And they...came after me." Her eyes closed.

Belinda continued to watch her for a few seconds.
Moira's breathing seemed regular, and none of the flashing
machines around her bed were emitting alarm-like sounds. She
was just sleeping.

Moira's explanation sounded farfetched, but plausible;
and maybe she was right? True enough, both women were
attached to Kirby. A link for sure.

John said from the door, "I guess we better go. Give
her more time to recuperate." He sounded disappointed. "I
dragged you here for not much new info."

Belinda followed him, engrossed in her own thoughts
and new conjectures. Up to this point she had been so certain
the key to Lana's murder was understanding the deceased
woman herself.

Now she re-evaluated--maybe this was about Kirby.

"So that's why I flew up here," Tessa concluded. "You
and Bernard are my cousins." Her voice cracked with emotion.

"And all I have." She dug in her sweater pocket for a Kleenex. "Gillian doesn't have time for me, and Gavin...Gavin just doesn't give a damn anymore." Tears came in a flood.

Belinda and Tessa were in Belinda's suite, sitting next to each other on her window seat, their backs to the night outside. Naja was asleep in the middle of the bed.

Belinda patted her cousin's knee. Not overly comforting or familiar, but even that small gesture felt strange and awkward. Even as children, "the terrible" Tessa had never bared her inner self like this to her or Bernard. Closeness with Tessa was new territory for her; and she wondered if this was genuine emotion on Tessa's part--then was immediately contrite. People did change.

But what to do next?

The sky was jet black, the moon only at a quarter, and a building cloudbank overshadowed even that sliver of light. It wasn't raining again, but a cool breeze flowing through Belinda's slightly raised window felt and smelled like another storm was approaching.

When Tessa had knocked on her door at midnight wanting to talk, Belinda had let her in. What else could she do?

For sure, Belinda knew she and Bernard were kind and generous--sometimes to a fault. She considered it the "best" within them; and if asked, would have directly attributed this part of their character to Glory Jones' genes and upbringing.

Consequently, telling Tessa to go away because it was so late was not an option Glory would have approved of.

But *now*, half an hour later, having heard the disappointing details of a marriage going bad, a daughter not meeting expectations, a mid-life dealing its inevitable existential blow--an extremely tired and weary Belinda wished that just this *once*, she had hardened that Glory Jones heart of hers.

Eventually, Tessa blew her nose and continued, "I want to stay here. With you and Bernard. Don't know how long. Just..." She was seemingly on the verge of breaking down again, but paused and gulped a breath. "Just until I figure out if Gavin and I still have a future." Then, with a dejected little sigh and her shoulders slumped, Tessa turned and looked out the window into the blackness that was Cedar Valley and waited for

Belinda's reply.

What to say, what to do?

In addition to being generous-hearted, Belinda also considered herself fairly self-aware. Especially when it came to knowing the flaws in her personality, facing them head-on, and if warranted, trying like heck to overcome them. Or at least minimize their negative impact on her life.

Selfishness in particular. She knew this demon well. Tonight, right now, when Tessa needed her, selfishness was holding her tongue, and cautioning her heart. For Belinda also knew that in lockstep with Glory Jones' instilled goodness, self interest ran deep and hard through her being. She considered it a major flaw, maybe even her Achilles heel.

She had always done what she wanted throughout her life. True, she had always taken Bernard into consideration, but they were so simpatico it had never been an issue.

Clive "The Bum" had attributed her "bloody egocentricity" to her Leo birth-sign. Clive had found easy answers for most things.

How had I ever loved him? Belinda wondered as she sighed softly. Her cousin was probably asking herself the same question about Gavin.

Poor Tessa.

A loud clap of thunder, nearby it seemed, caused both women to jump. Belinda hadn't seen any lightning, and evidently Tessa hadn't either.

She patted her cousin's hand again, this time with more resolve--even though the prospect of Tessa moving into Cedar Valley Residence was turning Belinda's stomach queasy, and the taste in her mouth had gone decidedly sour.

Westminster chimes marked twelve-thirty on the antique mantel clock on her dresser, and accentuated the silence between them.

She needed to give her cousin an answer.

She didn't want Tessa to stay.

She didn't need the added aggravation and stress.

No, she only wanted to find Lana's killer. Baby-sitting her cousin through an L.A.-style divorce was not on Belinda's agenda.

She said, "Of course you can stay, Tessa. As long as you want. Our home is your home." As Belinda heard her words materialize into the world, she figured she was making a mistake--but somewhere Glory Jones was smiling.

CHAPTER SIX

Friday

As soon as their waitress was out of earshot, Melissa
Norris said, "I want to thank you again for meeting me on
such short notice. And especially so early." She pulled off her
stylishly cut leather jacket. "Warm in here."
Belinda thought the temperature was close to being just
right; indeed they could crank the thermostat up another notch.
"No problem." Belinda smiled encouragingly.
"Actually I was going to call you myself."
The two women fell into a surprisingly companionable
silence as they waited for more coffee.
Reminiscent of Tuesday afternoon when they'd met in
Covington, an eternity of only three days ago, Kirby's sister-in-
law was again dressed impeccably. This morning, her demeanor
was calm and bland, her less than compelling countenance
pristine--and so far revealing nothing.
Melissa had ordered the French-toast platter, and
Belinda, the all American classic--eggs-over-easy, bacon, hash
browns, and toast. Both women also ordered orange juice and
coffee refills.
It was 5:00 A.M. Friday morning and the sun had yet to
sneak a peek above the Cascades.
Belinda had chosen their meeting place. She wasn't a
fan of chain restaurants, but for some reason she had a soft spot
for the IHOP in Issaquah near Lake Sammamish State Park. Lots
of comfy padded booths, congenial waitresses, and the hazy
restaurant air was always thick with old-time-diner aromas of
percolating coffee, browning bacon, toasting bread--and seemed
to wrap itself around her like a warm blanket. Comforting and
safe; and at this hour, the place was near empty.
And quiet.
In the past, Belinda had always found this particular
IHOP a sympathetic and restorative environment, and this
morning in particular, she felt both her body and soul needed

coddling.

After dealing with Tessa at midnight, then waking at 3:00 A.M. from inconsequential but stressful dreams, she had spent her morning so far wallowing in self-indulgent pity. *And* she still hadn't figured out who had killed Lana, *and* she was cold to the bone.

Even though it hadn't rained, last night's temperature had dropped to an unpredicted and unwanted forty degrees-- accompanied by howling winds and intermittent thunder and lightening--and she had neglected to turn up the thermostat in her suite.

Not even a hot shower before leaving the Residence had vanquished her chill.

She and Melissa were sitting in a window booth, and despite her now warm, comfy, and reassuring surroundings, a quick glance outside into lingering dank darkness prompted Belinda to pull her jacket in closer and clasp her warm cup tighter. Fortunately, she expected their breakfasts to be hot, greasy, and scrumptious.

That was what her body needed. For her mind, Belinda needed more information if she was ever going to pull this murder investigation off, and to that end she hoped Melissa also liked her favorite IHOP. Liked it enough to reveal something new. Maybe, just maybe, Melissa had additional information about Kirby. Or Lana. Or Walter even.

A busboy reappeared and refilled their cups with hot steaming brew.

"This smells like Seattle's Best," Melissa said. "One of my favorites. A little lighter than Starbucks. Walter, on the other hand, loves Starbucks."

What an odd thing, Belinda thought, being able to tell the difference like that. Yet, she didn't consider it out of character for Melissa to be a connoisseur of coffee aromas. Belinda, however, had not dragged herself out before dawn on such a miserable morning to discuss the nuances of designer coffee. "So, Melissa, what did you want to tell me?"

Melissa laughed outright, hearty and unrestrained. "You don't fool around with chit chat, Belinda." In concert with the broad and engaging smile that had so suddenly appeared,

Melissa's eyes were twinkling with mischief and warmth. "Or maybe the early hour has turned you so blunt?" Then, with an amused and pleasant sigh she dropped back against the booth's padding. "I guess that's one of the things I liked about you when you came to the house the other morning. Your forthrightness."

Belinda felt her cheeks warm. "It's just that I'm anxious to find Lana's murderer."

This was a different Melissa than the one she had talked to Tuesday morning in Covington with her husband Walter. Indeed, Belinda had already stashed them both away in a neat little unimaginative and humorless "suburban yuppie couple" box.

Damn. *Why do people have to be so complicated?*

Belinda took her jacket off. At last she was warming up.

Melissa's smile left as fast as it had appeared. Now she leaned forward across the table, brow furrowed, eyes serious and intent, "I need you to understand about Walter and Kirby."

"Okay."

"Olive has always favored Kirby. You know that, right?"

Belinda nodded.

"But you see, Walter always understood. He never begrudged Kirby Olive's love."

Since Melissa didn't seem put-off by her bluntness, Belinda asked straight out, "Where was Walter the Monday morning Lana was killed?"

"He was with me." Melissa's tone was insistent, almost pleading. "Don't you see, he couldn't have done it."

"The two of you were at home?"

"Yes, yes. I'll never forget that morning."

"Because?"

Melissa blew out a deliberate and melodramatic sigh of resignation. "Because it was the biggest..." She inhaled deeply. "The biggest *fight* we've ever had."

She couldn't miss Melissa's distress over the word *fight*. Evidently disagreements between her and Walter were not allowed? Too uncivilized? "You and Walter don't fight very often?"

"*Never.*"

Belinda doubted they *never* argued, and Melissa's vehement insistence and childlike tone were a surprise--but her words and emotion rang genuine. Melissa probably did believe she and Walter got along great. And a facade of genteel companionability might be very important to Melissa.

Instinct told Belinda to wait.

After a few seconds, Melissa said, "Well, almost never."

She couldn't hold back a bemused smile. For sure, she and Clive "The Bum" had fought all the time near the end. Now, however, was not the time to revisit her own failed marriage.

Melissa laughed lightly herself. "I guess no marriage is perfect." Then she inclined her head slightly and directed her expertly made-up and disconcerting violet eyes squarely on Belinda. "You know, you smile easily. You're either a very happy person or a born cynic." And like earlier, Melissa's eyes also suggested a touch of mischief. "Which one is it, I wonder?"

Belinda ignored Melissa's provocative question, and instead of taking her comments at face value, perversely decided Melissa was flattering her so she'd accept Walter's alibi.

Well, it wasn't going to work.

"Were you at home or out?" Belinda asked. "And what where you fighting about?"

"We were at home." Melissa closed her eyes for a second, seemingly remembering. "In the backyard. Commander was with us. Our German Shepherd. You remember him, right?"

Belinda again just nodded.

"It was about Olive. I know I shouldn't be so hard on her, but sometimes the woman is just so friggin' pious. And that awful purple motif and that monstrous handbag."

Belinda was determined to keep a straight face, but it was difficult. She managed, though, to hold her silence again and wait for Melissa to continue.

"Always losing stuff out of it." Melissa rolled her eyes and waved one immaculately manicured hand derisively. "And her bag is so huge it's always falling over, or being knocked about."

"What exactly were you arguing about?"

"Money. Whether we should give Olive more financial help with Kirby's defense. I said no. Walter was wavering." Melissa looked at her watch.

Belinda didn't miss the flicker of gold and diamonds--lots of diamonds. No wonder Olive was hitting them up for money.

It was finally getting light outside and Belinda could see the day was starting with a clear blue sky--not a cloud in sight--and she wondered if this predawn meeting with Melissa had been worth it. For sure, she had found Melissa an unusual and intriguing person.

But so many different *Melissas*. The stylish and well put-together Yuppie professional--the ingratiating and aspiring new friend--the childlike happy-home-and-spouse-defender. Belinda was left guessing--who was she was dealing with?

An interesting new friend?

Or maybe a murderer?

For Belinda was well aware that while she pushed to give Walter an alibi, Melissa was also establishing an alibi for herself.

Olive seldom cried. Never had, all her life.

This morning though, as she stood in front of her bathroom mirror, she just couldn't stop the tears. Every time she thought the flood was over, she'd dry her eyes and wash her face. But then, her eyes would well-up again.

It had started when she returned from church, and she just couldn't seem to stop the flow or eradicate the underlying emotions.

Her apartment was nice, spacious and airy, painted in varying shades of purple, and most importantly connected to Kirby's house--but still separate, with her own private entrance, kitchen, and bathroom.

Without Kirby around, it meant nothing. She might as well be living in a cardboard box.

Why hadn't Belinda Jones called last night or this

morning? The answer was obvious and so painful.

Failure.

Her only remaining ray of hope was the Adam Mason-Martin kid. He had called and left a message while she was at sunrise Mass. Something about rethinking Kirby's defense? But that had been obvious from the first, now hadn't it? As soon as she could stop the flow she'd call him back. Maybe he would succeed where the Jones woman was failing.

Olive washed her face one more time. Maybe the flood was over?

Well, at least she knew she had tried her best, and at great cost to herself. Could the Blessed Virgin be punishing her? Hadn't she done enough and prayed long or hard enough?

Now she had lost a prized possession and was about to lose her son. And there was nothing left for her to do. Or was there?

A memory returned, vivid and earth-shattering for Olive in it's remembrance.

Of course! Maybe there was one more thing she could do to keep from losing it all.

A hand-engraved wooden sign resting stylishly on a wrought-iron stand in front of the entrance to Cedar Valley Residence listed dining hours, proclaimed the current status of openness, and encouraged visitors to come right in.

Most did without further ado.

However, at 8:00 A.M. Friday morning, Belinda, having returned to Cedar Valley Residence from IHOP, walked through the foyer discussing with Miss Shirley the suitability of a replacement impressionist print scarf Belinda wanted to order for the Dear. At that same moment in time, Lois Michael, despite the welcoming sign, opted to gain entry to Cedar Valley Residence by using the heavy brass door-knocker with determination and vigor.

Surprised, Belinda opened the door to the woman standing authoritatively on the veranda. "Hi," Belinda greeted her, while Miss Shirley took a step back.

Belinda didn't immediately recognize Lois, but did know they had met before, for the woman's demeanor and appearance were quite memorable and unmistakable. Jeans, T-shirt, heavy-duty walking boots, rigid jaw, and irises and hair, both black and hard like coal.

For no readily apparent reason, Belinda fleetingly wondered at the confluence of the three of them, at that moment in time, at that particular spot in the residence.

Déjà vu or premonition? She wasn't sure which.

"Come on in, we're open." Belinda, though physically warm by this time, overcame an urge to shiver and inclined her head ever so slightly toward their entry sign.

Lois allowed a tight little smile as she entered. "I'm here to see either you, Ms. Jones, or Mr. Jones." She handed Belinda a King County business card. "We've met before."

Belinda accepted the proffered card, but the woman's arrogant and peremptory tone of voice instantly piqued her anger--which in turn brought recognition. The business card wasn't necessary.

Damn. The King County Inspector had returned, and Jorge hadn't finished replanting.

"I'm here about the raspberry bushes. We gave you forty-eight hours..." Lois abruptly let her thought go, and time paused as she stood silently for several moments and peered at Miss Shirley. "It...it..." she sputtered. Still, Lois was unable to speak--seemingly only able to stare at Miss Shirley as if she'd seen a ghost.

Belinda was bewildered and unsure what next to do or feel. Should she still be angry? Or just the opposite, maybe happy? Not knowing what to think or say, if anything, she just stood there, staring in amazement at Lois Michael, who in turn seemed mesmerized by the sight of Miss Shirley.

Finally, Lois found her voice, and asked, "Auntie Aldea?"

Auntie Aldea? Belinda mentally parroted.

Miss Shirley, looking genuinely puzzled, reacted to all this by becoming more flustered than usual--shifting her gaze back and forth between Belinda and Lois, while simultaneously pulling on the edges of the vivid red scarf currently draped around her shoulders. She was also making unusual clucking sounds with her teeth.

"Mother thinks you're dead," Lois finally managed.

Belinda was beginning to comprehend. Miss Shirley's identity was being revealed.

Her heart wanted to sing with joy. So what if the bearer of such good news was a thorn-in-the-side jerk.

Belinda quickly suggested they go sit in the parlor and figure this all out. They accepted her offer without objection, but Belinda lagged behind the two women and pressed the kitchen intercom button on the reception area desk. "Bernie," she whispered urgently into the receiver, "get out here right away. It's Miss Shirley. She's been found. And," she pleaded, "please, please, lock Buster and Naja up in Martha's suite."

As Belinda replaced the receiver and headed toward the parlor herself, she realized she hadn't mentioned to Bernard that Miss Shirley's savior was Lois Michael.

Mischievousness on her part? For sure.

After assuring herself Miss Shirley, Aldea Michael actually, and her niece Lois were reconnecting successfully, Belinda decided she could slip away. Indeed, Bernard was sitting on the settee next to Miss Shirley holding her fragile hand as the specifics of her true identity were unfolding. She was in good hands.

Belinda smiled watching them, and knew it would be a long time before she and Bernard would migrate from *Miss Shirley* to *Aldea*. Maybe in time, but for now, she was still their *Miss Shirley*.

Not that Belinda wanted to miss the story, but she needed to talk to Geri Keyes, Lana's former housekeeper again. Her instincts said Geri hadn't killed Lana. Before she could accept that as a definitive truth, however, she needed to experience the woman again.

It was time to start culling her suspect list.

She could still see the painting on Geri's wall, so

sensitive and beautiful; and Belinda was now certain it was a portrait of Lana. Not something a murderer would still have hanging in such an honored and visible place.

Yes, she decided, she had time for a drive back into Kirkland before lunch.

She would drive the minivan and sneak Naja and Buster out through the back to ride with her. It was cool enough they could wait for her in the van.

No point waving a red flag in front of Lois Michael's nose: and what had Jorge been up to anyway? He had a full crew. Seems like they should have found time to move those bushes by now.

This time, Geri seemed glad to see Belinda and invited her on through the living room back into her condo's kitchen.

Not surprisingly, her kitchen walls were tan, accents and appliances were tan; while stainless-steel covered her counter and cabinet surfaces. Even the alcove table where she offered Belinda a seat was chrome. The two matching chairs were padded; the color, however, was egg-shell.

If nothing else, Belinda thought, *she's consistent.* Geri's obvious disdain for clutter and accompanying fondness for a monochromatic color-schemes was intriguing; and she wondered if Lana had provided Geri that "spot of color" every life must need.

"Coffee?" Geri's voice was thick and scratchy.

A cold, Belinda wondered? More likely, Geri's flow of tears had continued into the night. Still, she had to be sure. "I'll pass. Can't have more than a cup. The acid you know." Belinda waited for Geri to pour herself a cup from a sleek tan colored espresso machine and then take the chair across from her.

"I'm surprised you're back," Geri said after a sip.

Steam was still rising from her cup. The aroma was delicious. *And Melissa*, Belinda bemusedly conjectured, *could probably identify the brand.* Which prompted her to ask, "You don't know Melissa well, do you?"

"No, only what Lana would tell me."

"You and Lana were close?"

Geri looked down at her cup and sighed lightly and softly, "Yes. Yes we were." The timbre of her voice was now weak, dejected.

Grief. Belinda knew it was, but still, she asked, "Were you and Lana lovers?"

Geri looked up directly at Belinda, the expression on her face stronger and more challenging than when Belinda had arrived. "You're guessing," she said.

"Yes. I'm guessing." Belinda leaned forward earnestly toward this woman she hardly knew. "But you see, Geri, you're the only person I've talked to who actually misses Lana. *The only person to show grief.*"

Geri brought her hand to her mouth, trying to hold her emotions at bay. She did manage to nod her head in agreement with Belinda's statement.

"You loved her," Belinda said quietly. "And now she's gone."

"Please, please," Geri begged Belinda as tears welled in her eyes. "Catch the bastard who killed my Lana." Geri's tears sadly turned to sobs.

On her way back home to Cedar Valley, Belinda used her time in the car to take stock.

The sky was still clear, the temperature pleasant, and for the time being, last night's threatening storms still had failed to materialize. Nonetheless, Belinda had lived in Puget Sound long enough to know the rapidly changing face of mother nature when confronted with the Cascade mountain range.

For now though, it was lovely. A little before lunchtime, traffic was light and the roads dry--easy driving, and I-90 roadsides were glorious with end of summer greenery.

"Enjoy it while you can," Belinda said to Naja who was sitting royally in the passenger seat next to her. Buster, as was his habit, was hunkered down as close to her minivan back seat as he could press himself.

As she headed out of Issaquah, the drive itself brought

thoughts of Moira. It must have been horrible Wednesday night. The curves in the darkness, the rain, the slick roads. Belinda considered Moira quite lucky. She could easily have died in the crash. At least in the hospital, she had a chance to make it.

However, Belinda couldn't ignore that except for Kirby, Moira had no alibi for the time of Lana's death. Lovers vouching for each other--not strong. And Moira had an obvious motive. Get rid of the wife so she can have Kirby to herself. In fact, she could have driven herself off the road. But Philly, why kill him?

Further thought on her suspect list brought Belinda to the realization that she was glad to rule Geri out as Lana's murderer. For some reason she couldn't yet identify, she liked the woman despite their diametric tastes.

Walter and Melissa both had motives, albeit weak ones. Olive's blatant favoritism would be hard to take. But killing Lana was an awfully oblique way to get back at Kirby. No monetary gain had surfaced, except that maybe Walter would inherit with Lana dead and Kirby on death row. She didn't know the terms of Lana's and Kirby's wills, but she thought it far more likely Olive was the beneficiary. And again why kill Philly? Melissa probably knew about Kirby and Moira--but why would she care who Lana was sleeping with?

Todd Johnson--now he was a good candidate. He could have easily killed Lana because she had dumped him. Then he killed Philly because... Again Belinda was stuck.

She was certain Philly, Moira, and Lana were connected. Motive-wise though, Belinda just couldn't make it work with any of her suspects.

Not even Jake West. She certainly didn't like him, but murder and attempted murder?

Belinda sucked air in between her teeth and made a clucking sound out the corner of her mouth.

Oh sure, there was still Pete Naldeen and Bull Morton. But like the police, Belinda just couldn't fathom why they'd want to harm any of the victims.

"Motive. Motive. Motive," she explained to Naja and Buster. "That's the key to these crimes, pups."

Then again, she could just be a very poor detective, and an even worse judge of character. Maybe Kirby Norris was sitting right where he needed to be for murdering his own wife. But, he certainly couldn't have killed Philly and run Moira off the road. He was in jail, now wasn't he? An accomplice for Kirby? Or two murderers with separate motivations?

"Screw it!" she finally decided and turned her thoughts to enjoying the ride with her canines and the scenery on I-90.

When Belinda arrived back at Cedar Valley Residence, still confused, but most of all ravenous, she didn't bother going upstairs to freshen-up; rather, she headed straight to the dining room.

Once inside *The Cedars*, Belinda was greeted by warm aromas of simmering olive oil, garlic, and tomatoes. Spaghetti, she hoped.

Bernard used ultra-thin angel hair pasta (*capelli d'angelo*) which he ordered from several special suppliers in the Campania region of Italy, and topped it with thick rich Bolognese sauce--"*Sugo Alla Bolognese*"--the dish read on their menu. It was one of Belinda's favorites.

Her culinary nose also detected what she considered one of the most heavenly aromas of all--Martha's fresh baked French baguettes.

It was late for lunch and she prayed there was food left.

Oddly, Morris LeBeau, his wife Anna, Vera Price, Phoebe Farmer, and Miss Shirley were sitting at their usual table by the window, and it appeared they hadn't eaten yet. They usually arrived for lunch early. Kaitlin, not unexpectedly, was absent.

Seeing them all there together was a comforting sight; and Belinda headed straight toward her little group of residents.

Spaghetti would replenish Belinda's body, and her friends would renew her soul.

Morris stood upon seeing her approach, waved her over, and pulled a chair up to the corner of their table between him and Anna. "Sit down Belinda, we've got a lot to tell you."

He was smiling. Belinda hoped that meant nothing else had been stolen.

Morris sat back down. "The most extraordinary thing happened this morning."

Belinda almost blurted out that she knew about Miss Shirley, but caught herself as not to spoil his excitement.

Miss Shirley dropped her head and blushed.

"Aldea is filthy rich! And she wants to continue to stay here," Morris said.

What? Belinda felt like her jaw must have dropped like a cartoon character as she looked around at all their smiling faces. "Rich?"

Miss Shirley looked up sheepishly at Belinda.

"And," Morris continued in a tone verging on idolatry, "we've made a financial *arrangement.*" He winked conspiratorially at Miss Shirley. "It's quite generous. We've been talking about it for a couple hours."

"We went past our usual luncheon hour," Vera stated quite properly.

Next they all waited a moment for Belinda to absorb their news; then Morris finished up. "Therefore, Anna and I will be able to remain at this wonderful place. And Aldea, though she has many alternatives, will stay here too."

Belinda felt a tear escape, but quickly brushed it away under a veiled cough. When she did speak, she knew her voice sounded husky with emotion. "This is unbelievable how this has turned out. Who would have thought Lois Michael would be your niece, and you Miss Shirley..." Belinda suddenly remembered the crime and accompanying hullabaloo two years previous. "Aldea Michael. The toothpaste heiress. You have a ranch out on Edgewick road, right? And a mansion in the San Juan Islands some place?" Belinda's eyes widened as her remembrances and comprehension grew. "Miss Shirley, you're *that* Aldea Michael! The woman who was kidnapped a couple years back and everyone thought was dead."

Miss Shirley shrugged her shoulders apologetically, "Yes, Dear, that's me. I can only guess about what happened. Lois wants me to go to a shrink and dredge it all up. I'm sure it's all unpleasant and I won't do it of course. Some things are best left buried, don't you think? I will of course inform the authorities that I am no longer missing."

Belinda wanted to ask her tons of questions, but not now. She also speculated *Aldea Michael* might turn out to be a tad spunkier than Miss Shirley; and there were definitely some twist and turns still ahead. She doubted all was settled for her dear Miss Shirley.

Further, Belinda figured, fortunes the size of Miss Shirley's didn't just sit for a couple years without spats among relatives and legal intrigues developing. She couldn't remember if the Aldea Michael she had read about had had any children. No, she didn't think so. That would be yet another complication.

"And," Miss Shirley said--answering one of Belinda's unspoken questions--"Don't know why I had so many houses. Who needs all those places to live? Don't have any children of my own evidently, so I told Lois she should move into the ranch, but I think most of her friends are in Seattle. Who knows..."

At that moment, Miss Shirley had such a winsome look on her face, it was hard for Belinda to accept she was in her mid-seventies and coming out of a two-year bout of amnesia.

"But Lois," Miss Shirley added, "did say she'll extend your time for a month. Now, isn't that nice?"

"Wonderful." Belinda agreed. What she actually thought was Lois should have dropped the whole damn thing.

Morris, however, was not as reluctant to speak his mind. "Hump. Shouldn't be bothering us at all." He narrowed his eyes and looked at Miss Shirley. "One day soon, you and I will have to have a little chat with that niece of yours. Fascist type if I ever saw one. If it weren't for Cedar Valley Residence she would never have found you. Typical, typical."

It looked like Morris was about to go down one of his "injustice in the world monologues", but Anna put her hand over his and said, "Now, now, Morris. This is a happy moment for Miss Shirley--Aldea. We don't want to spoil it."

Morris humped his reluctant agreement just as Mary Ann appeared at Belinda's side and placed an overflowing basket of crusty French bread and whipped garlic butter in the center of their table.

"Are you eating here, Ms. Jones?," Mary Ann asked. "I'll bring you a setting. Everyone's having spaghetti and Mr. Jones is just starting to plate their entrees." She pushed her glasses up on her nose and smiled encouraging. "Wouldn't be hard to add one more."

Without hesitation, Belinda accepted Mary Ann's offer, pulled her chair in closer, put her elbows on the table, let her shoulders relax, and allowed herself a big smile.

She could be depressed later.

These moments she should enjoy.

Morris, however, couldn't be completely squelched. "Alright, heck with King County. But Belinda, tell us everything about your investigation." He lowered his voice. "Getting close to nailing poor Philly's killer? You know we can help if you need us."

Belinda thought for a bit. And in the end decided she *shouldn't* be discussing any of the details of her investigation with her residents, but what the hell? Maybe talking everything out would help.

Besides, the rest of the dining room was empty, and she could see Bernard and Martha helping Mary Ann bring their lunches over. Heck--they could sit down too, there was room. Then they could all have a luncheon "pick-the-killer" party.

Then Belinda laughed, louder than she might have wanted, but with obvious pleasure. *Dear, dear Bernie*, she thought watching her brother approach, *must have read my mind.*

He was carrying several bottles of red wine.

CHAPTER SEVEN

Friday Night

While Belinda was off interviewing suspects Wednesday and Thursday, Bernard and Martha, when not engaged in restaurant duties or fending off Lois Michael and Devlin Stephens the architect, had been plotting and planning.
Secretly.
And tonight their plan went into action.
In preparation, Bernard had dutifully passed on his afternoon power nap, made sure dinner was easy (pot roast and macaroni and cheese), and rushed, with Martha and Mary Ann's help, to get the kitchen cleaned up early and all the prep completed for Saturday morning.
He had almost spilled the beans at their little lunch party, but Martha nailed him with a keep-your-mouth-shut look before he could blab.
Now, Martha was already in position when he crept from his suite in stocking feet--silently he thought--and furtively made his way downstairs. He moved through the foyer and dining room, then out to the kitchen by way of nightlights and memory. He heard no sounds besides his own shallow breathing--but one. There was a soft clank from behind the entrance stairs--which he ignored. No time for minor house-concerns--their plan was afoot.
Outside it was still quiet. No rain, no thunder, no lightening--yet. Just the blackness of a quarter-moon night.
As for the two canines, supposed "watchdogs" for the Residence, Bernard knew Buster was asleep in Martha's suite, while Naja was unaccounted for.
Once Bernard slid through the kitchen's swinging doors, it turned pitch black, but he dared not switch on the light.
A nervous whisper cut through the darkness. "Psst! Is that you Bernard?"
"Yes." He moved forward, feeling his way from table to table toward Martha's voice and their rendezvous point, the

pantry entrance. "Do you have a flashlight?"

"Yes," Martha answered. "But I don't want to turn it on. And you?"

"Yep. I brought the high-beam."

"Did you go outside?" she asked, still whispering. "I thought I heard…"

"Shh!" He stopped and stood wooden-man still, waiting, listening for a couple seconds. "I think I hear something." His voice was barely audible.

This was it--it would all come together now.

They remained silent, waiting, for several moments. It felt like an eternity.

Finally, Bernard heard the sound of padded feet approaching in the darkness. Then, a couple seconds more--he felt her presence inches away.

"Gotcha!" Bernard declared triumphantly while switching on his flashlight toward where he thought their prey stood.

Two startled hazel eyes stared back into his blinding light. *How could I have missed hearing or smelling them*, those eyes seemed to ask, while her ears flopped and her tail instantly dropped between her hind legs. Tonight's prized treasure fell from her mouth--a watch on a leather fob.

"Naja." Bernard said. It seemed so obvious now.

Martha inhaled a short gasp and brought her hand to her mouth. "I'll be darned."

Naja, self-proclaimed queen of Cedar Valley Residence had been found out.

While Bernard and Martha were embarking on their clandestine operation, Belinda, though in bed trying to fall asleep, found herself tossing and turning. Lunch had been grand, and her late afternoon nap had been delicious.

Now that it was nighttime, however, she was paying the price for overeating, drinking wine, and napping in the afternoon.

Earlier in the evening, before officially calling it a day, around ten or so, she had taken a peek at the night outside her window and knew the sky was eerily black. It might have been drizzling, though she couldn't hear the patter of rain, or see any telltale flashes of lightening. Amongst all that dark dampness, a quarter-moon sliver, now high on the horizon, was peeking through what had to be dense opaque clouds and possibly rain. Miraculous, Belinda thought.

During that same time, Belinda thought she heard a noise she couldn't recognize *outside* the residence; and in an extremely unusual and overly cautious move, she slipped into the office, unlocked their bottom desk drawer and moved Glory's aged I.J. .38 to her nightstand.

Definitely not a good night to be out and about, she concluded--an excellent evening to stay warm, dry, and safe inside. Who knew what might happen weather wise? It could pour any second.

She was aware Theresa Bacera and Janice Tanner were still out, evidently unafraid. But she was neither their age, or their keeper. The porch light was always on, and they had their own keys. That would have to be enough.

Awhile later, however, on hearing a few thumps and bumps *inside*--old buildings often creaked and wheezed, and her beloved Residence was no exception--Belinda pulled the covers up closer and decided this time to ignore the world beyond her suite.

She needed a good night's sleep. Tomorrow would be a big day.

For after talking it all out at lunch, Belinda now knew who had killed Lana and Philly; and it was the same person who had run Moira off the road.

She should have figured it out earlier.

However, now knowing the truth did not bring elation. Indeed, it saddened Belinda greatly.

An even better reason to pull the covers up closer.

*   *   *   *   *

Tessa had fallen into a fretful half-doze, half-sleep on the couch in her sitting-room while watching a recorded episode of *Criminal Minds*. Scary and creepy stuff, but she had been addicted to the show from its first episode.

She heard footsteps on the stairs, but like-minded with Belinda, wanted to ignore everything beyond her suite. Besides, Tessa very much doubted a serial killer like the one she'd just seen profiled on TV was roaming around the halls.

What business was it of hers anyway? This place belonged to Belinda and Bernard. Let them deal with it!

Yes, she was a guest--and it was *their* responsibility to protect their guests.

But then again, maybe she just might go show Belinda the genealogy matrix she was putting together. Maybe even tell her about her parents and John?

Belinda hadn't seemed to mind when she'd barged in before at midnight. And it wasn't even that late yet.

Her great-grandmother was sleeping in the bedroom, while Kaitlin was wide awake in the sitting room, headphones on, listening to French tapes and reading David McCullough's *1776*. But even so twice engaged, she heard the front door downstairs click closed: her hearing, despite Vera's cautions, was excellent. She paid no heed, however. Irregular French verb inflections and happenings at Fort Ticonderoga were far more interesting.

Maybe in a little while, she would go get a soda from the refrigerator in the common room at the end of the hall. She had brought several six packs of "Jolt Cola" with her.

A couple of those, and she could read all night.

Miss Shirley and Phoebe were asleep in their separate suites and dreaming the dreams of the "just." Miss Kitty, instead of her regular nighttime feline prowling, was fast asleep on Morris' chest, rising and falling gently with his breathing-- while Anna slept at their side.

The murderer of Lana and Philly waited outside for over an hour; first until the public areas of the Residence went dim, then until the suite lights went out. It was necessary to circle the Residence several times and use binoculars to adequately spy on all the suites.

It had been close once, when Belinda turned on her light and looked out her window. What with that damn moon-- inordinately bright for it's puny little size--the killer had waited, silently, almost right under Belinda's window until it was obvious she had retreated back into her suite.

Kaitlin, the stupid child, evidently refused to go to sleep- -which extremely irritated the murderer--who then watched, waited, and waited some more for the Price suite to go dark.

"Probably listening to that horrid music, rotting her brain," the killer hissed into damp night air.

Finally, the killer couldn't take the risk of lurking around the building any longer. It was critical to get *it* back; and the killer knew it had to be *tonight*.

What a terrible mistake, losing *it* like that!

Even plodding Belinda Jones would eventually connect the dots.

Thank goodness she had a key. Not that breaking and entering was out of the question.

Besides, though she was enveloped in her bright colored rain slicker, she was becoming chilled to the bone. Her feet felt like ice, and rain was imminent any second. The time had to be now.

Her .38 was fully loaded, and she patted her side for its reassuring presence; and even though her slicker was thick, she was further emboldened by the gun's weighty presence in her jacket pocket underneath.

As she entered Cedar Valley Residence, the front door creaked, even though she had been particularly careful to open it barely enough to slip through. "Oh no," she whispered and prayed no one had noticed the creak, or her voice.

From here on, she thought, it should be easy--everyone asleep in their rooms, even the *offending* one. She hadn't figured out yet what to do about that--how to get it back from her-- without more violence. If she had to, however...

But first, she had to get upstairs unnoticed.

Fortunately, she sensed Bernard moving toward the foyer before he saw her, and she was able to duck into the stairwell.

What was the silly man doing anyway? Creeping around in his own place in the dark?

She was warmer now she was inside. It would be nice to dump the rain-slicker, but intruders don't take the time to change clothes. Anyway she was tough, not about to die of pneumonia from a little coldness.

From the foyer it didn't take her long to silently make it to the top of the main staircase--where the moon surprised her yet again. The brightness of a minute shaft of moonlight finding its way through the skylight dome was quite remarkable in its intensity, and an unwelcome piece of bad luck.

Then, a third surprise--the second floor hallway was lined with wall-scones--dimmed, but lit just the same.

"Damn," she cursed, audible only to herself.

Illumination or not, she was close. She knew where Kaitlin's door was, to the left, then on the right; not much farther.

She had just made it along the railing boarding the open area that rose through the center of the residence when Lana's murderer came face to face with Tessa as she exited her suite, genealogy charts in hand.

"Who the hell are you?" Tessa demanded loudly and in a tone that clearly said she'd never before seen anything like what now stood before her. Her charts fell to the floor.

What hit Belinda's senses first was the intruder's scent. Then she heard Tessa's startled voice down the hall--and she

was instantly awake and keenly aware she had miscalculated.
Badly.

Tomorrow would not be soon enough to unveil a
murderer.

She grabbed Glory's gun and rushed out into the
hallway.

Belinda could feel her heart pounding and hear her own
staccato breathing--but couldn't control either. Instinct and
adrenaline took over.

She had her grandmother's gun, but for some reason,
Glory wasn't at her side offering sage advice.

She would have to act on her own.

What Belinda saw as she stepped into the hallway, gun
drawn, was Olive Norris' back. She was turned at an angle
toward Tessa, and pointing a handgun point-blank at her.

Tessa was smartly decked out in the palest of yellow silk
PJ's and matching slippers--and her designer outfit combined
with the look of outrage, fear, and incredulity on her face, would
have been comical if the situation wasn't so dire.

Essence of lavender was strong in the hall--and Olive's
purple rain-slicker added to the surrealistic scene.

It wasn't supposed to happen like this.

"Olive! Stop!" Belinda shouted. "I have a gun too." She
willed her voice to sound commanding and ruthless. *"And I
won't hesitate to use it."* As Belinda spoke she took cautious mini-
steps toward Olive's back.

In a blink, as she moved closer, the scene shifted. She
watched helplessly as Kaitlin, earphones still on and *1776* in her
hand, stepped out of Vera's suite.

Olive glanced at Kaitlin. "Just the little thieving tramp
I wanted to see," she said, the tenor and cadence of her voice
even and grandmotherly--her words and their deliverance eerily
incompatible. Olive shifted the muzzle of her gun from Tessa to
Kaitlin. "I'll kill the brat, Belinda. Drop your gun. And please
come over here where I can see you."

A polite request, ruthlessly delivered.

To her horror, Belinda could see on Kaitlin's face that
she was not about to stand still and do nothing. Instead, Vera's
Goth wannabe great-granddaughter snapped at Olive, "Go to

hell, you weird old purple biddy," and swung her hardcover *1776* sideways in an attempt to knock the gun out of Olive's hand.

She missed.

And Olive shot Kaitlin.

Belinda watched in paralyzing fear and disbelief as blood gushed from Kaitlin's shoulder.

There was a Felliniesque quality to the *mise-en-scène* before her as Kaitlin grabbed at her wound and dropped to her knees--blood oozing through her fingers. Even in the dimly lit hall, Belinda could see the look of surprise and horror on the girl's heavily made up face--while ruby-red blood saturated her stark black attire.

And underneath it all, Belinda saw a scared teenager about to bleed to death right in front of her.

What to do! What to do!

Tessa, her hands covering her mouth in horror, took a step back; then after an infinitesimal pause, reversed tack and rushed over to Kaitlin. "You animal," she yelled at Olive.

Olive shifted her weight, and looked like she was going to now shoot Tessa, or possibly Kaitlin again.

Belinda half charged, half lunged toward Olive--while Olive whirled around to face her. And even though seconds counted, her subconscious registered Bernard or Martha calling her name somewhere in the distance--dogs barking--a cat yowling--and Vera's startled voice from somewhere in her suite calling Kaitlin.

She had to save Vera's great-granddaughter. She *had* to.

Oh God! And any minute her other residents would be rushing out into the melee.

Belinda had managed to come within five feet or so of Olive, and now stood--her gun pointed at Olive, and Olive's gun pointed at her.

Up close to Olive, Belinda was surprised by what she saw. Nothing had changed since their first meeting less than a week earlier. Before her stood a short round woman with a puffy oval face and a substantial bosom; wearing sensible flat shoes, purple pants, and a purple rain-slicker with the initials O. N. in scroll on it's right front panel. The expression on her face--

benign.

"I just want what's mine. That silly looking girl tried to attack me. I only shot her in self defense."

Belinda didn't know what Olive was talking about, but she could see the very real gun Olive was pointing at her. The light was too dim and she wasn't close enough to know what *kind* of gun--but she guessed it was the Colt .38 Kirby had bought her. Would Olive have to cock her revolver? No, she decided, probably double-action.

Her own gun was double-action, but old; and she had only shot it once before.

Olive demanded, "Drop your gun, Belinda."

Tessa charged into Olive from the rear. The impact hardly made a dent against Olive's sturdy presence--indeed Tessa appeared to bounce off her back--but the gun did fall from Olive's hand. Olive made a move to retrieve it.

"Don't you dare," Belinda yelled. "Leave the gun right where it is. I don't want to shoot you." Then she shot a warning bullet into the ceiling of her beloved Residence.

Olive pulled herself up straight and took a step forward, her voice still calm, controlled. "You won't shoot me. You don't have the nerve. I'm the one that hired you, remember? Besides, the Blessed Virgin is on my side. I bet you don't even go to church, now do you?"

Tessa grabbed Kaitlin's book from the floor. "Stop you crazy woman or I'll bash you on the head."

Olive laughed. "With a book?" She took another step toward Belinda. "Now give me the gun," she said calmly. "You really shouldn't shoot holes in the ceiling and point guns at innocent people. It isn't the Christian way, you know."

Naja came charging up the steps, took a four-legged ready-to-spring stance next to Tessa, and growled menacingly at Olive.

In a milli-second of clarity and self-acceptance, Belinda realized Olive was right. She wasn't going to shoot or command her dog to attack a short, crazed, purple-encased old woman.

Instead, in one continuous and smooth motion, Belinda switched her gun to her left hand and as hard as she could, delivered a sucker punch squarely into Olive's nose.

Stunned, Olive covered her face with both hands, stumbled backward, and uttered some kind of expletive--but whatever the word, it was lost behind her hands.

In a few more seconds Bernard, Martha, and Buster came bounding up the staircase just as the remaining sleepy-eyed residents of Cedar Valley Residence also haphazardly stepped and stumbled out into the hallway to investigate.

Olive, though clearly surprised and hurt by Belinda's blow, wasn't ready to give up. Despite her injury, she lunged forward to retrieve her gun.

Fortunately, Morris LeBeau had rushed into the middle of the fray. Immediately he assessed the situation--and quickly put his foot on the .38 before Olive could reach it. "Now, now, we'll have no more of this nonsense," he said with authority--even though his large frame was shrouded in a floor length red nightshirt and topped with a matching red Dickensonian-inspired sleeping hat.

Naja didn't move, but emitting a low growl between bared teeth, kept her eyes on Olive. Buster, last on the scene, ran over to Belinda, his tail wagging, suggesting he thought this a grand new game.

Belinda wanted to laugh and cry. She managed to do neither.

Belinda forced herself to slow down and take several deep calming breaths--hopefully decreasing the adrenaline flow still raging through her body--and providing additional oxygen to her brain. She needed to quickly order her thoughts.

It was not enough just to have subdued Olive. She had to also outwit her.

The breathing seemed to work a bit, and time did seem to return to normal as she watched Bernard rush off to the office.

"I'll grab our first-aid kit," he yelled over his shoulder. "And I'll call nine-one-one for Kaitlin."

"And call your Uncle John too," Martha called to his disappearing back. He waved his hand in acknowledgement before disappearing into the office.

Belinda's heart, despite Bernard and Martha's now helpful presence, was still pounding at a rate that scared her.

Another slow deep breath.

Vera was kneeling on the floor next to Kaitlin, cradling her great-granddaughter and pressing a sofa pillow from their suite against her wound. Kaitlin still looked scared, but the bleeding had slowed and she didn't look as terrified as when she was first shot.

Just looking at her, Belinda didn't think Kaitlin was going into shock, but still, she wished the medics would hurry up. *No sound of sirens yet.*

Phoebe, also in a long nightshirt like Morris, her bleached hair wrapped tightly in what seemed like hundreds of little multi-colored curlers, was at Vera's side.

Belinda requested Morris to escort a recalcitrant Olive downstairs to the parlor. She figured Morris, even in his outlandish bedtime gear, presented an intimidating presence; and clearly, he had no intention of letting Olive get away.

In the end Olive begrudgingly acquiesced.

Both Anna, modestly cocooned in a pale-blue cotton robe, and Miss Shirley, sixties style tye-dyed psychedelic pajamas peeking from beneath her traditional thick down robe, insisted on following Morris and Olive downstairs to the parlor.

Belinda fleetingly reflected it wasn't taking very long for Miss Shirley *the caterpillar* to morph into Aldea *the butterfly*.

Martha, with Naja and Buster following her every move and step, took it as her task to run around the Residence flipping on light-switches in all the public areas--upstairs and down.

Belinda took yet another calming breath.

With the lights coming on, in a matter of minutes Cedar Valley Residence came back to life and shifted into a realm of physics and human behavior Belinda could again recognize.

Two people killed, another almost maimed, and a teenager shot right in front of her eyes--these events belonged in another universe--not in her little world.

Where's Tessa? She had seemingly disappeared into thin air. Belinda's concern, however, was premature and short lived. Within seconds Tessa reappeared from her suite, now regally clad in a floor length swaying silk designer robe and two-inch heeled slippers. Her cousin was now *dressed* for the occasion.

If Tessa was an indicator of anything, Belinda concluded with one more deep breath, maybe things were returning to normal.

Well almost normal.

She still had a murderer to deal with.

Belinda finally went downstairs after all the others, including Bernard, who having done his telephone duty had rushed off to follow Morris. When Belinda arrived in the parlor, she found Olive in an armchair, flanked by an empty armchair to her right, and Morris to her left on the sofa.

Belinda sat down in the chair next to Olive.

Anna, Miss Shirley, Tessa, and Martha had arranged themselves randomly in seats around the room.

Bernard had chosen to stand, wide-legged with his hands in his pockets, across the room in front of the fireplace, and directly facing Olive. Belinda found the expression of distaste on her brother's face surprising and quite uncharacteristic. But then, she knew how much he hated physical violence. And in his own home, for goodness sakes.

"You can't keep me here--" Olive protested, but her words were stopped by the unexpected and surprisingly loud opening of the front door.

Theresa Bacera and Jorge Villareal rushed in. Both were dressed in jeans, black sport shoes, T's, leather jackets, and baseball caps.

Belinda had a clear view of the foyer, and the pair's head-movement sweeps of the foyer didn't pass her unnoticed. Neither did she miss their professionally alert demeanor, nor the fact that both Theresa and Jorge had their right hands to their sides and hidden underneath jackets.

Sidearms. Belinda was sure of it.

Theresa, and to Belinda's sensibilities still on alert, came over to the parlor entrance, and asked authoritatively, "What's going on? Everything okay?"

Jorge had remained in the foyer, still looking around, but trying to act casual about it.

Belinda, despite the circumstances couldn't help

inwardly smiling. *This* Theresa Bacera was definitely a different person from the eager to please woman she knew. Undercover agent? FBI? INS? Something to do with illegal immigration, she was sure. And her beloved gardener an agent to boot. But now was not the time...

Olive stood. "I'm leaving now. You can't hold me." At last, sirens in the distance. Getting louder. Sounded to Belinda's ear like an ambulance, rather than police.

Theresa looked inquiringly at Belinda, then Bernard.

Bernard said, "This woman shot Kaitlin who's upstairs. I've already called nine-one-one and Sheriff Thomas."

Belinda was amazed at how calm her brother and Theresa appeared. While she still felt out of control--despite her deep breaths.

She watched in awe as Theresa calmly looked back over her shoulder toward Jorge and evidently communicated instructions without words, for he immediately headed upstairs.

Theresa then looked at Olive. "We should wait for the sheriff, don't you think, Mrs. Norris?"

Olive dropped back into her seat with a displeased grunt.

Thunder clapped, sounding close, but no one jumped.

"You killed Lana Norris and Phillip Towers," Belinda stated without preamble. "Look at me Olive. Look at me!" She could hear the anger in her voice, but there was nothing she could do about it. Time was short--her uncle would be on the scene any moment.

Olive turned in her seat to face Belinda.

"And you tried to kill Moira." Belinda could feel her adrenaline-fueled ire trying to take over. *No, I have to stay in control.*

"Now why would I do that?" Olive asked. "And frame my son? I would never hurt Kirby." Olive smiled strangely. "Even you must know that."

"What I know," Belinda said, charging full-steam ahead, but in a calmer tone, "is that you killed your daughter-in-law because she was having affairs--defiling your Kirby--defiling your sense of morality. All your talk about Kirby was only part of the story. So much of this horribleness is due to *you* and your twisted sense of morality."

Miss Shirley whispered, "Oh dear," and covered her mouth with both hands.

The sirens were growing louder--insistent. Then they abruptly stopped.

"What silliness," Olive said, her tone and manner now turned haughty and peremptory.

Two medics rushed into the foyer with a gurney. Jorge reappeared from upstairs and took charge of escorting them to Kaitlin.

Belinda prayed, *Please let Kaitlin be okay. She's just a kid.*

Olive continued, "I admit, I do have a reputation for being an upright and moral person, but that doesn't make me a killer. Besides, this *is* the twenty-first century. And some things I cannot change. Even with Jesus' help." Her disdain for modern morality, intentional or not, was palpable.

"An affair is a *sin*. Is it not?" Belinda demanded.

"Of course." Olive rolled her head as if stretching her neck.

"What is having an affair with another woman? A *sin* beyond the pale. A damnable offense. An eternity in Hell. Am I right?"

Anna exclaimed, "Oh my."

Olive clasped her hands tightly in her lap. "I will admit Lana had some answering to do to The Blessed Virgin. That's a long way, however, from my killing her."

What the hell, Belinda decided, it was now or never. Too late to turn back, and once Olive got in the hands of a good lawyer--who knew what would happen.

"Good God," Belinda said, still sitting next to Olive, but aggressively leaning toward her. "You come to see me in the afternoon, then you go out and kill a helpless and homeless man who just wants a few bucks." Belinda shook her finger accusingly at Olive. "Just because he *saw* you on the trail." At the thought of Philly, Belinda felt a hot rage rising within. It was a surprise experience.

She could strangle the woman with her bare hands-- right there in her beloved Cedar Valley Residence. She should have *shot* her. A punch in the nose wasn't good enough.

Bernard said, "Camouflaged as some giant doting purple mother-bird, just trying to get justice for her son. A son she herself set up." He spat the words out in disgust. "My giant lizard," he added sotto voce while shifting his gaze to Belinda for several seconds.

So, Belinda realized, *my dear brother wasn't as composed as he looked.*

"You have nothing on me," Olive hissed.

Belinda said, "To drug, strangle, *and* shoot someone are premeditated acts of simmering hatred." She forced herself to watch every nuance of movement in Olive's face and body. She would have to outwit this evil woman. "The murderer had to be someone close and who knew the family residence and habits--like Lana's coffee--brewing her a fresh pot and lacing it with Librium. And how else would Max end up back in his yard? The murderer would have to care about Max getting home." Belinda's eyes narrowed from outrage. "Not that I think you *actually* care about Max. But he's Kirby's dog, and you do care about Kirby, I'll give you that."

"Pure speculation," Olive said, and turned to Morris. "If you don't let me leave this place, now, I will have you arrested for false imprisonment."

Morris' response was a short, hearty laugh.

"And," Belinda said, "Kirby claimed he kept his car locked. Who else had a key besides Lana? *You.* There was no sign of forced entry into Kirby's car. And how could a gun possibly get into the wheel-well of Kirby's trunk if Kirby, you, or Lana didn't put it there?"

"Kirby regularly serviced his car, any mechanic could have made a copy of his key."

Belinda leaned even closer to Olive--she felt like she was only inches away from the woman's face. "You encouraged Kirby to take out the life insurance policy on Lana."

"So what." Olive shrugged. "It made good business sense."

"And who else would know about Moira? No one but you and me. That morning Kirby told only *us.* You were the only one with a reason to kill Moira. No one else. *Just you.*"

Belinda dropped back into her armchair, still angry, but

exhausted.

"But why would I care about the silly woman?" Olive said, seeming to take Belinda's physical retreat into the depths of her chair as encouragement she could still win this battle.

Belinda came back to life, "Because her being with Kirby that morning ruined it all." Again Belinda emotionally and physically challenged Olive by leaning in toward her and steadfastly holding Olive in her stare. "You had it planned so nicely. Kirby would have the perfect alibi--surrounded by twenty or so of his colleagues all morning. But then, your silly son decided to go off and *gratify* himself on the very morning you needed him to have a solid alibi."

Olive started to say something, but clamped her lips tightly shut and crossed her arms over her ample bosom.

"I wouldn't be surprised if you didn't bump off your own husband. But that's for others to decide," Belinda said.

Olive raised an eyebrow, but her tone was controlled. "Interesting theory, Ms. Jones. I have to give you credit there. However, you don't have any proof for such nonsense."

On the surface, Olive's delivery remained confident, but Belinda could finally hear a hint of fear underlying her words.

"Yes we do," Bernard said as he stepped forward, then started removing items from his jacket pocket and placing them on the coffee table between him and Olive. "It seems Naja has been, shall we say, collecting? First we have one chewed up silk scarf," he said, enumerating the items. "So sorry about it's condition Miss Shirley."

Miss Shirley gasped, and Naja crouched down and started a noiseless slink toward the rear of Belinda's chair. Sanctuary, she evidently hoped was behind her beloved mistress.

Bernard continued, "A pen set," and placed a leather case next to the scarf.

"I'll be darned," Theresa said from the doorway.

"An antique pipe." Bernard laid it next in line.

Belinda saw Morris smile.

Next, Bernard conjured up a velveteen sachet and inclined his head toward Phoebe. "Your brooch."

Phoebe wiggled her shoulders with delight.

"And here's Janice's watch." He took a deep sigh, for fortification or in regret, Belinda was no longer sure what her dear brother was feeling.

Bernard next lifted up high for everyone to see, a purple pouch from his other pocket with the letters "O.N." embroidered in scroll on one side. "One antique wedding ring." This item he didn't put on the table, but replaced it in his pocket. "I touched the bag, Mrs. Norris, but when I saw what was in it, I stopped. It's Lana's ring. The one she was wearing when she was killed."

Olive brought both hands to her mouth, partly masking her reaction.

Bernard stepped back. "With your fingerprint, smeared in Lana's blood. You can see the print easy enough, won't be hard to miss." He rocked back and forth a couple times on his heels. "A very nice print I think, and Lana's DNA, of course."

Bernard allowed himself a small, wry smile before continuing. "I'm not a CSI, and this isn't Las Vegas, but I'm quite sure the Washington State Police Crime Lab will be able to identify the print and profile poor Lana's blood."

Olives eyes were fixed on Bernard's pocket. "Proves nothing," she said. "Of course, I've touched it. It was mine before Kirby asked for it."

Belinda took the lead and carried on the thread. "But not with Lana's blood under your print." The significance and import of two other events suddenly became clear to her. "At the bank. You knew then you'd lost the ring. The teller thought she was picking up on your grief over Lana, when it really was your panic over losing the ring."

Olive sat frozen, now looking past Belinda and Bernard, her hands back in her lap, clamped tightly together.

"And you knew Kaitlin was suspected of the thefts. You heard it Monday morning. Right here in this parlor."

Anna spontaneously declared, "It was *us* she heard." Then she looked regretfully over to Morris. "Oh Morris, our loose talk might have gotten Kaitlin killed."

"I hope Vera will forgive us," he mumbled in penitent agreement.

"And Anna's keys," Belinda finished. "She left them in the parlor Sunday and you helped yourself to them Monday.

Keys I'm sure Sheriff Thomas will find somewhere on your person."

Olive moved her hand toward her jacket pocket even though her gun was still on the floor upstairs. An involuntary reflex, Belinda guessed--feeling for her keys.

"Hold still," Theresa demanded.

Olive dropped her hand, defeat and acceptance finally overtaking her.

At last, Belinda heard police sirens in the distance; and oddly she thought, no one spoke again until Sheriff John Thomas arrived.

Indeed, an eerie silence descended upon and encapsulated Cedar Valley Residence parlor until the moment he eventually walked through the front door. Then, everyone wanted to talk at once.

Surprisingly to Belinda, it took only about fifteen or so minutes for her uncle to sort everything out, call for back up from the State Patrol, and deliver a searched, handcuffed, and sullen Olive Norris into their hands, along with Anna's set of keys, and Olive's ring, pouch, and gun.

But before John himself could leave, the front door opened yet again and Janice Tanner returned home from work--barely a second before thunderous booms rocked the skies and let loose a torrential downpour.

"What's up?" Janice asked from the parlor door as she took in the scene before her. "Did I miss something?"

EPILOGUE

Monday again...

Kirby completed the last of his required paperwork and walked away from King County Jail at precisely 8:00 A.M. on Monday morning.

It had rained the previous night, leaving the morning air fresh and laced with the distinctive scent of Fall; and as Kirby stepped out onto Fifth Avenue, he greedily breathed-in and savored this new September day--a free man again. Just as his mother had prayed for.

Olive, of course, was now lost to him forever; and no one else was waiting for him in her place. Not Belinda, not Moira, not Senator, not Adam--not even his brother Walter.

Fortunately, no reporters, either. *I'm old news, thank God.* His life was again his own, he hoped. But Kirby knew much had changed, much would change, and he could only guess at the level of interest awaiting his story down the road.

For now, he faced this first day of the rest of his life, alone. That circumstance did not make him unhappy.

He decided to walk a bit before catching a cab to King County Impound where his Volvo awaited him. And as he walked, the jailhouse fading to his rear, he was overcome, quite suddenly and overwhelmingly, with an emotion that almost brought him to his knees on the sidewalk.

Grief.

For the first time since Lana's murder.

Their marriage had been far from idyllic, and with affairs on both sides, well, he didn't want to even think about that part. But Lana had been his partner in life for fifteen years.

Then, for the first time since her death, he wondered what had been on Lana's mind that other Monday morning in August. The morning his mother had killed her.

He could almost picture Lana, in shorts and T-shirt, wearing those large rimmed sun glasses she loved so much, and walking confidently as she always did. Healthy and alive. What had she been thinking about, he wondered--when that bullet had ripped through her brain?

Poor Lana. He had once loved her deeply and

completely, and now she was gone.
Forever.
Tears streamed down his face.

And one more Monday...

Belinda stood on the sidewalk in front of the steps to St. Francis, protected by a broad black umbrella creating a tiny island of dryness in a raging sea of wind and rain.

Over the weekend, she had led the way for a memorial to recognize and remember Philly, including helping plan the service and organizing a carpool. His passing, Belinda had insisted, needed to be marked on the calendar of time.

It was barely ten in the morning, and after only two days of clear weather, Cedar Valley skies were again in turmoil. Dark heavy clouds were marching relentlessly upward and onward through the Cascades to the drum-roll and fanfare of body-rattling thunder and intermittent flashes of lightening.

In their wake, sheets of rain were drenching man, beast, and countryside.

"It always rains at funerals," Belinda had said to Bernard Sunday night.

And he had declared, "But this isn't a funeral. It's a memorial."

Whatever you called it, Philly was still dead this morning, and it was raining like hell. Sure, Lana and Philly's murderer had been caught, and she had been involved in bringing Olive to justice. Belinda, however, couldn't find consolation in being right on the minor issue of rain, or more importantly, on revealing Olive for what she was.

At least Moira and Kaitlin were going to make it. Could have been much worse.

Miss Shirley had been *found*, and Calvin "Senator" Pope was retiring as of yesterday. Adam she thought, had made a good decision and had handled Calvin with amazing delicacy and respect for such a young man.

She had seen Adam enter the church this morning, and now wondered where he was sitting. It would be nice, even comforting to sit next to him. For Belinda was not blind to the rising interest her heart was taking in the young attorney-- despite the admonishments of her mind. Glory, unfortunately, had not yet made her opinion known.

Still, Belinda sighed dejectedly, her breath swallowed up into the rain-soaked air surrounding her.

For some reason this morning, *neither* her surfacing romantic inklings toward Adam, *nor* happy endings for others, *nor* even successfully freeing Kirby, were enough to comfort.

It was not a new thought for Belinda that "happiness" was an illusive and relative state of being. Still, where this morning was the happiness she expected to be feeling now that this investigation was over--and a romantic adventure lay ahead for her?

Ironic when you think about it: just last week at the Washington Corrections Center for Women in Gig Harbor, even Olive had told Belinda *she* was finally happy. "After all, Belinda," Olive had said. "Aren't I in charge of keeping the altar in the chapel in good condition? I even have a budget for flowers." Olive had then smiled beatifically as if being in jail for the rest of her life was the culmination of a life well lived. "With the flowers, I can have purple all around me. Now isn't that nice?"

Remembering that visit, and despite the rain and her miserable funk, Belinda was nearly moved to smile as she re-envisioned Olive's chubby face and gleefully lunatic eyes.

"Talking of flowers reminds me," Olive had added. "I've had some time to think about a few things." She then nodded her head sagely. "I grossly underestimated your abilities. Otherwise, I certainly wouldn't have hired you. I've even forgiven you for hitting me. And I do hope there're no hard feelings about the raspberries."

"Raspberries?" Belinda had asked.

"I hated calling the County, getting the government involved. But I was responsible at St. Francis for more than just the church, you understand." Again Olive nodded at the righteousness of what she was saying. "A lot can be said about a place by its grounds and surrounding neighborhood, and standards do have to be upheld. Those bushes at Cedar Valley Residence were looking just too, too tacky. And that lady, Lois Michael, if I remember her name right. She seemed so eager to help."

Crazy, treacherous, and murderous Olive was happy. Why wasn't she?

Belinda sighed again; and again the storm stole her breath.

Fortunately, a broad-brimmed black rain-hat both protected and hid Belinda's face, black leather gloves covered her hands, and an ankle length black rain-slicker shrouded her body. Indeed, Belinda felt a modicum of protection from the storm--but certainly not safe from the world or her own thoughts.

She pulled the collar of her rain-slicker in tighter with her free hand. Tessa had come to her room last night, after Bernard had left, around midnight yet again, talking nonsense about her parents, and claiming that only Uncle John knew the truth.

Belinda could see John's cruiser parked on the side of the church. Evidently he was on duty, and it pleased her he had taken the time. Was Katheryne with him? She hoped so.

But the hell with Tessa. No, she wouldn't ask John about what had happened between her mother and father as Tessa suggested. Just as Miss Shirley had decided about her two years of amnesia, *some things were better left alone.* She would not let Tessa and her resentful trouble-making ways and trumped up intrigues change the way she saw her own life.

The past was the past. There it would stay.

At least she had finally called their architect Devlin Stephens and committed to move forward on the addition.

Their entire Residence contingent had arrived together this morning in both residence vans, Bernard driving one, and Martha the other. It pleased Belinda that Janice, who took the day off from what Belinda now knew was a secret DOD Black-Box assignment at Boeing, had also come along.

While back at the Residence, a generous spread reminiscence of old-time wakes awaited their return. Belinda was hoping plenty of food and drink would transform grief into a "jolly good send off."

She had watched Bernard and Martha, carrying black umbrellas even larger than hers, shepherding them all through the deluge into the church--and at the end, expecting her to follow. They were now all waiting for her inside, her small family, and those who felt like family.

For this moment in time, however, Belinda still couldn't move forward, preferring to continue standing in the rain, unwilling, and possibly unable to join the service. The church doors stood wide open, inviting almost, the inside illuminated with bright lights and candles, with Bernard in the doorway waving her to come inside and join them. Inside, where it was bright, warm, dry.

And death was being revisited.

How romantic and dramatic it had sounded at first--being a detective. She, Belinda Jones, would bring justice and order to the incredibly messy business of murder and mayhem, guilt and innocence.

As more thunder rolled, the crux of Belinda's concern--borne on the wave of last week's reality--hit her hard and deep within. Another person had died, two more had almost died, and *she hadn't stopped it.* Now, all that was possible for her to do was mourn Philly, and comfort Moira and Kaitlin at Harborview hospital.

In the wake of this flood of realizations and emotions, Belinda suddenly felt incredibly naïve and vulnerable. She had been playing at being a detective, but this had not been a game.

No, not a game.

A flash of memory surfaced as she brought back a snatch of conversation just a few days earlier in her Uncle's office:

"*I think I want this to be who I am, Uncle John.*"

"*A detective you mean?*"

"*Yes.*"

Belinda hadn't been a child for decades now, but this moment, this place, she certainly felt like one. Afraid to face a reality she had partly chosen and partly been dealt, wishing for a world that wasn't the one she lived in.

She shivered--the wind was getting stronger, growing

and shifting, driving pellets of rain underneath her umbrella and hitting her rain-slicker. Her feet, already cold and damp, were now getting soaked.

Belinda couldn't ignore this. It was turning into another hell of a storm. Yet she was unable to move forward and join the others even though she could still see Bernard in the church doorway--illuminated from behind, looking like an angel.

She could even smell incense through the dampness, and hear an organ and singing maybe. A requiem mass? No, she didn't think so.

Memorial, not a funeral--remember?

Not that it made one damn bit of difference what she or anyone else called what was about to happen this morning. She had eagerly spearheaded the planning of Philly's memorial; but now, Belinda hated she was being forced to remember and grieve anew. To re-examine her own life and acknowledge her own failures.

Then, she felt a comforting caress followed by a hug from across the years, and across the barriers of time. Glory Jones was back at her side. Belinda's mind knew it wasn't real, her grandmother was long deceased, but her heart and soul felt Glory's presence just the same. *"Bella,"* Glory comforted and encouraged, *"you can do this. You can do this. You can. You can."*

Bernard's voice, barely audible through the pounding rain and her own groundswell of emotions, finally penetrated her consciousness. He was calling to her, "Belinda. Belinda."

Thank God for Bernie.

Slowly, with resolve born from sad acceptance, Belinda stepped forward toward the lighted church, Bernard, Adam, and her future.

Acknowledgements

My heartfelt gratitude and thanks go to my editors--
Mike Foley, Virginia Moody, and Jean Jenkins--and very
importantly to my agent and editor extraordinaire, Kitty
Kladstrup.

To my friends who generously answered my questions,
thank you for being there when I needed you. To name a
few, Nancy and Gene Wilson, Mary Hollis, Janice Maloney,
DeAnn West, and Gail and Jay Dobberthien.

A fortifying constant has been the unfailing encouragement
and support from my reading group members--Phyllis,
Mary, Janice, Luvenia, Cindy, Paula, Vonnie, Jan, and Kay.

To Joyce, Myron, and Steven, thank you for caring and being
such wonderful cheerleaders.

And without Lawrence, my living encyclopedia, historian,
and best friend--nothing would be possible.

Printed in the United States
129796LV00002B/1-48/P